PLACEBO EFFECT

GARY RUSSELL

BBC BOOKS

Published by BBC Worldwide Ltd,
Woodlands, 80 Wood Lane
London W12 0TT

First published 1998
Copyright © Gary Russell 1998
The moral right of the author has been asserted

Original series broadcast on the BBC
Format © BBC 1963
Doctor Who and TARDIS are trademarks of the BBC

ISBN 0 563 40587 2
Imaging by Black Sheep, copyright © BBC 1998

Printed and bound in Great Britain by Mackays of Chatham
Cover printed by Belmont Press Ltd, Northampton

This one is for all the *Doctor Who* followers who were at Furze Platt Junior/Comprehensive 1972-6, but particularly Jon Petter, Danny Roberts, Tim Firman, Alex Bridgeman, Steven Young and Martin Jay, who, I assume, all had the good sense to grow out of it!

Still - I'm glad I never did!

Introduction

There is a school of thought somewhere that equates the Borg from *Star Trek* with the Cybermen from *Doctor Who*. And superficially there are a great many similarities. However, I believe the Borg owe just as much to the Wirrn (or Wirrrn as the novelist Ian Marter revised them – brrr, verrry crrreepy that). That unrelenting self-drive to survive, to dominate and then learn. Whereas the Cybermen would take humanity and convert it to their likeness, the Wirrrn would rather absorb it, or 'assimilate' it as our Trekking bad guys would say. On top of that, as Seven of Nine is forever pointing out, she carries the knowledge of the entire Borg Collective in her head, quoting species numbers and medical facts relating to the many different races the Borg have assimilated. So it is with the Wirrrn, as viewers of *The Ark In Space*, the Bob Holmes masterpiece in which they made their television debut, will recall. When the Wirrrn absorbed Technician Dune, so they immediately had access not just to his individual knowledge and skills, but to the entire history of humanity or as much as Dune knew. Assuming he had, at some point, skimmed through a pretty detailed encyclopedia or had an A1 education, well, the Wirrrn knew everything they needed to know. So forget the Borg as the ultimate 'Resistance is futile, you will be assimilated' bad guys – *Doctor Who* via the Wirrrn was doing this fifteen years earlier. Now, add to all this the obvious insectoid paranoia encouraged by the *Alien* movies and you have the Wirrrn of this adventure for the Eighth Doctor and Sam Jones.

A quick round of thanks here – to Steve Cole at BBC Books who so good-humouredly nodded at me when I said I wanted to do a

Nimon-versus-Macra story. And equally good-humouredly smiled when I said, 'Oh, all right. How about the Wirrrn and the Foamasi?'

And to the other Eighth Doctor authors, particularly Peter Anghelides, John Peel, Kate Orman and Jon Blum, who answered my questions, queries and other irrelevant e-mails.

Grateful thanks also to: Trey Korte for the theology discussions; John Binns for the 'qualityness'; David Bailey for scans; Nick Pegg for having a surgeon for a father; David McIntee for patience and, of course, Johnnie, without whom...

A nod of appreciation to the folk at Gallifrey '98, Especially Rhonda, Jill, Shaun, Chad, Eric and Ingrid. And everyone at Marty's surprise party.

And a 'save big money' thanks to those who sat in the hotel lobby on the Sunday night after Gallifrey '98, discussing weird American store adverts. Particularly Kathy Sullivan, Gary Gillatt, Greg Bakun and Michael Lee. It was very surreal but by far the most relaxed and pleasant few hours of an entirely wonderful weekend. And as for that green goo in the plastic tube...

Plus a special hug for Andrew Pixley, whose contributions to *Placebo Effect*, indeed all my novels, are subtle things that float around my subconscious simply because of many happy hours spent talking *Who* and enjoying doing so because we love this unique concept in drama for what it truly is/was/should be again – just a damn good television programme.

Gary Russell
March 1998

Chapter One
Something Wicked This Way Comes

Quite some time past...

No one knows exactly where they came from. Legends on some planets believe they came from another galaxy, another universe perhaps. Other planets offer up the idea that they were created by the same giants for whom the universe is nothing more than a rose garden, a garden needing a blight of sorts to keep the rest of the life therein in check. And some planets simply don't care about their origins – just that they exist, they threaten and they seem to be unstoppable.

One thing that all these planets agree on is that the Andromedan Galaxy would be a safer, more pleasant and peaceful place if this blight were to be eradicated. Millions of bloodstones had been exchanged for weapons that proved ineffectual. Millions of lives had been fruitlessly laid down in an effort to fight them. And millions more lived under the constant threat of extinction – or worse – under their relentless pursuit of galactic supremacy.

How could anyone hope to survive the onslaught? How did you destroy an enemy whose body was so hardened that even a diamond-edged knife could not cut through it? How did you defeat a foe that could live as easily in the harsh, gravity-less areas of space as comfortably as in the heat of Tyrexus or the harsh arctic wastes of Livista? How did you thwart an enemy who picked clean the planets of the Phylox system in less than five days, killing or 'converting' everything they encountered?

No one throughout the Andromedan Galaxy had any answers,

but from the furthest reaches of Coscos and Salostophus to the rimworlds of Golos and Vysp, every living creature breathed a sigh of relief when the enemy left the Andromedan Galaxy behind and moved on to the rich pickings of what lay beyond. The Andromedans knew nothing of the galaxy that lay beyond, but they hoped and prayed that somewhere among the billions of planets it housed, a champion would arise to take on their apparently unstoppable foe and find a weakness, exploit it and eventually destroy the enemy, once and for all. Because if they failed, then that galaxy, then the next and the next and the next, would surely fall, leaving the entire universe dominated by just one malevolent, relentless, self-preserving species.

If they had the means, they would have sent out a message, a cry of despair, a plea for help. Just one word, guaranteed to bring fear to any who read it.

Wirrrn.

Chapter Two
Face to Face

A little more recently…

The shuttle was due in two hours. Not long enough by any means, but that was life. Never enough time to do all the important things like packing extra underwear in case you fell in a pond, or extra caps in case the sun burnt the top of your skull and you'd run out of blocking gel.

Never enough time…

Dr Miles Mason zipped up his holdall and gave his office one last look. The locum, a Dr Bakun, would be arriving in the morning, but for the next two months, this practice was no longer his, and that made Dr Mason a little sad. He'd spent most of his life savings creating this small business and, successful as it was, leaving it in the hands of another panicked him far more than it should. Nevertheless, business was business, and this new venture was an opportunity to get a very important tag-line on his CV. With a final stroke of a leaf on his rubber plant, Dr Mason turned and left his office.

'Well, Miss Rutherford, see you on my return.'

His receptionist beamed up at him. 'Good luck, sir. I'm sure you'll have lots of fun and very little work to do.'

He nodded and looked up as a buzzer sounded. 'That'll be the cab, then. Au revoir.'

He felt Miss Rutherford's beady eye on his back as the glass doors slid aside and let him exit the small building and walk out into the harsh sunlight of Cape City. He shielded his eyes to check the cab, and, yes, it was driven by Ntumbe – just as he had requested.

Ntumbe jumped out of the little vehicle, causing it to wobble slightly as the antigrav compensators allowed for the shift in internal weight. It wobbled a couple more times as first the luggage and then the two men added their bulk to it.

'Shuttle dome, sir?'

'Yes please. I'm very early, but you know me. I like to get there in good time.'

Ntumbe smiled. Ntumbe always smiled, come to think of it. Dr Mason had never seen him cross, even after an accident he'd had when his previous cab was shunted by a cargo loader. Something about the clean South African air no doubt made for a higher quality of life. Certainly Mason had felt happy since moving here eight years previously, from his old, rather suffocating job as a junior partner in a major Chicago practice.

'Heard from your son, sir?'

Mason shook his head. 'Not for ages. Last I heard, Matt was on his way to Io with the others in his division.'

'Nice to have a major for a son,' Ntumbe said. 'My son wants to be an astronaut one day like yours. I told him he'd be better off staying on Earth. Earth needs people right now, don't you think, Dr Mason?'

Mason nodded. 'Since the expansionists got into power, I've been feeling that too many people are heading to Mars or Saturn. If we're not careful, the administration won't be able to support itself because everyone they've trained properly will be offworld and we'll all…' Dr Mason trailed off. 'Sorry, Ntumbe. Soapbox time again.'

Ntumbe laughed. 'Not to worry, Doctor. If you didn't talk about it, I'd worry. Think you were sick or something. Nothing worse than a sick doctor, eh?'

Mason nodded and the cab glided through the gates of the Shuttle Dome. He pointed towards Bay Σ. With a nod of acknowledgment, Ntumbe turned the cab into the bay and Mason got out, hitching his holdall over his shoulder. He leaned back into the front of the cab, jabbed his card into the slot on Ntumbe's dash and winked slowly. He waited as the red light turned to green. It had recognised his retina print and accepted his credit transfer. With a cheery farewell wave, Ntumbe and his cab skittered away.

Mason wandered into the Dome entrance and started looking for the right queue for the shuttle. Twenty thousand years of civilisation, with wars, invasions, empires and declines – and still humankind queued for everything.

'Excuse me. Dr Mason? Miles Mason?'

Mason looked at the stranger who had touched his arm. He was no slouch when it came to alien species (which was just as well, bearing in mind where he was headed) but he simply didn't recognise the race of the person in the dark-grey uniform. It – he? – had a dark, bluish skin with a tinge of green, and a couple of tusks jutted out of yellow-spotted, membrane-lined, bloated cheeks. He couldn't spot a mouth (but, as the alien didn't appear to have trouble speaking, he assumed there was one somewhere) but the nose was an elephantine affair about thirty centimetres long. The eyes were two large red ovals that blinked slowly on a domed forehead. Mason acknowledged his identity, and the stranger offered a smallish hand, which Mason shook, cautiously.

'My name is Labus. I'm a huge fan of your work and –'

Mason whipped his hand away suddenly. It was burning – whatever this Labus's skin was made of, it wasn't designed for contact with humans. A thin greenish film covered his palm and he casually wiped it on his jacket. Labus (male, Mason decided) looked alarmed, and his trunk-like nose receded into his face, leaving a lumpy nodule in its place – which at least provided Mason with a view of Labus's tiny slit-like mouth. Mason then put his hand up, to show it wasn't damaged. 'I'm so sorry, Labus, but your skin is rather… warm to the touch. It took me by surprise, that's all.'

Labus seemed to relax. His trunk extended itself again, and his eyes seemed to widen a fraction, which Mason hoped was a sign of pleasure. Or, at least, not open hostility.

Labus indicated a nearby lounge. 'Could I buy you a coffee before your journey?'

'Well, I do need to check in…'

Labus produced a ticket from inside his grey jacket. 'Already taken care of.'

'Are you from Carrington Corp?'

Labus shook his head, and indicated his order to a service droid. 'Although I am affiliated to them. But yes, I have been sent to meet you. My… associates have followed your work in xenobiology with great interest.'

'Yes, well, some xenospecialist *I* am. First rule is "Don't whip your hand away rudely on first contact" – and I messed that up.'

Labus laughed, and Dr Mason found himself smiling. But his hand still stung somewhat.

The droid arrived with a jug of coffee and two cups. Labus poured and passed one to his guest. 'Tell me about your trip to Micawber's World, Dr Mason…'

Across the way, another figure watched the conversation with extreme interest.

At his feet was an attaché case. He lifted it and rested in on the table, deliberately aiming one corner at the conversation across the way. The tiny recorder inside couldn't possibly pick up the sound – even if it tried, the local ambience would drown it out too much and, no matter how good a job was done on filtering, they'd never be able to get a good enough recording. But at least by videoing the human doctor's side of the conversation, a degree of lip-reading would be possible back at the labs.

Someone was going to be paying him a lot of money for this information.

'You're not Suki Raymond!'

J. Garth Wilcox swallowed. A few seconds earlier, the thing facing him had been Suki Raymond, his loyal adjutant and personal assistant and secretary and dogsbody and gopher and...

And now she was a considerably larger green reptilian thing with rotating eyes, spiky whiskers and three-clawed hands.

'How astute of you to notice. Sadly, poor Ms R – how can I put this? – fell out of favour some weeks back.'

Wilcox frowned. 'Nonsense, she was here yesterday.'

'No. I was here yesterday. And the day before that. And before that. And –'

'Oh, God... Sunday night?'

'Oh yes, indeed. Oh that was certainly me. Oh wow, Mr Wilcox, just how do you humans do that thing with your –' Eerily, the inhuman... thing was speaking in Suki's voice. Some kind of vocoder no doubt.

Wilcox let his head fall into his hands and then let himself droop across his white vinyl desk. 'No, no, no, no,' he murmured, somehow trying to imagine that when he lifted his head up, his lovely neat office on the eighteenth floor of PharmaChem and Medico Inc. (Ganymede office) would be as it should be, with Suki Raymond sitting cross-legged on the white stool in front of him, tapping out notes on her little datapad, nodding serenely, and licking those very luscious lips every so often.

He looked up.

The room was in disarray. Drawers and filing cabinets were ripped open. His computer screen was cracked. The holos of his wife and two daughters were spluttering slightly as their combined function matrix was being disrupted by an upturned chair.

And facing him was every businessman's nightmare, green skin rippling with each breath, leaving a very slight damp patch on the carpet.

'How do you do it?' he asked eventually. The million other questions in his mind about how long his department had been infiltrated, how many secrets, deals and financial transactions were no longer confidential, how poor Suki had met her end and just how he had had sex with said green reptile last Sunday seemed bizarrely irrelevant at that moment. And far too awful to consider rationally – especially the last question.

'Our skeletons have hollow bones with double-joints every few centimetres. This means we can compact our natural forms quite comfortably inside a full replica-human bodysuit for up to eighteen hours at a time.' The creature sniggered. 'It's actually rather pleasant, like rolling in jelly for a while. Much of our body is liquid, our organs are small and our tails retract. Anything else you'd like to know? We're rather proud of our abilities. Makes industrial espionage so much more fun.'

'What did you do it for? Why do the Foamasi government need my department's secrets?'

The Foamasi sniggered again. 'Government? Do I look like a government representative, Mr Wilcox?'

'I… I don't know,' Wilcox whispered. 'I wouldn't know what a Foamasi government representative *should* look like.'

'No, I don't suppose you do. Rest assured, I'm not. I represent an… independent group very interested in acquiring a large piece of your business, Mr Wilcox. Subtly of course. No one need know. About our deal or last Sunday.' The Foamasi waddled across the room, its bulk making little noise as it did so, and flopped into a luxurious white leather armchair which swivelled. The Foamasi kicked with a clawed foot, sending itself spinning, seeing the whole glass-built office in one 360-degree turn. 'Wheeee! This is fun. D'you do this often, Mr Wilcox? Give yourself a good view of

Ganymede City from up here? Or did you do it as part of your most energetic frolics with the unfortunate Ms Raymond?'

Wilcox shook his head slowly. 'This can't be happening...'

Suddenly he was out of his seat – the Foamasi had crossed to him in a split second and was holding him against the glass with one paw, a claw pressing against his neck.

Wilcox could feel a stab of pain as the claw broke his skin.

'I'm getting bored now, Mr Wilcox. I have enough on you to bring your little empire down.' The Foamasi paused and cocked its head. 'Come to think of it, I've probably got enough to bring the whole company down, but your department will do. For now.' He dropped Wilcox back into his seat. 'All I want you to do is sign a document passing financial control over to poor Ms Raymond.'

'But she... she's dead?'

'I'm not. And, as you may have observed recently, I make a remarkably good replacement.' The Foamasi moved towards the door linking Wilcox's office with Ms Raymond's. 'You have twenty seconds, Mr Wilcox.' And with that the Foamasi was gone.

Think! J. Garth Wilcox, you did not get where you are today by not thinking. Should he tell head office and admit he had been duped? No, perhaps not. A quick call into the office of the Guardian of the Solar System? Get him to put his special agents on to the case? No, they probably had thousands of unsolved Foamasi cases pending. The Foamasi had spent ten centuries gaining the power and political sophistication that made them feared throughout the galaxy. The SSS didn't know where to begin.

God – what if his wife found out about last Sunday? What about the kids...?

Suki Raymond walked into his office from her own, smiling. Hell, the likeness was uncanny. The walk, the smile... But then, if this Foamasi had assumed her position so long ago, the smile and walk he recognised as hers were probably his. *Its!*

'Sign this, please, Mr Wilcox.' What looked like Suki held out a datapad. 'It confirms that financial dealings for PharmaChem and Medico Inc. (Ganymede office) now fall directly under my purview.'

Shakily, Wilcox pressed his thumb on the pad. A green light winked, indicating it recognised the signature.

'Now this one, please. This passes forty-nine per cent of the decision-making over to me. Any more than that, and people would become suspicious.'

'Like they won't anyway?'

The Foamasi laughed again. 'I've made sure that enough people are aware of our... torrid little dalliances, Mr Wilcox. Nothing you do will surprise them now.'

He signed, resignedly.

'And this one breaks your marriage contract with your wife. They will receive a healthy monthly payment from you, and it cites me – or Suki – as co-respondent in the cause for the breach. It also makes me your new wife, thus passing fifty per cent of everything you own to me as well.'

Without pausing, he signed.

'And finally, this one.'

'What is it?'

'Sign it,' the Foamasi shouted suddenly. Jumping, Wilcox thumbed it, as he had the others.

'That was your suicide note, Mr Wilcox. And, as your secretary, not only do I have that forty-nine per cent of the business but, as your new wife – or distraught widow – I inherit your shares, making me Director of this division *in absentia*.'

Wilcox let this sink in. 'My suicide note?'

'Goodbye, Mr Wilcox. Thank you again for Sunday. Most... charming.'

The Foamasi reached over and shoved Wilcox against the glass wall. As his head smacked against it, he heard a sound like a thunderbolt. Was it raining?

As the glass behind gave way and Wilcox felt the rush of wind around his ears, he looked up, and saw a glorious day, the artificial sun warming the city, the blue, cloudless skies reminding him of his childhood on Earth.

Then he hit the causeway eighteen storeys below.

Chapter Three
The Whole Price of Blood

Contemporaneous...

Dust.

Sam tutted. Just like, she realised rather disdainfully – and somewhat alarmingly – her mother.

She dragged another finger across a different TARDIS wooden surface. More dust.

She recalled that once upon a time, probably in a galaxy far, far away, the TARDIS's alleged owner, the Doctor, had commented that the TARDIS cleaned herself. Frequently. Sam could certainly remember more than one occasion when a cloud of smoke, accompanied by loud bangs and a few sparks, had gone off around the central console making the darkened interior look like bonfire night meets the ghost train. And within moments, the acrid smell was gone, the TARDIS having expelled the fumes, smoke and bits of broken wood and metal into the ether. Or the space-time vortex. Or wherever she expelled such things.

But now the TARDIS had a good coating of dust.

Sam wandered into the main console room and saw the Doctor slumped in his favourite easy chair. She was wearing one-piece overalls, stained with oil, petrol and a few splashes of water. In her breast pocket was the Doctor's sonic screwdriver, an adjustable spanner and a broken spark plug. Sam carried a tool-box in her right hand and a broken gearbox in her left, dripping oil on to the polished wood floor. No doubt there would be a stern word or two about that later.

A steady clicking noise nearby told her that once again the Doctor had fallen asleep playing his old vinyl records. Sam had given up trying to get him to invest in a Bang and Olufsen digital sound system a long time ago. After all, the scratchy black records did have a certain charm about them, much like the TARDIS itself. For all its wooden surfaces, springs and levers, brass adornments and Heath Robinson stylistic touches, she knew that it was one of the most fantastically futuristic space craft imaginable.

Even now, she could still remember the awe, not to mention initial disbelief, that something resembling an old police box out of *Dixon of Dock Green* could really be infinitely bigger on the inside than out and travel through time and space.

But what the hell! In the three months since she had become reunited with the Doctor after her 'short break' (his words) on Ha'olam, they'd had a few short holidays, visited a dozen or so museums and nipped back to Tudor England to return a lace handkerchief the Doctor said he accidentally nicked when he'd been older.

Sam was no longer the young schoolgirl she had been when the Doctor first took her away from Shoreditch, but she still hadn't lost her excitement at seeing new things and places. The freedom they shared, the ability to travel anywhere in time and space, well... it was something she promised herself she wouldn't take for granted again.

'Hello?' She poked at the sleeping Doctor with the gearbox.

To all intents and purposes he was a human male in his midthirties, possibly from somewhere north of Watford Gap. He had long, wavy, light-brown hair, beautiful eyes that seemed to change colour with the tides and a nicely structured bony face.

Oh, there had been times...

The Doctor woke up, and smiled at Sam. And at such close range, Sam couldn't help but be swamped by those eyes, which were like curtains to the universe, the link which said that, despite the physical appearance, the Doctor was old, wise and experienced. A Time Lord, who knew more than most, cared more than most and tried harder than everyone.

'Good morning, Sam. You're up early.'

Sam sighed. 'It's teatime, according to the TARDIS clock. You wanted to be woken at teatime, remember?'

He peered at her left hand. 'What is that?'

'The gearbox from the Beetle. Sneaky of you, moving it into the garage back there.' She tossed her head back, letting her still-growing hair flap in the general direction that she meant.

'My Beetle, young lady, has a brand-new automatic transmission. While you were away, I had it serviced. Whatever you have there is not its gearbox.'

Sam looked at the lump of metal in her hand. 'Ah... I thought it seemed a bit odd. Some of the connections didn't seem to make sense. I thought you'd done your usual jury-rigging and cocked up again.' She gave the Doctor a big smile. 'What if I said "Oh, whoops" and we pretended this conversation never happened?'

The Doctor removed the sonic screwdriver from her pocket, inspected it, then slowly returned it. 'And I thought we talked about making you one of these for your own use, eh?'

'And I'm still waiting. But I wanted something to do and teach-yourself-motor-mechanics seemed fun. Besides, you've got stacks of books on it, so I can't go wrong if I follow the instructions. To the letter.'

The Doctor was up instantly, long legs carrying him across the room towards the TARDIS console. He reached the databank portion of the console and twisted a small dial. Behind him, the vast library of books which seemed to stretch away into the depths of the TARDIS was illuminated.

He stared into the library. 'You've been helping her, haven't you?' he said, apparently to no one. 'When I wanted to play with cars and hovercraft and motorbikes all those years ago, you couldn't have been less helpful if you'd tried.'

The lights dimmed slightly. The Doctor cleared his throat. 'Yes. Well, apology accepted.' He turned back and looked at Sam from across the TARDIS console. 'Just don't try working on the TARDIS, all right?'

Sam pretended to agree. Trying to understand how the TARDIS worked fascinated her, and learning car mechanics was actually just the first step on the ladder to finding out how to repair it. *Her*. And to do all the things the Doctor always said he'd get round to but never did.

Sam stroked the TARDIS console. She never tired of trying to understand it, or being delighted by its simple beauty – especially as each of the six sides was reflected by a themed area just off the main room, a design she considered very practical and, rather like the Doctor, decidedly eccentric. For instance, the co-ordinate panel was opposite a massive wall of clocks, each of different shape, size and format. The panel that detailed their destination was overlooked by an ornate archway with a small pebbled area, complete with park bench, ornamental fountain and a small church organ. Other walls included a huge filing cabinet and a blank wall, against which rested the bust of some old man the Doctor reverently referred to as Rassilon. He seemed to be some figure out of Time Lord history who was both beloved and feared by today's Time Lords. Somehow Sam had gathered he was a mate of the Doctor's as well, but she didn't want to begin trying to figure that one out.

Sam didn't understand much about the console. The Doctor had told her the rudiments of programming co-ordinates in, and how to open the door ('after checking the atmosphere outside'). And she knew how to slide the domed ceiling back to reveal a marvellous holographic matrix screen which could display whatever you wanted to see on it.

She did so, just to find out where they were.

The familiar blue-and-gold infinity – a multitude of stars, planets, asteroids and space – told her nothing. After all the time she and the Doctor had been friends, she could recognise the odd star system just by looking for recognisable constellations or tell-tale planets, but their current location was a mystery. They were simply parked in space.

'I suppose if we got in the way of a Number 9 galactic tour bus, the TARDIS would move herself away,' she muttered.

'Of course she would.' The Doctor emerged from his library, which accordingly plunged itself back into darkness, robbing Sam of the view of the endless racks of books and datafiles in there.

'Got it!' He held up a small blue paperback triumphantly. 'Knew I still had a copy.'

Putting down the tools and the gearbox that wasn't a gearbox, Sam took it, glancing at the front. '*How to be a Best Man and Ensure the Wedding Goes Well in a Hundred Easy Lessons*.' Sam laughed. 'Who's getting hitched?'

'Two dear friends of mine. I haven't seen them for a while.'

Sam raised an eyebrow. 'Anyone I know?'

'No. No, I don't think so. They... travelled with me for a few months.'

'How long ago?'

'Ah. Well. Promise you won't get upset?'

Sam's other eyebrow raised. 'Oh yes? This sounds good.'

'Remember not long after we first met, and I dropped you off at that Greenpeace rally in Canada?'

'Uh-huh.'

The Doctor smiled. Sheepishly. 'Well, you know that while only a few hours passed for you –'

'You'd been gone nearly a year of your time. Yes, I remember.'

'Well, I met them then.' The Doctor took the book back. 'After we parted, they stayed together. Very romantic. I suppose.'

Sam smiled. Once upon a time – probably not that long ago as far as the Doctor was concerned – she'd have been upset. Jealous even that someone else encroached on her time with the Doctor. Took away its uniqueness. Now? Now that was then. Sam was pleased with herself actually. The Doctor had been aware that she'd had a bit of a crush on him back then, but that had now comfortably turned into something better. Deeper. A real friendship based on trust, reliance and good fortune. Forged in the fires of... well, of all sorts of things, not least adversity, or whatever that old saying was.

'So, just what did you get up to at that time? Who are these people?'

The Doctor shrugged. 'Met up with some old friends. Saved Earth from alien invaders. Hung around with an old archaeology chum. And at some point met Stacy and Ssard.'

'Ssard?'

'A Martian. An Ice Warrior. Nice chap, very proper. Make Stacy a wonderful husband.'

'Having kids'll be fun, I'd say.'

'Stacy can't. Side-effect of something that happened while we were travelling.' The Doctor frowned at the memory.

'Hey, does she blame you for that?'

'No. No, I don't think so. Why?'

Sam shrugged. 'You obviously do. If she's getting married to this Ssard bloke and they want you to be the best man, there's obviously no problem. Let's go.'

'Are you sure you don't mind? I could drop you off somewhere and then nip back and pick you up afterwards.'

Sam laughed. 'That embarrassing, am I? Likely to eat all the jelly and ice-cream then burp loudly when they ask for any just cause to stop the wedding?'

The Doctor looked horrified. 'No! Nothing like that. I just thought –'

Sam tapped his nose with the book. 'I haven't had the

opportunity to get dressed up in... well, years. Where are we going?'

The Doctor produced an invitation from his inside pocket. 'Micawber's World, it says here.' He reached over to the console and pressed a couple of buttons. Sam looked up as the hologram shifted to another part of the galaxy, focused briefly on one area and then zoomed in. A small grey planet took 3-D shape up there, and some text she couldn't read because it was in Gallifreyan scrawl began running up the side.

'Translation?'

The Doctor nodded. 'Well, basically, Micawber's World is an artificial planet, built around a tiny asteroid, tripling its size. It's one of the Leisure Planets, and according to Professor Thripstead's *Guide to Having Fun in the Milky Way*, it's one of the most sought-after holiday locations in the galaxy.' He screwed his eyes up a bit. 'It hovers just between Pluto and Cassius and –' he reached out to the switches and twisted and twiddled a bit more – 'in the time frame we want, it is owned by Carrington Corp.'

The Doctor reread the invitation, then the scrolling text above them. 'Ah, good timing, Stacy.' He smiled at Sam. 'It's playing host to the Galactic Olympic Games right now.'

'Right now being?'

'Late July, 3999.'

'Earth time?'

'Ah, you see, by now Earth is the centre of the Galactic Federation and so, without too much bother, the rest of the galaxy has adopted Earth's dating system. Most places even operate on the basis of a traditional twenty-four-hour clock.'

'Who set up the Federation then?' Sam thought this was quite interesting. A hint that peace had finally been realised, even if it was a few thousand years too late for her liking.

'Oh, you'll enjoy it, Sam. Set up by Earth, where the central administration is based, overseen by the rather pompously named Guardian of the Solar System.'

'If it's a federation, why does it need a guardian as well?'

Sam smiled as the Doctor put his hands behind his back. It was a sign that he was about to go all teacherly on her and pass on his wisdom and impart his knowledge. A couple of years ago that would have annoyed her, too much like 'old Pain' in her maths class, but now Sam found it quite endearing.

'Consider it similar to the United Nations on Earth. The Galactic Federation is there to protect, preserve and serve, while attempting to bring all the planets under one common roof. But the Guardian is like, say, your American President, Billy: he's associated with the Federation but Guardian of a subset, in this case your solar system.' Sam could see he was enjoying his own lecture as well. 'And rather like President Clinton,' he continued, the Guardian has his fingers in many pies around the place, making him slightly more important to the galaxy than, say, the Admin-proctor of Earth or the Colonial Deputy of the Mars colonies, who are more akin to the Thatchers, Chiracs and Mandelas of your time. Are you following this?'

'Oh absolutely, Doctor. It's fascinating. Please tell me more.'

The Doctor gave her a look through half-closed eyes, as if daring her to poke fun more obviously, so he could be sure of her irreverence. 'The Federation's headquarters are on Io, which has become a wonderful sort of interspecies university. The whole kit and caboodle is based on the idea of people spending all their time just being awfully nice to each other. Shall we go?'

'Sounds delightful, Doctor. Give me chance to find something splendid to wear and I promise not to catch the bouquet when Stacy chucks it away.'

The Doctor smiled at her. 'Of course. Be there in, oh, ten minutes?'

'Give me twenty. Got to look my very best if we're going

somewhere where everyone is "awfully nice to each other", OK?'

'Are you scared of the dark?'

Cartwright sniggered. 'Yeah, and I put it on the application form. That's why I'm here.'

But Salt was serious. 'Some people are just frightened of it. Some are frightened of heights. Or spiders. Or hypos. Irrational fears – everyone has one.'

Cartwright eyed his companion with a mixture of sardonicism and impatience. 'You're weird, Ed. Real weird. C'mon, we've some mapping to do.'

Ed Salt shrugged, and stepped aside as Cartwright shoved past him. Cartwright nipped down the slender rock passage, slapping one halogen lamp against both sides of the wall every five metres, just as he'd been doing for three hours now. With a shrug, Salt aimed a tiny instrument at each one as he passed, rotating his body with practised movements in the confined space, activating each one remotely, testing its eight-year battery source. Naturally, each one lit up and stayed lit as he followed Cartwright. Space Security Force halogen lamps never went wrong. Space Security ensured that no piece of equipment, no matter how large or small, ever became faulty. It just didn't happen. Procedures ensured that nothing left Stores without being given a one-hundred-per-cent guarantee of lifetime success – it was the way things worked in Space Security.

So both Salt and Cartwright were somewhat surprised when a couple of the halogen lamps some way behind them went out.

'Hey, Jaypee, did you see that?'

Cartwright shrugged. 'Maybe they fell off the walls. Perhaps we've been given the wrong type of magnetic clamps.'

Salt pulled one of the lamps out of Cartwright's satchel, examined it and shook his head. 'Nope. The right design for the iron ore in these walls.' He looked back and sighed. 'Guess we'd better try and refit them or the techs will be whinging for the next three weeks.'

Cartwright grunted knowingly. 'Yeah, and we'll have the unions bleating as well.'

The two men slowly trudged back up the tunnel, heads bowed as it was too small to stand comfortably upright.

'I hate this work, Ed. Have I told you that?'

'A few trillion times, JayPee, yeah.'

Salt reached down and picked up the nearest fallen lamp. He shone his torch at the back, trying to see why the magnetic clamp was faulty.

Nothing. No sign of decay or damage. No reason at all why it should fall off.

'Unless someone deliberately yanks 'em down, these things should stay up for years.' Cartwright said what was going through Salt's mind.

Salt nodded. 'Weird, JayPee. Well weird.'

Shrugging as if it really didn't matter, Cartwright shoved another dropped light back against the wall. It stayed tight.

And then, further on, where they had stopped a few minutes earlier, the last set of lights they had put up went out. Or fell off. Or whatever. Behind them, another load went out.

The two soldiers were in darkness bar the one light Cartwright had replaced and Salt's flashlight.

'Jean-Paul?' Salt spoke quietly. 'Jean-Paul, would this be a good moment to tell you I'm quite freaked out by this?'

But Jean-Paul Cartwright said nothing. He was listening, holding his hand up for silence. Salt frowned. He could hear it, too. A shuffling, sort of scraping sound.

From behind them and in front. Moving towards them. Boxing them in.

'I thought this place was deserted,' Cartwright said pointlessly.

Salt did not answer. He was pulling his night goggles from his satchel and holding them up to his eyes.

And seeing what was making the noise.

Quartermaster-Sergeant Dallion waved impatiently at Agent Clarke. 'Peter, how are things going?' she asked.

Clarke shuffled over, wearing the portable mass detector like a papoose on his chest and tapped on the tiny keypad. A hologramatic globe appeared to hover just above the PMD, a series of tiny white spots moving slowly under its surface.

'Bailey and McGeoch are in Sector Seven, Sarge. Smith and McKay in Sector Eight, with Morris and Pirroni in Four.' Clarke frowned suddenly. 'That's odd, Sarge.'

'What is, Agent?'

'Well, Cartwright and Salt ought to be in Sector Two, but they're not registering.'

Dallion shrugged. 'Two's right down near the core, Pete. Could well be shielded from the PMD.'

Clarke nodded slowly. 'I guess so.'

Dallion took a long drag on her cigarette and leaned her chin on her hunched-up knees. She, Clarke and a couple of the others were pretty bored of waiting by the borehole entrances. It was all very well for SSS Admin to request them, but she wanted something to do. Sending her agents down tunnels to put lights up seemed a hell of a waste of resources. She and the others were well trained, forged together as a fighting unit. OK, so wars weren't exactly common these days, but nevertheless they'd spent a lot of time earning their famous black uniforms. Rummaging around tunnels didn't seem a productive deployment of human resources.

They were sitting on a ridge inside the planet, waiting by the first of five boreholes down which her men had gone. The ridge stretched back the way they had come and quite some way into the gloom in front. It was quite a wide ridge, and about four metres deep, which was just as well since the drop immediately in front of them had no visible bottom. And although Dallion knew it must have, she also knew it was a pretty hard one, far enough down to turn a falling human soldier into a red puddle.

As a result, she and the agents were pressed against the rock wall behind them. To her left Klein and McCarrick were playing chess, with holographic Mayorga versus Gamarra, while their cook, Carruthers, was adding boiled water to tiny capsules and still managing to make the food taste better than it did at HQ. That just left Fenton, who had gone back to the surface to radio HQ – their carrier beam was too distorted under the rock.

'Maybe it's like the radio,' she murmured. It was to herself really, but Clarke, nodding and fussing around his machine as if it was his own personal baby, disagreed. 'No, Sarge. This thing should work in any locale. Especially as the guys are all wearing tracers.'

He gasped suddenly. 'This is ridiculous!'

Dallion caught the tone of his voice and was beside the hologram globe in a second. 'What now, Pete?'

'Well… well, I've lost Pirroni and Morris now.'

Dallion tapped her wrist communicator. 'Dallion to Pirroni, come in please?'

Nothing.

'Dallion to Pirroni. Dallion to Morris. Come in!'

Nothing.

Carruthers was there now. He tried his own. 'Carruthers to Pirroni. Marco, are you there?'

By now even Klein and McCarrick had given up their game and were trying to raise their comrades.

A curse from Clarke sent a shiver down Dallion's spine. 'Who now?'

'Bailey and McGeoch.'

Klein adjusted his communicator. 'Klein to Bailey. Are you there, Steven? John, can you hear us?'

Two more lights winked out on the globe. Dallion didn't even ask. 'Smith? McKay?'

Nothing.

Klein shrugged. 'No one else is down here, surely?'

Clarke shook his head. 'If they are, they're not only shielded from the PMD, but they're shielding our guys too.'

'Is that possible?'

Carruthers was frowning. 'Surely the portable mass detector can't be blindsided?'

Clarke threw his hands up in despair. 'God knows. I mean, it's hardly top of the range equipment these days. Yeah, it's possible.'

'How?'

'Like chucking a blanket over you, really. Something that can't be registered on our stuff covers up our guys, so we can't read them.'

'But –' Dallion was stony-faced – 'as you said, no one else is down there.'

McCarrick tried not to let his panic show. 'No one we're aware of, anyhow.'

Dallion stood up, pulling her blaster from its holster and checking the charge. The others did the same.

'Carruthers, you and Clarke stay here.' She looked at Clarke. 'Monitor us, Pete. We'll keep talking all the way.' She indicated the second borehole. 'Smith and McKay were nearest, we'll try there first.'

McCarrick led the way, followed by Dallion, with Klein nervously bringing up the rear, doing periodic 360-degree turns as Carruthers and Clarke watched them dwindle into the darkness.

'Shouldn't there be lights down that tunnel?' muttered Carruthers. 'I thought that's what the guys were doing down there.'

Pete Clarke didn't answer. He was too busy listening to the constant reports coming in from QS Dallion, and watching the tiny spots on the hologlobe that marked their progress. And praying to God that they didn't suddenly cut out.

* * *

Reverend Lukas gently laid his hand on Phillipa Iley's shoulder. Behind them were the clean, white buildings of the spaceport.

'Do you feel better for our walk, child?'

She nodded.'Much, Father. I find travelling so far unpleasant. It is so much better to arrive in a place, somewhere new, ready to do the Goddess's work.'

'Indeed,' smiled Reverend Lukas, indulgently, a hand smoothing out the folds of his long, black robe.'Indeed.'

A young man, hitching up his own robe with one hand, trying to keep his hat on with the other, was hurrying towards them.

'Is there a fire, Jolyon?'

'No, Father.'

'Then is this haste necessary? It is not seemly to serve the Goddess in a way so undignified.'

Jolyon Tuck bowed his head slightly, catching his breath. 'Forgive me, Father. I apologise, but I felt you should know that the wedding has been brought forward a day. It takes place tomorrow.'

Reverend Lukas absorbed this information, smiling. 'Excellent. We should be able to perform the Goddess's bidding and be on our way to another crusade within a few days.' He nodded as he saw Jolyon take Phillipa's hand affectionately.'I shall retire to my quarters and prepare for the ceremony we are to perform tomorrow. In the meantime I shall leave you two to enjoy the sights of this world.'

Phillipa and Jolyon smiled their gratitude and walked off. Reverend Lukas picked up his suitcase and walked towards the accommodation end of Carrington City, searching for the low-rate rooms he had hired for himself and his small flock. With the two youngsters off enjoying themselves, he only had to wait for Kyle Dale and his group and they would all be there, ready for the big day.

It did not take long for Reverend Lukas to navigate the well-laid-out streets and pathways, past the green grassy knolls, beautiful fountains and gleaming buildings, before he found his hotel, the Mirage. Before entering, he glanced back at the section of Carrington City he was in.

'Truly a Utopia for the next millennium,' he said. 'Such a tragedy.'

Removing his hat, he hoisted up his robes and climbed the few steps to the glass doors, which slid open to admit him. He crossed the polished floors to the reception area in the centre.

Around him, lush green plants dotted the floor and entranceways to the elevators. He could see through the smoked glass walls the glass tubes that connected the upper levels with the other areas. A cool breeze was artificially pumped across the vast room, a welcome respite from the slightly humid air of the city outside. Artificial energy sources were all very well but even in these days of such so-called miracles, they still couldn't get the weather perfect.

'Good afternoon, ma'am,' he said to the receptionist. 'My name is Lukas. Reverend Lukas. I believe I have a suite of rooms in Delta Sector booked in the name of the Church of the Way Forward.'

The receptionist, her burnt-orange skin and three stubby fingers clearly marking her as a Cantryan, tapped her keyboard. A series of numbers appeared in the air between them and she nodded as they appeared.

'Suite 904, Father.' She glanced at a set of smaller numbers, and then pointed to them. 'Your credit will run out in five days, I'm afraid.'

'Not a problem, ma'am. We will be leaving the evening after next, if that's all right. We'll be transferring to the Olympic barracks, then.'

The receptionist adjusted the booking. 'Not a problem, Father. We hope you enjoy your stay. If you require any of the services we offer, a full description of how to get them is in the suite's datapad. When do you expect the others in your party to arrive?'

Reverend Lukas smiled. 'In their own time, but before supper tonight. I will remain in the suite until we are all gathered.'

'Do you require a booking in one of the restaurants?'

Reverend Lukas shook his head. 'We will travel to the poor sector and help there in one of the gratuity kitchens.'

The receptionist frowned, then smiled. 'Oh, I see. But actually, Father, there are no poor sectors in Carrington City. Nor gratuity kitchens. No need for them – everyone here has everything they need.'

Reverend Lukas took this in. 'I see. Truly the Utopia the brochures promise. In that case, we will order some small amount of fresh fruit and vegetables in our suite.' With that he took the tiny ID card the receptionist held out and headed for the elevator that would take him to Delta Area.

Everything was just perfect.

The church was not exactly what Stacy Townsend had in mind when she planned the wedding, but as neither she nor Ssard could afford the space flight to Earth or New Mars, Micawber's World was a good substitute.

Ssard was sitting on a pew, flicking through a brochure, grumbling pretty much as usual. Stacy knew this was a good sign – Ssard was happy and content only when there was something, no matter how insignificant, to grumble about.

'Why they cannot supply electronic brochures, I cannot understand,' he hissed.

Stacy draped herself over his shoulder, squeezing the outer body shell tightly, knowing that the pressure would transfer to the softer reptilian skin beneath, sending all sorts of tingles through Ssard's body. Not that he acknowledged this very often, but Stacy knew, and that was enough for her. She loved this large, hulking reptile to death. Green scales, silly helmet ('A Martian must look ready for action at all times,' he had said when she suggested he take it off now and again) and all.

'It's part of the charm of the Church State, Ssard. Tradition. You of all people should understand tradition.'

Sensing he was flummoxed by the logic, an amused Stacy released her grip and moved around the pew to drop on to her knees before his. 'Please, I know Christianity means nothing to you, but my faith is, well, important to me. And bearing in mind neither of us actually comes from this era – thank you, Doctor – I need something to hold on to. It means a lot to me if we can be married by a priest in a Christian church. I just wish my parents were here to see it all. They'd have loved all this. And you.'

Ssard nodded. 'I understand, Stacy. This is all a little strange, that is all.'

Stacy smiled. They had had this conversation before. On New Mars, marriage was a brief ceremony, established when the participants were young, and predetermined. Keeping bloodlines pure and all that. Pretty medieval in Stacy's view but in the few years she and Ssard had continued their lives as part of this Galactic Federation, she had learned that the sheer diversity of cultures, races and creeds made the galaxy seem a much larger and far more interesting place. Stacy was working in an office on Antares, sorting out applications from the outer planets wishing to join the Federation. Ssard had a job in the Martian Commission on Io, helping locate some of the fringe Martian groups who wanted out of the peaceful coexistence that Martians shared with the Federation members and demanding a return to their independent, even warlike, past. As someone who originally came from that past, Ssard had some sympathies with the groups, but nevertheless rationalised that living in the fortieth century meant fitting in with the modern way. Stacy always reminded him about Romans in Rome, but knew Ssard hadn't the foggiest idea what she was talking about.

Now they had travelled to Micawber's World, where one of the few off-Earth Christian churches had been built by Carrington Corp and hired out for traditional weddings.

The tall building, constructed entirely from stained glass, was not quite the olde-worlde stone church Stacy had envisioned getting hitched in, but what the heck! It would serve the purpose nicely.

'Hello, Stacy.'

She did not turn around immediately, although the smile that broke across her face was heartfelt. She had played this scene through her mind so many times...

She let out a breath and then turned. 'Hello, Doctor. You haven't changed.' She hurried to him and gave him a massive hug. 'Still as punctual as ever.'

'We've missed it?' the Doctor was aghast.

'No, silly. You're early!'

Ssard saluted the Doctor, right arm across chest. The Doctor returned the greeting, offering a slight bow as well. 'Ssard, how are you?'

'I am very well, thank you, Doctor. It is a... pleasure to see you again.'

The Doctor coughed. 'We're not early, actually. We wanted to have a look around the Olympic Stadium.'

'We?'

'Yeah, "we".' Stacy watched as a young woman walked into the church behind the Doctor. She was quite tall, shoulder-length blonde hair parted in the centre, wearing an all-in-one beige tracksuit, and carrying a small satchel. She wasn't stunningly attractive, nor was she plain. In fact she was, Stacy was pleased to note, frighteningly average. Rather like her.

Stacy smiled. 'You're Samantha Jones?'

Sam's eyebrows raised. 'Yeah. Right. How did you... Oh, I get it. He told you about me when you travelled together, right?'

Stacy nodded. 'But he said you were... younger.'

'I was. I've been on this gig a while now.'

Stacy nodded, offering her hand. 'Time travel, eh? Who needs it. Life's confusing enough as it is.'

'Too right, Stacy. Good to meet you. How long since you last saw the Guv'nor, then?'

'Just about two years, give or take a few months. Oh, Sam, it's so good to meet you at last.'

The two women slowly walked away from the Doctor and Ssard, who seemed to be swapping stories already, and headed further into the church. After a few moments of idle chit-chat about Micawber's World, Stacy glanced back at the Doctor.

'How is he? Really.'

Sam shrugged. 'OK, for the most part. Gets a few moods, but on the whole, he's all right.'

'Part and parcel of the hero bag, I suppose. Cosmic angst and all that.' Stacy sighed. Remembering...

'Yeah,' Sam agreed. 'But he's strong. He gets through it all. Always there with the right words, the soft shoulder and the fresh Kleenex to cry into.' Sam smiled. 'He's pretty damn fab, actually.'

Stacy smiled. 'You know, I thought I loved him once. Thought he was the greatest thing since sliced bread. He saved my life and I transferred so much on to him. Don't tell Ssard – he wouldn't see it as the innocent thing it was.'

'Really?'

'Yeah. How about you?'

Sam paused, then grinned. 'Nah. Not my type.'

Stacy just nodded knowingly. 'Yeah. Right.'

Another pause and then the two new friends burst into laughter. 'Oh, all right, then,' Sam admitted. 'A slight crush. I mean, really minuscule. Like atom-sized, OK? But don't tell him.'

Stacy shook her head. 'My lips are sealed. Honest. But I'm glad he's got you around. Keep him in order. When we parted, I said to Ssard that my only regret was not being sure how he'd cope alone. I should have known he would have gone back to collect you. He talked about you a lot.'

Sam seemed to glow at this. 'Really? Cool. He missed you two a lot as well, you know. That's why I'm glad we came, I wanted to meet you. I've heard… so much about you in the last few years.'

Stacy threw an arm around Sam's shoulder. 'That's nice. I often wondered if he'd bother mentioning our time together. Wasn't that long really.' Stacy hugged Sam a bit tighter. 'This is going to be fun, you know. It's a small service – we still don't have many friends out here, but the ones we have are good. I'm glad we can add you to the list.'

Sam nodded happily. 'Yeah. It's going to be great.'

Events Co-ordinator Sumner was fretting. Why did nothing go as planned for him? What gods had conspired to not only give him this appointment which he never really wanted (only filled in the application form because the fire-breathing man-munching dragon he called 'the wife' told him to) but also to ensure it was a living nightmare.

'Mr Sumner? The latest tourist activity reports.'

Sumner stretched out a thin hand (my God, when did I last eat?) to take the datapad from his obsequious, but very efficient, assistant, Madox.

Madox was typical of the clerical and service personnel supplied by the Federation. Tall, bald, beaky nose and wearing a long blue smock that hung from his permanently hunched shoulders down to his ankles. Madox rarely smiled, rarely expressed an opinion and ate even less than Sumner. Madox was one of a cloned species, the Teknix, as they were known. Sumner found them creepy and unpleasant to be around. They spoke little, smiled less and, Sumner was convinced, had an aroma of staleness about them. Did they sleep? Did they need to?

Sumner wasn't given to paranoia, but he still held a belief that in many ways the Teknix were employed not so much by the Federation, but directly by the office of the Guardian. His eyes and ears. Always listening and looking for knowledge to pass on for political reasons.

Madox waited for Sumner to tap in his signature code and began to walk away with the datapad.

'Hold up,' Sumner said quietly. 'Madox, let me see the visitor data again, will you?'

There was barely a breath before Madox was beside him again, the relevant data on the pad's screen. Sumner scrolled through the characters.

'This one.' He pointed at a file. 'Bit odd, isn't it? What are they doing on Micawber's World right now?'

'I shall ascertain, Co-ordinator.' Madox wandered off again.

Which left Sumner staring out of his office window at the verdant plazas below. The beautiful spires and domes of Carrington City, reflecting the artificial light from their glazed walls and roofs, towered over the tiny blobs of people moving around the walkways and glass tubes connecting the buildings. The odd taxi flew around the parking lots, delivering passengers to offices, hotels, ports and the like. Carrington City seemed like a paradise.

But Sumner had a sinking feeling that the forthcoming Olympiad may well change that, especially as *they* were on the planet.

The Doctor found Sam sitting in a park about an hour later, throwing small pebbles into a fountain.

'Penny for them?'

Sam didn't look up. 'What, the stones?' The Doctor just kept looking at her and she sighed. 'I like Stacy and Ssard, you know. She's got her head screwed on tight and, as green guys with scales go, I reckon Ssard's going to make her happy.'

'But?' The Doctor sat on the ground beside her, not catching her eye, but fiddling with some blades of long grass.

Sam sighed. 'But I had to lie to her.' She threw a pebble with more force than she intended, and it bounced out of the fountain and towards the pathway. A woman walking some strange pet muttered a curse, gave Sam a filthy look and walked on. 'You told her about me. Hell, you even told her where the demo was that you left me at. The smallest details. You know, she even knew that I came from East London, right?'

'Right.'

'You never talked about them to me. I told her you did, that you enthused about them as much as you do about chrono-displacement theories, interstellar cartography and the value of Majusian gold bricks to the Talute dynasties. But, Doctor, you *didn't*. You never even acknowledged their existence. I mean, they *were* travelling with you for almost a year. But when I came back, their rooms were empty. There was nothing to tell me that someone else had lived beside you all that time.' She slumped back on her elbows, and stared at the sky. 'I seriously considered staying on Ha'olam, you know. But if I had, would you have emptied me out of your life as easily? Would my room, my belongings, be locked away somewhere so that the next Sam, the next Stacy, the next whoever, would be unaware of *me*?'

'I'm sorry I never told you about Stacy and Ssard.' The Doctor was still picking at the long grass. 'My judgement at the time was that you didn't need to hear it. As time went by, it just became, well, irrelevant. I apologise, not just for the omission, but for making you lie to Stacy. And thank you for doing so. I sadly find it very easy to forget that in a life as long as mine has been, the people I meet are often changed by our adventures, sometimes not always for the best. I will promise to think about that more. And Sam?'

'Yeah?'

'I will always remember you even if the next Sam or Stacy or Victoria or Tegan doesn't.'

'Victoria? Tegan? Who the hell... Oh, never mind.' Sam lay back on the grass and closed her eyes. 'I'm just making mountains out of molehills, as usual. Ignore me.'

'OK!' said the Doctor cheerily. He stood up, brushing down his frock coat. 'I want to go shopping. Get some trinkets and meaningless baubles to commemorate the Olympics. Coming?'

Sam kept her eyes closed. 'I want to get Stacy a wedding gift. Something special. For all her happiness, she's feeling a bit... displaced. Know what I mean?'

The Doctor frowned slightly. 'Not entirely, no. Sorry.'

Sam shrugged. 'This isn't her time, her era. She's been legitimately dead for, what, fifteen hundred odd years? As far as I can see, that doesn't matter so much to Ssard, but Stacy misses her friends, her family. You're the only person apart from Ssard she has any real links to. Well, and me by default.'

'Go on.'

'Well... Oh I don't know. I just think she deserves something special. Something to make her feel more... human? More like she's really getting married. More connected I suppose. For all their love, Stacy must feel a bit as if they've eloped and got married in some Los Angeles We-Marry-U-Kwik church.'

'How about this?'

Sam lazily opened one eye and stared up at what the Doctor was holding. Two figures, holding hands, woven from the long grass, like corn dollies. They were unmistakably Stacy and Ssard. She laughed.

'I used to think you were a magician, you know. All this crap about science – never seen you near a test tube or Petri dish for more than a few moments. Only magicians could create spaceships bigger on the inside than out. Only magicians could take me to Victorian London or twenty-second-century Borneo.

And only a magician could create something as beautiful as that in five minutes.' Sam got up and took the sculpture, placing it carefully in her satchel. 'Thank you, but I'll tell them it's from the both of us.'

'As you wish, Sam, as you wish.'

Sam suddenly gave him a hug. 'I know I'm being selfish, Doctor, but I don't want to be forgotten. By you or anyone. Ever.'

'Immortality often has a high price, Sam. But I'll see what I can do.' He smiled at her. 'Now, let's go and magic up some Federation credits from the TARDIS ATM and hit those stores!'

Chapter Four
Throw Them to The Lions

'The Foamasi are a legitimate business consortium. There is nothing we can do to keep them out of the Games, sir.'

'Legitimately.'

'Legitimately. And, for that matter, illegitimately. The Foamasi do not make mistakes, sir.'

Chase Carrington sighed and deleted the letter he had been composing from his datapad.

Ms Sox, his companion, personal assistant, secretary, masseuse and confidante, tried to look sympathetic. This was not easy because, although she had a great deal of respect and admiration for Carrington, each time she actually looked at him, she felt... well, disappointed. Something to do with his abnormally egg-shaped head with a few tufts of grey... growth (well you couldn't really call it hair) at the apex. He wore silly little round glasses and had a perfect set of regrown teeth that gleamed unnaturally white and thus made him look more comical than attractive. Couple this with the brown liver spots that dotted his pale complexion and Ms Sox could never entirely shake off the concept of an aging Humpty Dumpty just waiting to fall. He was dressed, as he was every day, in a black pinstripe suit, double-breasted, the lack of collar being his only commitment to current fashion. Ms Sox had not seen his feet this morning but could guarantee that he wore light-brown loafers which someone had, presumably as a cruel joke, told him went well with the dark suit. No one at Carrington Corp quite had the courage to tell him otherwise. Including Ms Sox. Putting a brave face on things, she punched a couple of things up on her pad. 'But there is some good news, sir.'

'Oh, joy.'

'Yes, your acquisition of Grecian Corp has gone through successfully at last. The entire company is now a subsidiary of Carrington Corp. We have absorbed their debts easily, repaid the outstanding consumers and look to make eight times the purchase price from our marketing of their major asset.'

'The Olympics?'

'Indeed, the Olympics.' Ms Sox had allowed Carrington to fill that detail in by himself. It might make his day a bit more bearable to keep repeating those words, like some kind of money-making mantra. 'We now have all copyrights, trademarks and registrations related to the Olympics. On top of the money we normally make per month simply by renting out this place, we are in for a bit of a windfall over the next twelve months.'

By 'this place' Ms Sox was referring to the planet they were on, Micawber's World, the artificial satellite Carrington Corp had constructed to which thousands flocked every month to use its enormous resort facilities. In Ms Sox's opinion, something of a goldmine.

'What of the Grecian Corp board? I never liked that chairwoman. Did we manage to get rid of any... surplus stock?'

Ms Sox smiled delightedly. She didn't have much time for the Grecian Corp boss either. 'Eight of the board resigned immediately, including Mrs Nikolas. The other four were absorbed into various boards of our other interests. Only...' Ms Sox scrolled down her datapad. 'Only Plato Aristotle remained with an interest in the Olympics.'

Carrington nodded. 'Daft name but bright boy. He'll go far. I remember thinking he was the only one who understood the Olympics and all they stand for. Bearing in mind how many times over the years they've been in and out of vogue, I'm glad to have his insights still available. What is he in charge of?'

'Broadcasting arrangements, sir.'

'Oh. So he wasn't responsible for bringing in the SSS troops?' Carrington clearly did not like military types, and the Space Security Service were the lowest of the low as far as he seemed to think.

Ms Sox, however, did not share his distaste. She shrugged. 'That was me actually, sir. Can't have too much security at a time like this, Mr Carrington.' She scratched her nose. 'I mean we'll be playing host to a majority of the elected leaders and representatives of the Federated worlds, the Guardian, the Chair of the Federation and a handful of non-aligned dignitaries. To be frank, I insist on the presence of the SSS.'

Carrington shrugged. 'Ah well, Ms Sox. I know you and your security measures. I'm sure everything will be subtle and invisible. Last thing the Duchess wants to see is jackbooted thugs marching athletes around, eh?'

Ms Sox smiled. 'Everything will be perfect, sir.'

Carrington hauled himself out of his chair and turned to look out of his office window, at the summit of Carrington Spire. He looked down forty storeys at the neatly arranged blocks of buildings and parks below. To one side he could see the cluster of churches, to another there was a glut of shopping malls. 'In a few days, Ms Sox, Micawber's World will host a huge party, full of beautiful people all competing in an atmosphere of friendly rivalry. Apart, of course, from the drug pushers, the local mafia, some political movers and shakers and, no doubt, a couple of fleeing galactic criminals. The usual kind of stuff you get at these things, I suppose.'

'Precisely, sir.'

Carrington turned back to her. 'I still don't feel comfortable with a Foamasi presence. I don't... Well, I don't trust their motives. They have no one entered into the Games and no obvious reason to be here. We have no Foamasi businesses on Micawber's World – well, none we know of, but with the lax Federation rules on buy-ups and mergers…'

'Similar to the one we did with Grecian Corp,' ventured Ms Sox, possibly unwisely, she thought. Think before you speak, she told herself.

But Carrington just nodded. 'Oh, you're right, Ms Sox. What's good for the goose and all that. Still doesn't explain what the bloody Foamasi want.' He shuddered. 'They make my skin crawl, you know. Can't help it. Like Martians. Can't stand reptiles, never could as a child.'

'Really, sir?'

Carrington looked at her. 'Not terribly Federally Correct am I, Ms Sox. I'm sorry, it's nothing personal.'

'I understand perfectly, sir.' Ms Sox scratched her nose absently and sniffed. 'People on my world were equally sceptical about joining the Federation. There was a large antihuman, indeed anti-everyone campaign. Fears that the Federation would tell us what to wear, what to do. What shops could and couldn't open on what days. Even what ingredients could go into our confectionery. And as for outlawing any gwampa fruits that didn't have a perfect ninety-degree bend in them…' Ms Sox shrugged. 'But we got over it. The benefits outweighed the petty concerns. Without the Federation, Jadea had little chance of commerce or industrial future. There was a limit to how many times we could sell archaic speeders and straight gwampa fruits to each other.' Ms Sox stopped scratching her nose and moved her finger to the corner of her eye. 'So don't worry, sir. Everyone feels a degree of… discomfort around new and unusual species.'

Carrington harrumphed. 'Well, the bloody Foamasi have been around for centuries. Should be used to them by now.'

Ms Sox reached over and patted Carrington's arm. 'Yes, but you are confusing their existence with their business habits. I suspect it's the latter you really dislike. There are some very nice Foamasi around, you know.'

Carrington smiled brightly. 'I'm sure you are right, Ms Sox. What would I do without you?'

Ms Sox laughed lightly. 'Call up the Jadean embassy and find another secretary from the pool.' She clicked her datapad off. 'Time I was getting back to work, sir. Coffee at the usual time?'

Carrington nodded. 'Oh, and Ms Sox. I seem to recall, on the subject of irrational xenophobia, that the C of E is being hired this morning for a wedding, is that right?'

Ms Sox reactivated her datapad and checked. 'That's correct sir. A human lady and Martian gentleman. Scheduled for ten thirty this morning. Flowers as usual?'

Carrington nodded. He always sent flowers to weddings and funerals. Then he stood up. 'You know, I might head down there myself. Invitation only?'

Ms Sox rechecked. 'It appears not, sir. Traditional Earth C of E regulations. Open to all.'

'Excellent. Fancy going to see a wedding yourself?'

'I'd be delighted. I'll need to change. If I recall my training, human wedding ceremonies are meant to be a bit... posh?'

'Posh will do,' Carrington laughed. 'But don't go overboard. Don't want to outdo the bride, do you?'

'Oh no, sir. Absolutely not.' With a final frenzied scratch at the back of her neck, Ms Sox left Carrington's office.

Sumner was playing with his fork, moving his sausage around on his plate, soaking up the egg yolk and mixing it into the tomato ketchup. The resultant bizarrely coloured goo made him even less hungry.

There was a chime at the door.

'Come in, Madox.'

Madox, as bidden, came in. Talking. 'I have no more information of why they are here, Co-ordinator. Perhaps they are just coming to watch the games.'

Sumner accidentally shoved his sausage too hard and it shot off his plate, only to be neatly caught by Madox, who did not even grimace as his smock was instantly flecked with yellow and red goo. Without breaking his stride, Madox dropped the offending piece of meat into the recycling bin then crossed to the kitchenette area and rinsed his hand.

He was back in front of Sumner's desk in thirty seconds, as if nothing had happened.

A little sheepishly, Sumner silently placed his plate and fork into the same bin and tried to rearrange everything on his desk. As this consisted of a couple of executive toys, a datapad and a fixed communicator screen, that was both difficult and futile.

Madox said nothing, staring intently at his employer with his usual unflinching gaze.

'Are they perhaps entered into the games?' Sumner offered quickly.

To his surprise, Madox cocked his head slightly. Clearly an option he had not considered. 'A good question, Co-ordinator. I shall go and inquire.' Without waiting for an order, Madox turned around and walked out.

Sumner looked out of his window at the reflection of Carrington Spire in the SSS Administration building opposite. Somewhere above him, the mighty Chase Carrington had pretty young women to run around and do his bidding. Humans, Zonians, Jadeans... ah, Jadeans. Beautiful, green-skinned sirens whose merest glance could turn his legs to jelly... He shook his head. And what was he stuck with? Ten Teknix and, back home, Mrs Sumner with her blasted mother.

One day, Algernon Sumner would rise above the twelfth floor. Above the shared coffee room and snooker hall. Above the cupboard-sized WCs.

One day, he would be CEO of Carrington Corp. Or Sumner Syndicate as he would rename it. Then he would marry some

Jadean beauty and live life to its fullest, doing as little work as possible and having no worries, no problems and no headaches. Except wondering where he was to play the next round of golf or quoits.

Oh yes, Chase Carrington upstairs had it so easy.

SSS Commandant Ritchie was not having a good day. In fact, it was currently hovering just below 'pretty damn crap, really' and marginally above 'absolutely bloody disastrous'.

According to the reports he was staring at, Quartermaster-Sergeant Dallion had returned from her squads' exploration of the artificial cave system minus sixty-five per cent of her agents. And she offered no rational explanation for the disappearances. The same report also stated that various damaged lights, tools and one undamaged blaster had been recovered from the last recorded positions of Agents Salt and Cartwright.

He tapped his pad and the data vanished. Swallowing, he looked across the room.

Quartermaster-Sergeant Dallion looked back at him, impassively. Poor cow – Ritchie could tell that she guessed her career was finished, but she kept a stoic face on it. She, her family, her dependants were about to be deprived of SSS housing, education, everything. Her parents were in an SSS care home, being looked after by the best nurses and occupational therapists. All that should be gone by 1800 hours. Her kids would be collected from their school on Phobos and transported back to Earth, probably on a cargo shuttle.

'Well, Quartermaster-Sergeant, it's not very good, is it?'

'No sir.'

'Any comments?'

'No sir. I wrote the report exactly as I believe it to have happened. Sir.'

Ritchie nodded and glanced behind Dallion. Her agents stood

alert and to attention, not catching his eye. Loyal, of course, to their QMS.

'Agent McCarrick, do you have anything to add to Sergeant Dallion's report?'

A flicker of puzzlement flashed across Dallion's face, Ritchie noted.

McCarrick, to his credit, did not falter. 'No, sir. The sergeant's report must be right. Sir.'

'Have you read the report, Agent McCarrick?'

'No, sir. Of course not, sir.'

Ritchie sighed. 'So, how d'you know that the sergeant's version of events is correct?'

'I trust my sergeant, sir. Implicitly.'

Ritchie stood up and walked around his desk, snapping, 'At ease, agents,' as he passed Dallion. He waved them all towards him, creating a sort of conspiratorial huddle. Although he noted with a wry smile that even when 'at ease', Dallion's agents were as tense as ever, even if not at attention.

'Agents, eight of your compatriots are inexplicably missing in a series of man-made tunnels. They may be forty-odd-year-old tunnels, but I find it hard to believe anyone can get lost in them so completely. This isn't some unexplored Federation newcomer world, you know. I want an unofficial 'let's get together and talk about this entirely off the record' kind of kick-around of ideas. Frankly, this close to the Olympics, I could do without headaches like this, OK? Now, ideas anyone?'

For a moment no one spoke and Ritchie realised they were all looking to Dallion.

'At ease, guys,' she said quietly, and this time the five agents really did relax. Ritchie filed this observation away for future reference.

'If I followed the rules set down by the Guardian,' Ritchie said quietly, 'Sergeant Dallion here would be on a cargo barge back to Earth, the five of you spending the next six or seven years cleaning toilets and scrubbing floors.' He cleared his throat conspiratorially. 'Unfortunately for the Guardian, I don't give two tosses for rules and regulations where good agents are concerned. Now I don't pretend to know any of you very well, but I recognise Sergeant Dallion's commitment to her charges, and yours to her. Basically, the six of you have until the opening of the Olympics to discover what happened to your friends. As far as the SSS is concerned, you are all on report, pending an investigation due to begin in five days. What you do in that time is, of course, entirely up to you.'

He straightened up and walked back to his desk, sat down and reactivated his datapad. After a few seconds, he looked up, feigning surprise at their continued presence. 'Hello? Can I help you, agents?'

Dallion almost smiled. 'No, sir. Sorry, sir, we came into the wrong room. Just leaving, sir.'

Ritchie nodded as a muted but relieved chorus of 'Sir's echoed through the closing door, and then they were gone.

He sat back in his seat. 'Have I done the right thing?'

To his right, a panel in the wall slid back. Even to the most observant of people, the panel was well disguised. No one could have seen the join in the flat wall unless they knew exactly what they were looking for. Ritchie could not see the small corridor beyond, but knew it ran behind the small executive toilet block next door.

A Foamasi shuffled into his office, a clawed hand scratching just beneath its right eye. 'I think that went fine, Commandant. We will monitor them carefully and they will lead us to our prize.'

'At which point your promise will be carried out.'

The Foamasi nodded (at least, Ritchie assumed that was what the movement was – Foamasi did not really have necks as such) and again dramatically swished one of its arms around. 'It is just as much in our interest that Sergeant Dallion's people do not live to report their findings as it is yours.'

I'll bet, thought Ritchie, but kept that to himself. He regretted telling the Foamasi he required Dallion's death – but if the Guardian found out he was ignoring the rule book, his own career would be finished.

The Foamasi stopped as a shrill bleeping came from something in the pouch it wore around its waist. 'My apologies, Commandant, I must leave you for now. We will talk later.' And it returned to its secret corridor and whatever lay beyond that provided it with a quick escape route.

As the panel silently slid shut, Ritchie let out a breath. He then stabbed, a little harder than he should, at a comm button on his desk. He stared at his face, reflected in the black metal, while waiting for the answer. He was definitely looking drawn, and his hair was getting thinner. God, he'd only been on Micawber's World a few months. He needed to get back to Earth soon. This dealing, double-dealing and hush-hush stuff was not his forte.

His main office door opened to admit a Teknix, who bowed customarily. This was Krassix – the only Teknix in the building. Only Ritchie's most trusted staff even knew of his existence, and Krassix was very good at being seen by only those people. The light reflected off Krassix's head and Ritchie reflected gloomily that assuming he got out of all this unscathed, he'd be as bald as the Teknix was himself in a few years.

'Krassix, have the sergeant and her troop gone?'

'Indeed, Commandant.'

'Did they see you?'

'Of course not.'

Ritchie stood up. 'OK, the Foamasi are making their move. I want you to follow the Foamasi that are following Dallion's group. Got that?'

If there was any irritation in Krassix's voice at the suggestion he could not grasp this, it did not show, but Ritchie was sure it was there. 'Of course, Commandant. Whatever the Foamasi believe is beneath the surface of this planet will be ours, not theirs.'

'Thank you, Krassix, that'll be all.'

With another bow, Krassix left.

Ritchie was finally alone. Playing various groups off against each other and for what? He had no idea, but whatever it was, the Foamasi believed it was going to strengthen their power base in the solar system. So pretending to help them could only be good for Earth in the long run.

Ritchie swung his chair around and looked out of his office window. Directly opposite was Carrington Spire, the twentieth floor. Probably full of dull little civil servants doing dull little jobs, worrying about nothing but their pensions and pushing a datapad from one desk to another.

How he envied them.

Samantha Jones was feeling a bit narked. Again. And, as usual, a certain Time Lord was the cause of this.

But Sam's annoyance was nothing compared with Ssard's.

'He should be here. He is the best man. Whatever that means.' Ssard looked at Sam. 'I do not understand human customs, but it matters to Stacy. Therefore it matters to me.'

Sam thought Ssard looked ready to punch someone. So long as it wasn't her.

Fussing around the Martian, tightening his ceremonial clothing, was a Pakhar tailor, its diminutive furry body darting quickly around. Two yellow-and-purple-spotted horses, dressed in what clearly passed for Sunday best on their home planet, were standing on their hind legs by the doorway to Ssard's apartment, ensuring that Stacy did not accidentally wander in.

Bad-luck customs are the same the universe over, Sam decided.

Ssard had removed his traditional warrior exosuit for a slimmer, darker one-piece affair, with a breastplate, knee-height boots and sleek black gloves. A white sash went from left shoulder to right hip, while a red sash around his middle acted as a sort of belt. From it hung the box containing the ring the Doctor was supposed to be responsible for.

The small hamster-like Pakhar (funny how most alien races seemed to have some equivalent on Earth, Sam noted, wondering whether on the Pakhar home planet there were tiny humanesque mammals kept in cages, forced to run around wheels for exercise and eat straw) was getting more flustered by the minute. Ssard's impatience was making his job exceptionally difficult and, in desperation, the little creature jabbed the Martian with a needle in a particularly vulnerable spot.

'For the ten millionth time, I'm warning you, the next time you move, stamp your foot, wave your arm or breath deeply, I'll shove one of these where the sun don't shine. Got that, Mr Ice Big Brave Warrior?' The voice reminded Sam of Kenneth Williams on speed, never stopping, barely pausing to catch a breath. Sam smiled as he stared right at her. 'And you can stop that smirking, young lady. Ooh, I don't know, young people today. No sense of occasion. No sense of style, either. I mean, take your friend, the Doctor. I mean, that coat of his.' The fiery little Pakhar tutted. 'I mean, no sense of colour, no sense of style. I mean, I've come to accept over the years that the Doctor has no taste –' he took Sam's hand in one of his paws – 'but believe me, this is one of the worst. Then again, there was that multicoloured version a while back. Not quite sure where that came from. Possibly one of those Kolpashan fashion houses. I mean, always a season or two behind the rest of us, I say. *They* say they're ahead, 'examining retro', but no, they're behind. Ooh, I mean, they must think we were born yesterday.' Ssard coughed meaningfully, so the Pakhar jabbed him with a pin and ignored him. 'But you tell the Doctor to ditch that coat – hideous. Mind you, not as hideous as what the bloody nobs are wearing these days. Regency – whatever *that* is – seems to be back in vogue. Regency, pah!'

Ssard started to adjust his waistband until the Pakhar shrieked and jabbed another pin into him, swearing less than nicely and calling into question the Martian's parentage and hatchling dynasty.

Ssard sensibly just muttered an apology and stood still.

'Super. Lovely. Bless you,' muttered the Pakhar tailor. And then swore loudly as Ssard moved again.

'Doctor!'

Sam breathed a sigh of relief followed by one of anger as the Doctor sauntered into the room, grinning as if nothing was wrong.

'Sorry, am I late?'

'Very nearly,' hissed Ssard.

Sam took the Doctor's arm. 'Thank God you're here. Between Ssard and the furry tailor, we were going to have a bloodbath in here.'

The Doctor nodded. 'Sorry, lost track of the time. How long have I been away, your time?'

'Four or five hours by now.' Sam screwed her eyes up a bit, suddenly wary. 'Why? How long have you been away *your* time?'

The Doctor looked uncomfortable. 'Oh not long. Ish.'

'How long?'

'A week. Maybe two.'

Sam took a deep breath. 'Where?'

Before she could get an answer, two humans, clearly dressed for the wedding, came in. They were in their mid-fifties, dressed in some strange reflective silk, shot with a variety of colours and looking really impressive. The man was trying not to look alarmed at Ssard, while the woman was staring at the two horse-people.

The Doctor disentangled himself from Sam and crossed quickly to them.

'Mary, Christopher, may I present M'Rek'd and P'Fer'd? They are

Equinoids and are the ushers at the wedding.'

The humans tried to smile.

'H-hello?' said Mary.

'Hello, Mary,' said the male Equinoid, P'Fer'd. 'A pleasure to meet you. Welcome to Micawber's World.'

Mary just nodded, too stunned to reply.

The Doctor continued. 'This is Sam Jones, my travelling companion.'

Christopher shook Sam's hand. 'And you are...?'

Sam smiled broadly. 'Human.'

Christopher relaxed instantly.

'Why are these furless types here, Doctor?' squeaked the Pakhar tailor. 'They're in my way.' He stared at the Doctor with tiny black eyes. 'But then, they're friends of yours so they're bound to be in the way. Comes with the territory.'

'The charming little chap with the needle and thread is Frankie.'

'Yeah, right,' Frankie said, sticking another pin into Ssard to express his annoyance.

'And this is Ssard.'

Ssard looked down at Mary and Christopher, both of whom tried, unsuccessfully, not to shudder. But then Christopher offered his hand.

'Don't you dare move!' screamed Frankie, but Ssard ignored him, and took Christopher's hand. And bowed slightly.

'Ssard, may I introduce you to Christopher and Mary Townsend?'

If Ssard felt any surprise, he hid it well. Sam, however, did not.

'Townsend... Stacy's mum and dad?'

The Doctor smiled, his blue eyes wide with pleasure.

'But the web of time and all that?' Sam hissed.

'That,' the Doctor whispered, 'is why I've been away for so long. Putting other things in motion so that history won't notice their disappearance. Tricky, but can be done. By a master.'

'Oh, I'm sure it can. What worries me,' Sam retorted, 'is that *you* did it.'

'Oh bear of little faith,' quoted the Doctor, then returned his attentions to the new family. 'Stacy, by the way, doesn't know you're here,' he said to her parents.

Mary and Christopher Townsend were too engrossed in Ssard, their new son-in-law, to really listen.

Sam shook her head. 'I don't suppose they imagined their daughter would marry a Martian Ice Warrior. I guess it's a lot to get your head around.'

'That's the other reason I was nearly late,' the Doctor said quietly. 'I've been giving them a quick tour of the cosmos, showing them the alien races and updating them on Stacy's life. Alien contact was restricted to a few invaders and a couple of benign helpers in the twenty-third century. But they're nice people. They'll adjust.'

Sam nodded. 'Good, because I know that having them here is the best present Stacy could ever get.' Sam kissed the Doctor on the cheek. 'You're a nice bloke, sometimes.'

The Doctor shrugged. 'I try.'

Sam looked back at the confused humans talking animatedly now to the Equinoid couple and Ssard, while poor Frankie watched as his carefully pinned sashes and robes fell to the floor, ignored.

It was going to be the best day of Stacy's life, that was for sure.

Kyle Dale adjusted his long black robe and reset his wide-brimmed hat to keep the sun off his pale skin. He then tightened the yellow cord around his waist and tapped the side of his pebble glasses, altering them so that they turned a shade darker, polarising the effect of the sunlight.

Around him, the others from the Church were similarly preparing themselves for their vigil outside the stained-glass construct known locally as the Church of Earth. Reverend Lukas stood slightly behind them all, hands clasped behind his back, holding his sunglasses, apparently unaffected by the harsh light. Unlike his charges, he was not sweating under his robes either, Kyle guessed. Reverend Lukas never sweated. Probably too mundane. To the left, Jolyon and Phillipa were almost touching at the shoulder. Reverend Lukas would not like that. Then there were Maximilian Girard and his young friend, Veronique. To Kyle's right were the Reverend's longest-serving followers, the eternally young-looking Eldritch and Marcus. None of the others knew exactly how long they had been part of the Church, but they had certainly been there when each of them had joined up. Two or three others were scattered around – Kyle did not even know their names. They had joined them in transit – clearly Revered Lukas had called as many followers of the Church as he could for this big day.

So, here they were, grouped, silently waiting. Patiently observing the Church of Earth on Micawber's World, waiting to catch of glimpse of the couple who had hired it out for their wedding day.

A group of well-wishers from the planet had begun to gather. Kyle could see a multitude of people from different races gathered there, many of whom did not even know the couple, but had come because it was – according to the hotel's guidebooks – always an event worth witnessing. Kyle was glad they were there. Today they would see something they would never forget.

'Is anything wrong, Kyle?'

'Not at all, Father. Everything is perfect.'

Reverend Lukas ran a finger down Kyle's shoulder. 'Be patient, my boy. Your time is coming. Today, our work is here.'

'Yes, Father.'

Reverend Lukas always made everything right. That's why he was their leader.

Kyle noticed that Reverend Lukas was talking quietly to Eldritch and Marcus. They nodded and slowly walked backward, then away from the gathering crowd. Kyle watched them through his ever-darkening glasses as, without actually running, they moved swiftly around the rear of the crowd and then circled until they were at the side door of the beautiful glass church.

Waiting for their cue.

Reverend Lukas had it all planned perfectly. This was going to be a wedding to remember.

The speeder car got nearer the church, and Sam gripped Stacy's hand. 'Nervous?'

'Yup.'

'Ready?'

'Nope.'

'Going through with it anyway?'

'Guess so.'

'Good.' Sam felt the speeder car slow down. 'My God, look. You've got a fan club.'

Stacy let out a breath. 'Tradition apparently. Old Earth churches allow anyone to witness the wedding.' She swallowed. 'Has the Doctor actually turned up yet?'

'What? Oh... yes. He's with Ssard now. In the other car.' Sam stopped. 'In that one in fact.'

A speeder was parked outside the church, a robotic chauffeur polishing it, wearing the traditional cap and grey suit of a driver.

Their own chauffeur slowed down and, through the crowd, Sam saw the two Equinoids trot over. Equally comfortable on two feet or four, the Equinoids reared up and pulled open the shuttle's hatchway. The female, M'Rek'd, held a hoof out to Stacy, who took it and stepped away from the vehicle.

'I'm going to cry,' M'Rek'd said quietly. 'And it's not even my wedding.'

'Don't do that, my love,' said P'Fer'd. 'You'll spoil your make-up.'

'Ready to lead me down the aisle, then, surrogate Dad?' laughed Stacy.

But P'Fer'd shook his head. 'Afraid not, my lovely girl.'

Stacy stopped and Sam nearly cannoned into her. 'Why not?' Stacy asked throatily. 'What's gone wrong?'

'Nothing,' said a quiet voice from behind hem. 'We just thought it more appropriate if I did it.'

'Dad?' Stacy turned and looked at her father. And mother. And all three burst into tears as they hugged each other.

'Happy Wedding Day from the Doctor and me,' muttered Sam, holding back a tear or two of her own.

After a few moments, Stacy wiped her face. 'Oh my God, I'm so happy to see you and... and... God, have you met Ssard? Does he know you're here?'

'Yes,' said her mother. 'We've spent the morning with him, and a nicer... man... you couldn't have chosen. We like him a lot.'

Good on you, Mary Townsend, thought Sam. She knew that neither parent was entirely convinced by Stacy's choice. After all, kids were out of the question anyway, and not just because of Stacy's choice of husband. But her parents didn't know that. Then there was the fact that Ssard was not the most demonstrative of people. Ah, what the hell! It was Stacy's day and the Doctor had just put the icing on the cake.

What could go wrong now?

The Olympic Stadium was situated amid a two-mile circle of dust and shrubbery. Unlike the rest of Micawber's World, the surrounding area lacked the greenery and refinement of the major tourist attractions, and also housed the entrance to the underground tunnel system and a series of Power Blocks, buildings that supplied power to the Stadium. This was all part of the intended success of the Stadium – on leaving the desert-like area outside, visitors would enter a plush, hi-tech and verdant interior. It was even nicknamed the 7,438th Wonder of the Universe. There were not exactly 7,437 others, but to some wag at the holocam networks the phrase had made a good headline.

Carrington Corp had spent the equivalent of three planets' entire agricultural profits creating the massive bowl-shaped arena, at least four times the size of the traditional ones back on Earth, where the concept of a battle for excellence had sprung some five thousand years previously.

There was seating for a million plus, with eight massive holographic projectors so that those too far away to see the competitors as anything other than tiny ants could view the whole thing in glorious 3-D.

Below, in the actual games area was the traditional eight-lane running track encircling a massive lush green centre of fake grass that would need little upkeep during the six weeks of the event.

Despite the eighteen different races that had registered to take part, the actual events were pretty traditional, each planet seeming to have developed similar games. Obviously the species that tended not to be of the two-armed, two-legged variety had created their own special games, thus enabling everyone to have a good time despite their differences. The Arcturans were masters at many of these, losing only occasionally to the high-spirited defences put up by the physically challenged teams from Earth, New Mars and Jadea.

Holovid crews from a variety of planets and companies were arriving on Micawber's World alongside their teams or just to relay the events to a noncompeting homeworld that, nevertheless, had an interest in the whole spectacle.

The Stadium was about eighteen miles away from Carrington City. It was built on a rocky plateau, beneath which were the artificial catacombs put there by the planetoid's designers to enable good passage of air and strengthen the artificial surface. The Space Security Service were assigned to patrol the catacombs, set up lighting rigs (because the power sources for the holovid crews and their projectors would be stored there) and generally ensure their safety. The threat of terrorism from the likes of Galaxy Five or the Free Rasta VI was ever-present. In fact the FRS had threatened to destroy Micawber's World during its construction, but had been stopped, the terrorists exposed and incarcerated on Desperus, the solar system's artificial prison world.

The Foamasi standing at Gate 12 stuffed the guide book back into its pouch, having taken in all the information it needed.

With a quiet chirp to itself, it shuffled forward, its folds of scales and smooth skin rippling in the daylight. Its two protruding eyes affording it a unique view of the whole Stadium in one go. A claw scratched at its hard nose and its tail twitched at an itch on its back.

'I don't think this is very safe, you know.'

The speaker was a human male, aged about forty from what the Foamasi could guess. Its knowledge of human physiognomy was limited, but it had tried learning as much as it could.

The man was wearing a hard hat, and blue coveralls (although they did not cover his paunch particularly well). He carried a large datapad, which he waved in the Foamasi's direction. 'Most of my people are on lunch break, but even so, I'd prefer if we met at my place.'

The Foamasi opened its beaky mouth to speak and emitted a series of chirps.

As the human male sighed, the Foamasi realised its error and dug into its pouch, plucking out a voice-synthesiser disc which it triumphantly popped into his mouth.

'Terribly sorry, old chap. Bit of a bother, I'm afraid.'

The man sighed again. 'Oh for goodness' sake. You've been pilfering the human library again, haven't you. Nicking their voice synths of holovid actors. Who is it this time? Malcolm Guttridge?

Dennis Puzakha? No, don't tell me, Van der Cleele!'

The Foamasi scrabbled inside its pouch again, pulling out a data strip. 'Awfully sorry, old man, can't read your blessed type. Jolly unfortunate, sorry.'

The human snatched the strip of plastic. 'George Sanders? Never heard of him. Still, if it's before 2650, I'm out of my depth.' He looked back at the Foamasi. 'Anyway, it's stupid, inappropriate and dangerous. Why did you want to see me, "George"?'

The Foamasi scratched its nose again. 'Well, runs like this, old man. My friends are rather impatient, you know. Got to get moving. We've acquired a lot of the facilities, including your construction chums. But we need the final plans, all right? Have to know who has the contracts for the turf, the cleaning, the supply of the discus and of course the catering. All we're missing, really.'

The man shook his head. 'You want it all, don't you, "George"?'

'Naturally. We are Foamasi.'

The man stopped talking and waved frantically for the Foamasi to duck back under the Gateway.

With remarkable speed, 'George' did so. It watched as a tall human male with much darker skin than its contact walked over, laughing about something. He passed 'George's' contact a thermos of something.

The Foamasi was getting impatient. It had to report back to its Lodge before evening. Would this irritating new male human never leave?

Finally, he did so, still laughing, but before 'George' could move, its co-conspirator came to him.

'Catering is a human company, Elton Ward. They're on Bachius III, sorting out their stock. The turf has been supplied by one of Carrington's offshoots, so you're buggered there.'

'I see. Dashed unlucky, that, eh?'

'Yeah, whatever. The discus stuff I can't help you with – I have no contacts, nor do I need any, regarding supply of items once the games are under way. Oh, and the cleaning contract is with the Snarx, as you could have guessed.'

'Snarx, eh? Dreadful sorts, what?'

'Oh for goodness' sake, change your voice synth before someone shoots you out of pity. Now, where's my payment? You lot are three weeks overdue.'

'George' again shoved its fist into its pouch and brought out a credit chip.

The human ran his finger along the magnetic strip, placing his finger print on to it. 'Thank you. I trust we won't meet again?'

'Oh, probably not, old bean. Terribly sorry to have bothered you today, but you know what they're like back home, eh? Always fussing over nothing.' 'George' turned away, glad to have finished its business.

The trouble was, facing it were about twelve human males, dressed like its conspiratorial human contact. Only each of them carried something large, heavy and, in some cases, very blunt.

The Foamasi felt its pouch being tugged off.

'Sorry "old bean",' said the human from behind. 'That's business.'

The last thing the Foamasi 'George' saw was a blur of humans, including the dark-skinned one it had seen with the thermos, rushing at it. Then he felt something hit its head and the lights went out.

The ship was coming in to land at Micawber's World's solitary spaceport. It was a gleaming silver ship, long and sleek with raised fins and massive propulsion units at the back. The sides were decorated in various gold and platinum-embossed seals, as befitted a vehicle of its rank.

This was the FPS *Space Pioneer*, and it carried a group of *very* important Very Important People.

Via a control tower, messages were relayed between the

harbour pilots in their flitters bringing the massive craft into spaceport and the ship's captain, ensuring the safest arrival for these terribly special passengers.

They were seated in the spectacular dining room. It was red-carpeted from wall to wall, the cream walls decorated with large seals and crests, again in gold and platinum, while each velvet-covered seat had ancient carvings embedded around the legs and backs.

There were eighteen of them, mostly courtiers. Standing by a food replicator, immaculate in his regal finery, was Consort Ethelredd. His ever-watchful eye flickered intensely between his charges and the others. Always inscrutable, his face deliberately betrayed none of the scorn and derision he felt for his fellow travellers.

First, there was the dapper man seated at the far end of the largest table, Torin Chalfont.

'Nice ship this, isn't it? Only saying to the lads back at the office before we left, bit of an honour to get this gig, I can tell you. Still, I was the only choice, really. None of the younger journos understand the protocol, or have the... well, ability to get to the heart of the matter. And to understand how one should deal with situations like this, yes?'

Listening with ill-concealed boredom was Secretary Aigburth, his hand involuntarily resting on his ceremonial sword, as if preparing to slice the tedious older man in two. Torin Chalfont was famous for his boasting that he was friends with everyone of any social, political or show-business importance to his readers and viewers. Aigburth, like so many, tolerated him and let him continue to delude himself. He threw a desperate look towards Security Officer Gar, the large V'orrn, whose shaggy white fur-covered body was squeezed rather badly into his uniform. As always, Gar offered no response.

Also sitting at the table were Edyth and Cait, two young ladies-in-waiting who had spent much of the trip absorbing Torin's loathsome, and undeniably untrue, reports of his adventures of thirty years as a journalist. Ignorant and guileless as they were, the two girls could be expected to do no less than fall hook, line and sinker for his rubbish.

'Dreadful business of course, the old King going like that. Round the office, we had flowers and pictures for weeks. The mood was so dark, you could cut through the atmosphere with a knife. Tragic, so tragic.'

As the girls nodded eagerly, Ethelredd groaned silently. Torin's news service had been the first to celebrate King Garth's death, immediately pointing out the blunders he had made. The delegation to Corpos Delta, for example, where he had likened the predominantly herbivore people to cows back on Earth. Or his diplomatic mission to Hallion II, where he had informed the Earth natives studying there that he was amazed they hadn't grown wings like the native Hals, bearing in mind how loyal they were to their adoptive planet. Worst of all, he had visited one of the Uranian colonies after their very aged, very wise and very popular leader had passed on and told the royal court that they should be grateful – the young regent was an attractive young filly who would look much prettier on the stamps than her ugly father had done. Fine, except she was just nine years old.

Actually, that was not the worst thing. The worst thing was that the holovids, news services and WAV filers had been present at all of these and reported back verbatim.

If King Garth hadn't died when he did, one of his courtiers would probably have assassinated him just to shut the fool up before the reputation of the Earth royals was tarnished for ever.

Of course, no one had foreseen that with Queen Bodicha's mourning, and the young princes still at Eton, the only royal capable of travelling to Micawber's World was the Duchess of Auckland. Divorced from the Queen's son, Prince Artemis, the

Duke of Auckland (who was off on some vacational jaunt to shoot asteroids in the Saturn belt), the Duchess was as demented as they came. She had been plucked from a food mall by the Duke on a walkabout one day, and they had enthralled the solar system with their 'fairytale' romance. Seven years, and a set of twins later, they separated. Apart from a very comfortable financial settlement, the Duchess had taken to presenting holovid shows on wild animals, children's day care and the best way to teach old-age pensioners New Martian via the GalWeb. She exploited her royal connection to the limit – a series of unflattering books on her life as part of the court had made more enemies than friends, and more money than Ethelredd could dream of.

And so, here they were, approaching Micawber's World, preparing to open the first Galactic Olympiad for eight years.

And somehow, Ethelredd had drawn the short straw to act as the Duchess's adviser on protocol. And what had the stupid woman done? Invited Torin Chalfont to follow her around. The press were a bloody nuisance at the best of times, even at arm's length. This boring oik was a walking inducement to homicide.

If Secretary Aigburth didn't do it, Ethelredd had decided he would. Slowly.

The doors swished open, and Counsellor De'Ath marched in, his dark suit and white gloves almost as showy and affected as their wearer.

'All rise for the Duchess,' he announced with a notable soft R, head cocked slightly on one side. His voice betrayed everything you needed to know about him, and a lot you didn't. Fussy, mincing, precise and foppish.

In medieval times, Counsellor De'Ath's role would have been food taster. These days, he was more likely to try on her wardrobe, just to check that the colours didn't clash with the wallpaper. At least, that would be his excuse.

The rest of the people in the room stood immediately to

attention, bar the ladies-in-waiting, who took up positions either side of De'Ath.

The Duchess of Auckland tripped happily into the room, wearing a long midnight-blue dress that on a woman with a sleek figure would have been glorious. On the Duchess, it looked like a badly stuffed pillow.

It also clashed horribly with her tightly curled, lime-green hair. Ethelredd tried not to smile. He could imagine De'Ath deliberately choosing it. They had had 'words' the night before concerning De'Ath and one of the pursers. Ethelredd was sure that the Counsellor was now having his revenge. And the Duchess was stupid enough not to realise.

'Hello, everybody,' she giggled. 'Lovely dress, don't you think?'

A mumbled agreement from those with privilege enough to be allowed to reply made her happy. Especially when Torin bowed with enough exaggeration to make Ethelredd feel giddy.

'Marvellous, Your Highness, I must say. You bring a radiance and a warmth to the room sadly lacking before your entrance.'

The Duchess giggled again. 'Oh, Torin, you're so sweet. One really must get around to sorting out that bio- biogro- book thing you wanted to do, yes?'

Torin Chalfont clapped his hands. Ethelredd swore he could see the grease dripping off them. Maybe it was sweat. 'Heavens, yes, Your Highness. At your convenience, naturally.'

De'Ath intervened with a well-timed cough, nurtured through years of experience. 'Your Highness, the harbour pilots report that they will guide the ship down within five minutes. Please be seated until then.'

She sat, and Edyth and Cait tiptoed behind her, dropping to the floor either side of her chair, like well-loved puppies.

The Duchess then indicated for Torin to sit.

Secretary Aigburth waited to be told likewise, but was disappointed. He coughed.

'Yes,' snapped the Duchess. 'What is wrong, my Lord Aigburth? A chill, perhaps? You cough a lot these days.'

'My apologies,' the Secretary said softly. 'I did not mean to cause offence.'

She regarded him with a raised eyebrow, her head juddering slightly. Ethelredd could not take his eyes off the ridiculous hair. Since when did Royal Family members, divorced or otherwise, take to following the fashions of the music or holovid stars?

'Oh, do sit down, you silly man,' the Duchess snapped. 'You look like a... like a... a hatstand!' She clapped her hands together. 'Yes, a hatstand.'

'Indeed,' toadied Torin.

The Duchess smiled. Secretary Aigburth offered the sort of rictus grin normally seen only on corpses, and sat down.

Torin leaned forward, breaking all protocol by invading the Duchess's personal space. She did not seem to mind, and Aigburth clearly wasn't going to risk another insult, feeble as it might be, by correcting him.

'You know, Your Highness, as I was saying last night, you have to be careful. I do hope your entourage is sufficiently well equipped to protect you. These offworlds can be very dangerous, you know. I can remember when you needed real men to protect you on these little backwaters. Not just a few nonces in frilly lace sleeves and Regency jackets.'

'Really? Do tell.' The Duchess smiled at her favourite storyteller.

Ethelredd merely flicked an imaginary mote of dust off his red and white Regency jacket.

'You know,' said a camp voice in his ear, 'I have never felt more like starting a republic than I do now.'

Ethelredd shrugged. 'Well, Counsellor De'Ath, there are still the young twin princes. Hope for the future.'

'Dear God,' tutted De'Ath. 'May we be preserved from those two little brats. The gene pool had a leak when they were conceived.

I mean, her and Prince Artie... they're only one step up from frog spawn.'

Ethelredd was going to reply when he realised what Torin Chalfont was saying to the Duchess.

'I mean, we've suspected back in the office for ages. There are all sorts of rumours, Your Highness. They say even your... well, ex-husband's family could be involved. And we cannot trust the SSS. I mean, you must be on your guard. If they do attempt to... well, you know...'

'Kill me?'

'Assassinate you, I think the parlance is,' the reporter said. 'Arrange a little accident. I mean, there were those back at the office who warned me. "You're taking a risk, Tolly," they said. "That ship could go up in smoke between planets and no one would be able to find the black box, would they?" But I couldn't let my favourite royal down, could I?'

The Duchess put her fingers to her lips in horror. 'Kill? Me? Poor little moi? But why would anyone do that? I'm so harmless.'

Ethelredd could think of a few million taxpayers who would probably delight in seeing the Duchess's remains floating in space, and as many again who would pay to see Torin Chalfont's corpse beside her, but the last thing he needed was Her Royal Battiness getting paranoid.

'I think, Mr Chalfont, that is a ridiculous and rather unpleasant thing to say.' Ethelredd crossed the dining room until he stood between them. 'First, Her Highness is under our protection. And second, I don't think the Palace would take kindly to your gossipmongering. Least of all when you paint Her Majesty Queen Bodicha as some kind of murderess. I think this conversation ought to be saved for another time - preferably never - as Her Highness needs to prepare herself to meet the harbour workers on our arrival.'

Torin began to try to stare Ethelredd down, but quickly realised he was wasting his time.

'Yes, well, whatever.' He put his hand on the Duchess's arm once again. 'Must get ready to meet the proletariat, I suppose. Greet the great unwashed, eh?'

The Duchess let out a shrill, girlish laugh. 'Oh, Mr Chalfont, you are so sweet,' she added, and then leaned back, tapping Ethelredd's hand.

He bent down and she whispered into his ear, 'What's a prol - prolet - whatever he said?' rather too loudly, so that everyone could hear anyway.

'Your devoted public, Your Highness. The good people of the Galactic Federation.'

The Duchess nodded. 'Well, naturally we will greet them. That is why one is here, is it not, Lord Consort?'

Ethelredd agreed with the Duchess, then threw a quick look to Gar, who marched over and, without a word, eased Torin out of his seat and towards the door.

The reporter managed to hold back momentarily.

'A delightful dress, Your Highness. And such an honour to be amongst the first to see it worn so splendidly...' If Torin Chalfont said any more, it was through the soundproofed dining-room door. With any luck, Gar would forget his training and pull Torin's head off. But that was sadly unlikely. The V'orrn were too well disciplined for that.

'How awful. To think anyone in my own family could hate me so much they'd want to kill me.' The Duchess was sagging in her seat, looking faint. Edyth and Cait were flapping lace handkerchiefs at her face.

The Duchess grabbed Ethelredd's arm. 'My Lord Consort, you'll protect me, won't you?'

'With my life, Your Highness.'

As he returned to his position by the food replicator, De'Ath pursed his oversized lips and wobbled his head. 'Well, I hope for her sake it doesn't come to that. I can just see you skipping lightly to one side at the last moment, throwing up your hands and saying, "Oh, whoops, they shot the Duchess."'

Ethelredd merely smiled back. 'Just remember, Lord Counsellor, that to get to me before her, they'll already have gone through you.'

Startled by this untimely reminder of his own duties, De'Ath silently minced back to the Duchess, offering his own, equally insincere platitudes, but delivered with his usual style so that the Duchess couldn't see through them.

Ethelredd realised that the end of the games, only three weeks away, seemed like an eternity. Or a life sentence.

'Co-ordinator Sumner, there has been a murder. A Foamasi.' Madox punched more keys on his datapad. 'Oh, and the Duchess of Auckland's ship has landed.'

Sumner wanted to run away, screaming, leaving reams of paper and astonished secretaries in his wake. Sadly, he knew this would be pointless – paper was scarce enough this far away from Earth; the secretaries were all Teknix (enough said); and, above all, he'd soon be dragged back to his desk by well-meaning friends. And his wife (who, no doubt, would have singed him all over just by shouting at him).

Instead, he nodded at Madox as if this were the sort of news he received every day and poked at his executive toys, letting the distraction of one silver ball hitting another amuse him for a few seconds. 'Who was the Foamasi? Government by any chance?' That, at least, would have been neat and tidy. A quick apology to the Foamasi Temple, a shipping over of the body and the whole thing wrapped up.

'No ID at all, I'm afraid, Co-ordinator. Probably one of the Lodges.' Madox waited patiently for orders. If Sumner said nothing between now and home time, Madox would probably stand there. Patiently. All bloody afternoon. Teknix were like that – annoying but efficient. Where was the cruel hand of fate that had decided he should have to have Teknix working for him?

'Right. Get the body to the SSS building and tell someone over there to deal with it. I'll go and check on the reception suite for the Duchess.'

'Already checked, sir. It looks immaculate, if I may be so bold.'

Of course it's bloody immaculate, you bald git. Your bloody chums made it so. No Teknix in the universe would have left the room until it was immaculate. There won't be a thread out of place, a paper napkin misfolded or a fork slightly skew-whiff. Just once, why can't you drop red wine on the carpet, or pee slightly to the left of the urinal and hit the floor, or... or... anything but be so damn perfect?

Sumner just smiled up at Madox, hoping to goodness that his face betrayed none of these less than charitable thoughts. 'Thank you, Madox. Shall we go and greet Her Highness?'

Madox bowed slightly and followed Co-ordinator Sumner from his office, pausing briefly to speak to a female Teknix who nodded at him and walked away.

Sam ran out the church before anyone else, handfuls of rice substitute ready to chuck over the bride and groom. A couple of others followed suit – and, although none of them knew Stacy or Ssard, the fact that they were joining in with the tradition pleased Sam enormously.

Sure enough, the bridal party followed by the happy couple emerged and were showered with rice from every angle.

Stacy laughed as Ssard breathed half of it in, and Sam saw the Doctor wink at her and toss something through the air. Sam caught it and realised it was an Olympus camera. She took a few pictures hurriedly, assuming that despite its archaic outward appearance, like its owner, internally it was probably automatically focused, took great pictures and never broke down. Not much like its owner at all, really, but who cared? It was a happy day.

Stacy and her parents were all hugging each other and Stacy threw her bouquet over her shoulder. It was caught by Frankie the Pakhar tailor, who shrugged and started nibbling at the flowers, amid much cheering.

The Doctor was suddenly beside Sam.

'Trouble,' he hissed, keeping a happy, beaming face directed at the newly-weds.

Sam was immediately tense and looked away from the church, into the crowd gathered outside the small fence that enclosed them – half a dozen clusters of people, mostly cheering or clapping, from a variety of races, ninety per cent of which Sam wouldn't have been able to describe, let alone recognise.

'Where?'

'Nine o'clock.'

She looked to her left immediately and saw in the crowd four or five black-clad figures, all wearing long robes, buttoned at the collars. One of them had a white collar under his, and all wore wide-brimmed hats and dark glasses. She immediately recognised them as Clerics.

'You're frightened of a vicars' convention?'

'No. Just the two that are coming through from inside the church, when they weren't inside for the ceremony. That and the fact they've got large bags which could contain bombs.'

Sam stared at the two black-clad vicars the Doctor had indicated. She was still trying to shake the almost comical notion of a preacher with a five-pound Dalekanium bomb when, sure enough, the two newcomers took something from their bags.

'Everyone down!' yelled the Doctor.

Experienced as they were, Stacy and Ssard hit the ground instantly, the Martian using his own body to cover Stacy's parents as he yanked them over with him. The two Equinoids nudged into Frankie, flattening him, and most of the congregation looked around alarmed.

Three of them were immediately pelted, not with bombs, but with dye or paint. Shrieking and panicking, the crowd ran around. Outside the fence, the rest of the clergy did the same, apart – Sam noticed – from one, who stood, arms behind his back, observing everything.

Stacy was up, realising that no one's life was threatened, and before anyone could stop her slammed a very perfectly aimed kick into the shin of the nearest clergyman. He went down soundlessly, but this caused the others to swarm in, throwing their paint bombs at anything and everything.

A huge bag of blue dye caught Sam on her shoulder, soaking her cheek as well. Reacting automatically, she lashed out with her arm, catching a young clergyman on the chin with a crack. He fell motionless on to the grass.

'Stop!'

Everyone stopped.

The Doctor stood right at the centre of everything, not a spot of paint on his clothes, not one hair out of place. Quietly, he turned and looked straight at the clergyman who had not taken part in the attack.

Slowly the man walked through the gate and into the now multicoloured garden. He was a little shorter than the Doctor, but carried himself with the same authoritarian air.

No one spoke for a moment as the two men watched each other.

Eventually, the Doctor broke the silence. 'Good afternoon. Would you care to explain this?'

'It is afternoon, I grant you,' replied the newcomer in a soft, well-mannered voice. 'It is not good. In the eyes of the Goddess, this union is anything but good. It is unholy.'

Sam watched as Stacy began to splutter indignantly, but a flick of the Doctor's wrist quietened her. How quickly we all come to obey him, Sam thought.

'Unholy? In what way, Reverend…?'

'Lukas.' The Reverend removed his hat, revealing his cropped grey hair, and bowed slightly to the Doctor. 'Unholy because matrimony between alien species is unnatural. Over the last twenty thousand years, the human race has degenerated into a morass of corruption, decay and immorality. To allow this wedding to take place without a reminder that it is against the wishes of the Goddess, who has overseen our race since the dawn of time, would be unforgivably remiss of the Church of the Way Forward.'

'Way Back more like,' Sam muttered quietly.

'Not at all. Reverend Lukas is taking us forward, to a purity of life and soul that the corruption of the modern galaxy cannot despoil.'

Sam looked at the young man she had accidentally thumped a few moments before. He was nursing a red mark on his chin, but stared straight ahead at his leader.

Enraptured, Sam thought. Completely committed. Which they should be. She gave a final look at the young man and walked away, towards Stacy, who was helping her parents up from under Ssard.

'Our point has been made. We are not legally empowered to stop this wedding, but we are within our democratic rights to protest in a non-violent manner.' Reverend Lukas clicked his fingers and his group were at his side in a moment.

Sam moved to the Doctor's, just in case a kids-in-the-playground sort of fight started. She felt her heart rising in her chest.

Then pushing through the crowd towards them, came a man and woman. He was human, late fifties, in need of a few sessions at the gym to get rid of the waistline. She was slim, immaculately dressed, with a lime-green flesh tone, solid black eyes and long black hair. Both were splattered with the various dyes Lukas's gang had lobbed about.

The man stood in front of Reverend Lukas. 'Reverend Lukas? Church of the Way Forward?'

The greenish woman was tapping on her datapad, and whispered in the human's ear. He nodded.

'Staying at the Mirage? Delta Sector, I gather.'

Reverend Lukas nodded politely. 'And you are?'

'Chase Carrington. I own that hotel. I own this church you have just... redecorated. For what it is worth, I also own this planet.'

'I am aware of who you are, Mr Carrington. My apologies that you and your Jadean assistant found yourselves caught up in our democratic expression of our feelings.'

Carrington nodded. 'Sadly, Reverend, under the Galactic Federation's Charter – three nine three two – which I am bound by, I cannot stop your demonstration.' He dragged a finger through the wet dye ruining his white shirt and waved it at Reverend Lukas. 'If, however, my labs discover that there is a single trace element in the composition of this dye that is in any way, no matter how petty, an infringement of Import/Export Duty or Transport of Illegal Goods or, best of all, contains a base substance used in the preparation of any narcotic substance – and that includes a bloody aspirin – I will have you deported so fast you won't have time to go back to your hotel and pay my manager for his service. In the meantime, I would appreciate it if you would leave Micawber's World as soon as possible. Or this evening, whichever comes sooner.'

The greenish assistant – Jadean, was it? – triumphantly punched up a few more details on her pad, then frowned. She whispered something else into Carrington's ear, and Sam could already see a smile crossing Reverend Lukas's face.

'So, may we leave now? My congregation need to get cleaned

up.' Without waiting for an answer, the clergymen and women turned as one and walked away.

'Well, aren't you going to charge them?' Sam was furious. 'You can't let them get away with this. They've destroyed Stacy's wedding.'

The Doctor looked at Chase Carrington, who frowned and shook his head. 'They're booked in for the Olympics. And I don't have the necessary power to exclude anyone from that, unless they use firearms. And annoying as the Church is, I sincerely doubt that we'll find anything more troublesome than a few pots of paint at the hotel.' Carrington looked over at Stacy and Ssard. Stacy was fuming rather than upset. 'My apologies Mrs... er...'

'Warrior?' muttered Sam.

'Yes, well, Carrington Corp will fully reimburse you for this unfortunate incident.' Carrington whispered to his PA and she tapped in a few things. 'How many in the wedding party?'

'Nine,' said the Doctor.

The green PA nodded and passed her pad to Ssard. 'You are booked into the Carlton for 9 p.m. The meal is also on us, under Mr Carrington's name.' The PA turned to the assembled spectators. 'Please ask you cleaners to use credit code TEN-P, and Carrington Corp will automatically pay the bills. Thank you.'

'No, thank *you*. That is surprisingly generous of you, Mr Carrington,' said the Doctor. 'How nice to know that not all businessmen fit the stereotype of uninterested capitalist.'

The green woman turned and stared at the Doctor. And for a second, Sam thought she was doing more than that, staring inside him almost. It was a strange look, and Sam could not actually define what she felt about it, just that it seemed a bit... intrusive. The Doctor must have felt this as well, as he took a slight step back.

'How... interesting,' the green PA said quietly, then smiled at the Doctor. 'I'm sure we will meet again.'

'I hope so,' murmured the Doctor, but she probably didn't hear.

Stacy, Ssard and the priest from the church were trying to explain to two very alarmed parents that this was not the normal turn of events in the fortieth century, while the other wedding observers were making their way to their homes or hotels. The two Equinoids and Frankie the Pakhar made their excuses and said they'd meet in the Carlton bar at 8 p.m. The Doctor nodded his agreement and with a smile at Sam, suggested they sort out the bride and groom.

Stacy's parents were calming down slightly and the Doctor proposed retiring to the TARDIS to get changed. They agreed with this, and the Doctor asked Sam to take their guests back there.

'But what are...'

He put a hand on her shoulder. 'I'll meet you all in the Carlton bar at eight, all right?'

If it wasn't, it was too late. His long legs were carrying him far away from the church, in the direction taken by the green lady. Sam gave him one last look and turned her attention to ushering Stacy's parents towards the ship. But her mind was on other things. Why was the Doctor so keen to disappear? And who was the strange green-skinned woman? She'd given the Doctor a look that suggested... familiarity? No, not really. More like curiosity, as if she could sense he was not quite as human as he seemed from the outside.

Without any real rationale, Sam found that she did not particularly care for this green PA at all. She wondered if the woman was a threat; if she had set a trap, which the Doctor was blindly walking into.

And if that was the case, there was nothing at all Sam could do about it.

Chapter Five
Jigsaw Feeling

'You're late, Agent.'

SSS Agent Hedges looked daggers at the apparently irritated gate guard. 'Tough.'

The black glass doors slid aside as the large trolley was shunted forward by two black-clad SSS agents, with Hedges, armed, walking a few paces behind. The scientific and medical staff cast looks of varying degrees of interest at the body on the trolley as it travelled past them. To most it was 'Oh, a dead Foamasi. When's lunch again?' To some it was 'Oh, a dead Foamasi. Where's that come in from?' And for one or two newcomers, it was 'Wow! A dead Foamasi. Never seen one of those. Can I go watch the autopsy?' – to which an older and more experienced person would smile, knowing that after the fourth or fifth xenoautopsy those recruits quickly got fed up with watching the same entrails coming from different cavities.

Agent Hedges waved a couple of straggling medics out of the way as he guided his team through the labyrinthian corridors that laced the lower basements of the SSS Administration Building.

The trolley swerved slightly and was ushered through another set of sliding doors, white ones with a red cross, where it was allowed to stop. Hedges dismissed his two agents but remained with the body while three medics and a scientific team leader busied themselves with whatever they needed to do. One of the medics looked up as if noticing Hedges for the first time. Unlike the others, he wore skin-tight white cotton gloves.

'Where was it found?'

'About seven kilometres from the Stadium, sir.'

The gloved medic peered towards the dead Foamasi without actually moving closer, as if it was something he expected to see every day.

'Skull pulped pretty efficiently. Oh well, I suppose we better find out if it was dead already.' He clicked his fingers and a small flying drone about the size of a baseball shot towards him, turning on its own axis constantly.

'Case nine oh three oblique delta red. Begin recording. Time and date stamp.'

++CONFIRMED++ chirped the floating ball.

The gloved medic looked at Hedges again. 'Any ID?'

Hedges shook his head.

'All right, Agent Hedges, that'll be all.'

That was the scientist. Hedges nodded his acknowledgement and smartly marched out.

The scientist turned to his colleagues. 'If you need me, I'll be sorting out the reports on this. Any help with an alternate ID would be handy.'

The medics all nodded, although one muttered that this would be Micawber's World's first John 'the Foamasi' Doe.

The scientist turned to go but was stopped by a figure standing in the doorway.

Tall, human, with long but neat hair. Bizarre attire, highly irregular for the SSS Building, but with piercing blue eyes that indicated an intellect. Those eyes were scanning the room, taking as much in as possible.

'Who the heck are you?'

The stranger smiled. 'The Doctor. Why, who are you?'

Ignoring this, the scientist asked for his ID.

The Doctor shrugged. 'No ID. Sam carries it. Sometimes. I'm very interested in your patient, however. Saw him being wheeled across the service area outside.'

'That is a restricted area,' protested one of the medics.

'This is a restricted area, too,' added another.

'Where's security?' asked the one who had programmed the remote recorder.

The Doctor just smiled. 'I have full authority you know. Chase Carrington is a personal friend.'

'So?'

'So, this is his planet.'

'And this is an SSS building. Carrington has no control or rights in here.'

The Doctor looked momentarily flustered, as if trying to remember something. Then he smiled. 'All right, how about I say I'm here by the request of SSS Headquarters on Earth? Dal Karlton, that's the chap.' The Doctor walked past the astonished scientist, and smiled at the floating recorder.

'Hello.'

++GOOD AFTERNOON++

'What do we know so far about our Foamasi corpse, my little friend?'

++VERY LITTLE. T-++

'Desist.' The scientist crossed back to the Doctor, standing between him and the remote. 'Describe your relation with Karlton?'

'Actually, I've never met him, and he wouldn't know me from Adam. But let's be honest: name me someone outside the SSS or the Guardian's office who knows his name?' The Doctor stepped sideways and again looked up at the remote.

'Initial prognosis?'

++NOW INVESTIGA-++

'Desist,' the scientist snapped harshly. 'Remote, total deactivation. Erase all record of case nine oh three oblique delta red.'

++CONFIRMED++

The remote shot back to the far wall and gently eased itself on to a bench and deactivated.

'Spoilsport,' sighed the Doctor and then turned to the dead reptile. He scooped up a pressure blower and began expertly easing small pieces of ruptured skull apart. One of the medics rushed over to stop him, but the scientist actually held him back.

'If he *is* associated with Karlton...'

The gloved medic relaxed and peered at what the Doctor was doing. 'You've done this before, Doctor.'

'An autopsy is an autopsy, no matter who the victim is. This is a particularly nasty case, though. Do you know if he was dead before his head was mashed?'

The scientist coughed. 'My medics were on the verge of finding out when you... arrived so unexpectedly.'

The Doctor looked up, and moved the pressure blower so it pumped a strong concentrated burst of air into the scientist's face. 'Oops. Sorry.' He moved it away. 'Look, why don't you go and talk to HQ and find out all about me? If I turn out to be an enemy agent, I'll surrender to the men in black out there. Otherwise, why don't you let me do this autopsy, eh?'

'Do it?' queried the gloved medic.

'I mean, help whenever asked, of course.'

The scientist gave his medics a final shrug and turned to leave the room.

'Oh, one more thing,' said the Doctor apparently engrossed in his work. 'Do you think this could be the work of the Church of the Way Forward? Only I just saw them demonstrating against a mixed-race wedding, and wondered if...'

The scientist shrugged. 'Not really their thing. Bunch of weirdos, seeking Divine Retribution of the Third Coming, or something like that. Most people stay well away from them. Including Foamasi.' He left the room. The Doctor waited until he was out of earshot before conspiratorially looking towards the three medics. 'Pen-pushers, eh? Everything must be signed in triplicate and all that?'

The three medics looked expressionlessly at him – perhaps they didn't have pens in 3999, he thought. 'Oh. Well, anyway, why don't you proceed. By the way, I noticed something trapped in the oesophagus.'

Immediately the more talkative medic began probing down the throat with his tiny torch.

The Doctor took a couple of steps backward and without taking his eyes off the now busy medics, reached out, scooped up and then pocketed the remote recorder. He walked forward again. 'Can I do something to help? I'm very easily bored you see.'

Without answering, one of the medics reached back, clicking his fingers and pointing at a strange metallic object on the sterilisation trolley that resembled a miniature crowbar. Grimacing slightly, the Doctor passed it to him.

Then he quietly slipped towards the doors and exited.

Two of the medics didn't notice his departure, but the most talkative one did. But as the Doctor disappeared from view, he merely nodded to himself and smiled.

Almost as if he had been expecting something like that to happen.

'I'm late. Again.'

The dinner table at the Carlton was going to be filling up right about now, and his place would be noticeably empty. The Doctor imagined the choice words Sam and Stacy would be using to describe him right now. He needed to get a move on.

He had been very lucky with the use of Karlton's name. He guessed that the scientist would be intimidated enough to check, which would give him some time too snoop around, as administration was pretty much the same the galaxy over and red tape still took a good age or two to cut through. Meantime, if he bumped into any of the SSS military types, he knew they'd be less amenable to his bluff.

He was aware that tiny hidden cameras were probably monitoring him, but as they were equally monitoring everyone else, he hoped that whatever watchers were watching, they weren't watching too hard.

He passed room after room, office after office, on floor after floor. He didn't really know why he was there, only that his insatiable curiosity had once again got the better of him. After following Carrington back towards his building, the Doctor had spotted an SSS vehicle hovering outside the back of the SSS Admin Building and, with his customary skills, he had found a hiding place that ensured he was well concealed but with a good view of what was going on.

And his presentiment had been right on the mark: they had been transporting something large and dead, which, of course, had been a Foamasi.

Foamasi weren't exactly top of his list of favourite alien life-forms – they were aggressive, money-grabbing lizards, whose entire culture was based around corruption, gang warfare and insidious corporate takeovers which hovered uneasily either side of the letter of whatever local laws they encountered. Foamasi lawyers were probably the best-paid Foamasi around, because they could usually guarantee to either find a legal loophole, or arrange for the local judge to be found in a compromising position with someone not considered conducive to popularity within their community.

That aside, the severity of the beating the Foamasi had taken intrigued him. This was more than a casual murder. This was a warning. And to make a warning of that scale to a Foamasi Lodge was akin to a declaration of war. The SSS would want to keep this quiet as long as possible.

He exited an elevator, and the holographic display floating just outside the doors told him he was on the thirty-sixth floor. He had selected the button at random and kept his eyes closed until he got out – he didn't want to spoil the surprise.

Trouble was, eighteen or so black-clad SSS agents were aiming a vicious-looking assortment of blasters at him.

'Sorry, wrong department. I was looking for haberdashery and underwear.'

'Don't move, Doctor whoever you are.'

'Smith.'

'Nice try.'

'Well, it worked two thousand years ago.'

One of the guards, a young one who looked as if he should still be at school, began frisking him but then stepped back, confused. 'Nothing. He's clean, Sarge.'

'Where's the recorder you took from Sterile Four?'

The Doctor shrugged. 'I have no idea what you're talking about.'

The leader of the guards aimed a small silver box at the holo device next to him. The floor number wobbled away to be replaced by an image of him reaching out and stealing the recorder while the medics worked on the dead Foamasi.

'Oh. That recorder. Here.' He slowly put his hand into his pocket and withdrew the recorder.

The young guard who had frisked him stared open mouthed. 'It wasn't... I mean, you all saw... I patted him down and it wasn't –'

The sergeant ignored his protests. 'Why did you take it?'

'It was more conversational than those people working on the Foamasi.'

'The Commandant wants to talk to you.'

'Marvellous. Saves me asking you to take me to your leader. I presume he *is* your leader.'

The guards separated and the sergeant and the young guard who had frisked him walked into the elevator, pulling the Doctor with them.

As the doors closed, and the sergeant punched the relevant

floor button, the Doctor nudged the younger man. 'Easy mistake. The pockets are adapted – not part of the original coat. I sewed in an extra dimension – you'd be surprised what else I've got tucked away in them.'

'Sarge,' the young guard said warningly.

'The prisoner is babbling, Agent. Ignore him. He's just trying to wind you up.'

'Doing quite a good job on both of you, I'd say,' the Doctor said sadly.

As the elevator started to slow down, the Doctor staggered back against the younger soldier, as if fainting. Instinctively, the younger man tried to support him, letting his blaster drop away, so it hung by its strap over his forearm.

'Agent...' began the sergeant, but the Doctor was quicker and he twisted sideways. In doing so, he accidentally knocked the young agent against the wall of the elevator and he slid down silently to the floor. The older sergeant tried to react, but in the confines of the elevator succeeded only in lifting his blaster up, knocking the nozzle into the wall and letting the barrel swing up and catch him a glancing blow on the chin. Apologising profusely, the Doctor gripped the sergeant's face and banged his head back against the elevator wall. A second gentle but forceful tap to the back of his neck dropped him completely.

The Doctor bent down and retrieved the recorder, replacing it in his pocket.

He was about to stand up when the elevator stopped and the doors opened to reveal another group of agents.

'Oh no, not again...'

'He's *never* on time!'

Sam was more disappointed than surprised. More importantly, she was actually worried. The Doctor could be thoughtless occasionally, sometimes a bit childish and frequently daft, but somehow Sam believed that he wanted to be here, to help celebrate Stacy and Ssard's marriage, and see them off on their honeymoon. But he had not arrived.

'He definitely knew it was the Carlton?' Frankie the Pakhar had suddenly stopped being an amusingly camp little tailor and become a rather serious and concerned friend of the Doctor's. 'This is unlike him, you know.'

'I know.'

'I mean, I can remember when he was that older guy with the white hair – he never missed an opportunity to knock back a couple of good vintages and taste the best greenery that Pakhar had to offer, you know.' Frankie smiled and rubbed his whiskers, which Sam had come to associate with signifying that a Pakhar was amused. 'I once left him a note in a bottle on Talin VIII, you know. It said, 'Meet you at Ca'nt'rs in five years from today.' And blow me down, he was there. Turned out he actually went every year on the same date as I'd forgotten to tell him when I actually left the message. But that's the sort of guy the Doctor is. Reliable, you know.'

Sam rather wished she'd known this 'reliable' previous Doctor, but just nodded at Frankie's story. She felt his tiny paw slip into her hand and squeeze. 'He'll be fine, love, you know. Have faith.'

Sam suddenly wanted to hug the little Pakhar. She didn't know why, she just did. But all she actually did was pat his paw gratefully. 'Go join the others, Frankie. I'll go and look for him.'

'Maybe he's back at the TARDIS, you know,' Frankie suggested. 'I mean, I got lost in there once and he got even more lost trying to find me. Mind you, he was that large guy with the dreadful coat by then – that one couldn't find his way out of a paper bag sometimes.'

As Frankie scampered back to their table, Sam left the restaurant and wandered into the walkway. Above her, a couple of vehicles hovered around, and a few pedestrians were hurrying into the rather portentous-looking shopping mall nearby – Sam liked the concept of twenty-four-hour shopping.

The walkways were lined with immaculate green grass and neat shrubs. The whole mall had a neatness to it without being formulaic. It was as if someone had mapped the whole of Carrington City out on a computer but then added a code to move every eighth bush and third building just a few degrees off the perfect grid, so that it looked less perfect, less likely to induce the misery and gloom that blighted the identical blocks of flats and estates built back in her own time.

Carrington City was very attractive, no doubt about that. It reminded her of those promotional films they used to show on telly about Milton Keynes or Docklands, where everyone smiled a lot and there was no graffiti, no urban decay, and lots of trees, glass buildings and litter-free pathways. Unlike those promotional films, the reality of Carrington City had mirrored those concepts rather nicely. Sam would have no objection to staying here a while, shopping (well, the TARDIS ATM did seem to have an inexhaustible cash flow in any currency) and watching the Olympic Games. If the Doctor had the right contacts, maybe they'd get front-row seats.

She waved down a courtesy bus, which took her for free to roughly where the TARDIS was parked. After she disembarked, she took a circuitous route back to the Ship – experience had made this kind of behaviour instinctive; she never ever let strangers see where the TARDIS was (unless it was pretty obvious, such as the time it had materialised on Rockefeller Plaza amid a bunch of shocked ice skaters) and always took the longest route back to it (unless being chased by Daleks, Zygons or Psionovores).

The TARDIS was there, tucked away behind a sweetshop that had closed for the night (obviously the malls had better pulling power for the tourists). She tapped on the door, but there was no answer. Taking the key from around her neck, she opened the door and the interior brightened up as she entered the console room. 'Hello?'

No reply, although Sam thought that the background hum of the Ship had grown a fraction louder. Perhaps this was the TARDIS's unique way of returning her greeting. 'Doctor?'

The hum dropped momentarily – she took that as the TARDIS telling her he wasn't home. With a sigh (she knew she'd regret doing this), she stared at the central column on the console. 'Look, if he comes back without me, tell him I was looking for him, will you? I'm sure you can find a way of doing that.'

The TARDIS hum rose again, then dropped back to normal.

Sam decided that she was mad – it was just a machine after all, and, no matter how many times the Doctor referred to it as a 'she', Sam had always promised herself she'd never do the same. Until now.

'Thanks,' she said and left the Ship, locking the door behind her.

'Don't move!' snapped a voice, and a series of rather harsh handheld flashlights caught her in their beams. Sam could just make out a blur of silhouettes and she shielded her eyes.

'Can I help?' she asked, trying to keep her voice level.

The beams lowered so that she was now standing in a circle of light. There were five or six of them, dressed in black and all armed.

'You are required at the SSS Admin Building. Now.'

'Oh, Doctor, what have you done now?' Sam muttered, just knowing this was his fault.

'It's late. Again.'

Ms Sox jumped slightly – she thought Chase Carrington had headed home hours ago. She moved away from the computer screen, hoping she didn't look guilty, and smiled at her boss.

'I know. I just wanted to wrap up a couple of things before

tomorrow. A couple of the staff are heading off to the Stadium tomorrow, guests of a some of the workers there. I'm ensuring we can spare them.'

Carrington nodded. 'Very conscientious, Ms Sox, but I think it's good for morale to let them go up and see the project. Makes everyone feel that they're contributing to the whole thing, rather than being stuck here all day.' He scratched at one of the tufts of hair that Ms Sox hated so much. 'Well, I'm off home. See you in the morning.'

'Good night, sir.'

'Oh, and Ms Sox?'

'Sir?'

'Don't stay too late again. Especially considering how late you were here last night. The project will go ahead on time, and even you need to rest now and again.'

Ms Sox nodded. 'Of course, Mr Carrington. Half an hour, and I'm off.'

Carrington turned to go and Ms Sox moved fractionally back to her screen.

'Oh, one last thing.'

Resisting the urge to shove the screen down her employer's throat out of sheer impatience, Ms Sox gritted her teeth, then smiled at him. 'Sir?'

'Did the Carlton look after our newly-weds?'

'Yes, sir, although I understand that they were two down eventually. I took the liberty of paying for their flight to Kolpasha, where they are having their honeymoon. The human's parents are travelling with them, before going on to one of the Deimos colonies. I haven't paid for them.'

'Fair enough. I think we've done our bit for public relations.' With a farewell smile he finally left.

Sighing quietly, Ms Sox returned to her computer screen. If Carrington had assumed that she was working, or playing Tetris, he was mistaken. On the screen was a highly illegal relayed image, beamed directly there from the supposedly security-tight SSS Administration Building.

She was watching the two missing dinner guests being shouted at by someone. 'ID bottom left,' she said quietly.

The image zoomed in on the speaker, the pixels rearranging themselves to keep the face perfectly focused. A line of text ran across the bottom of the screen:

COMMANDANT GARY RITCHIE

'ID top left, female.'

PRISONER GPR/64. NAME: UNKNOWN. STATUS: UNKNOWN

'Race?'

BIOSCAN INDICATES HUMAN

'ID top right, male.'

PRISONER GPR/63. NAME: UNKNOWN. STATUS: DOCTOR

'A doctor? Medical or scientific?'

UNKNOWN. PRISONER USES 'DOCTOR' AS GIVEN NAME

Ms Sox pursed her lips. 'Does he indeed. Now that's interesting. Race?'

UNKNOWN. BIOSCAN DOES NOT MATCH ANY OF THE 1,362 RACES ON THE GALACTIC FEDERATION DATABASE.

'Give me access to the database of the Galactic Federation.'

PASSWORD REQUIRED

'Override. Jadean Privilege.'

OVERRIDE UNACCEPTABLE

Ms Sox cursed. The Federation database was always doing this, just to frustrate hackers like her. Well, to be honest, it was doing it to protect the data itself, but at times like this, it always seemed as if it was done just to spite her. 'Keyboard.'

A holographic keyboard plopped into view in front of her and she punched a series of letters and numbers.

OVERRIDE ACCEPTED

'Delete keyboard.' The keyboard vanished. 'Box image from SSS.' The moving pictures of Ritchie interrogating his two mysterious prisoners shrank and shot into the bottom-right corner of the screen. Replacing it was the symbol of the Galactic Federation. 'Access people database – search parameters... oh, two hundred years.

ACCESS ACCEPTED

The image was replaced by swirling multicoloured patterns.

'Search. Keyword "Doctor", as a designated name. Ignore records of "Doctor" as a trade or description.'

Ms Sox turned her attention back to the tiny image of the interrogation while the computer database was further hacked into. Ritchie, poor man, appeared to be getting nowhere with his prisoners. She wondered what this Doctor had actually done to annoy the SSS Commandant so.

ACCESS – DOCTOR LOCATED

'Show.'

Over the next seven minutes, Ms Sox read about what appeared to be at least four different people called 'the Doctor', none of whom looked remotely like the one in Ritchie's office. But there were odd coincidences. The word 'TARDIS' appeared in all the entries, as did a note that he was almost always accompanied by young humanoid females. The most recent record was from 3984, when the Doctor was a guest of no less a personage than the Federation Chair himself.

'Interesting. Seconded to the planet Peladon... links to something called the "Ancient Diadem"... links to Pakhar... links to...' She shook her head. This Doctor certainly got about a bit. She racked her brain. Peladon, well, that was no longer part of the Federation. She'd never heard of the Pakhar Diadem thing. But the fact that he seemed to be a personal friend of the Federation Chair, as did two previous Doctors with different faces... hmm. Perhaps he was some kind of free agent. A glorified detective and master of disguise. Of course, that didn't alter the fact that one of these Doctors had appeared a number of times, more than fifty years between each appearance – and on three occasions, he'd also been involved with Peladon.

'Doctor whoever you are, you are a mystery. Normally, I like mysteries, but right now you're a pain. Still –' she closed her computer down – 'I'd like you to be *my* mystery and not that of the Space Security Service. Tomorrow, I think you and I will have a little talk.'

'They're late. Damn.'

It was very dark in this part of Carrington City, especially as one in three halogen street lamps was broken.

'Wait! Here they come,' said someone to the right of the first speaker.

'OK, coming into range...' He had the driver in his sights. But he had to wait for the car to hover lower – they didn't want it to crash, or there'd be alarms going off everywhere. Sure enough, the cab hovered and then landed.

The first shot neatly zapped through the front of the cab and sliced the driver open from the chest to the tip of his head. Before the body had fallen sideways, the second shot hit the other man in the side of his skull, pulverising his brain in less than a third of a second. His body toppled forward and on to the floor of the cab.

Immediately the killer's compatriots scurried forward, checking expertly that no one had seen anything. One jumped into the front of the cab and shoved the driver cleanly aside, operated the hovercar and, with the two fresh corpses still inside, took off. The other scurried back.

'Perfect,' he reported.

The killer nodded. 'We'll meet again in two days. We can assume that Typtpwtyp thankfully did not survive the Twin Suns Lodge's mission and so we can move our plan forward accordingly. Without his information, they can only guess at what they need to know, which suits us far better. Now I'll contact our Lodge and get more orders.'

His fellow Foamasi acknowledged his words and quickly went off in an easterly direction, swallowed up by the darkness, until it looked as if no one had ever been there. The Foamasi assassin then produced a small device, and aimed it at the street lights that were off. They came back on. The blocking signal to their generators was now inactive.

Despite the now well-lit street, the Foamasi assassin casually slung his weapon over his shoulder and scuttled back to his hotel. If anyone was to see him... well, no one ever wanted to get on the wrong side of a Foamasi with a gun, so they'd stay well away, and very quiet.

Now, *that* was power.

'We're late. Sorry.'

The medics examining the dead Foamasi in the sterile room looked up, surprised. They weren't expecting a relief team tonight anyway. They certainly weren't expecting the relief team to aim blasters and fire at them.

Two of the medics lay spread-eagled on the floor, surprised expressions on their dead faces.

The third medic, the one who had been interested in the Doctor earlier and who wore skin-tight white gloves, crouched down beside them. 'Can you get their bodies out of here easily?'

The three members of the 'relief team' nodded in unison. Two of them crossed the room, effortlessly picking up a body each and taking it outside. They, too, were wearing skin-tight white gloves.

The remaining one, his hands similarly attired, pointed at the dead Foamasi. 'Why is that here?'

The other medic shrugged. 'It was killed and the SSS wanted it examined. Why weren't you here earlier? I need to get out of here as soon as possible.'

'Do you have the formula?'

The medic laughed at the newcomer. 'Better than that, I have the drugs already prepared. This place spends so much of its time chasing its own shadows, they never notice anything going on under their noses.' He crossed the room and pulled open a drawer in a metal cabinet. He threw a small seven-centimetre disc over to the leader of the 'relief team'. 'The details are mostly on that. The rest are in here.' He tapped the side of his skull, then dipped his hand back into the drawer and brought out a plastic bag of pill bottles. 'This is the first batch. We should try them out on our new friends.'

The other two 'relief team' members returned.

'Time to go,' said the medic.

The four white-gloved men left the sterile room, and the dead Foamasi – proving once again that SSS security was not all it ought to be – vanished without trace. No one had seen them enter. No one saw them leave. And no one realised that the two medics were dead until the scientist they worked for found the partially disembowelled Foamasi on the sterile table the following morning, and a couple of agents located the two bodies, shoved clumsily into a waste-disposal chute.

Chapter Six
Are You Still Dying, Darling?

The Wirrrn had a plan, and so far, it was progressing very satisfactorily.

Whoever was actually responsible for constructing the infrastructure of Micawber's World had done their job very well indeed.

As artificial planetoids go, it was pretty much state-of-the-art. Indeed, even by 3999, no one had bettered the technology used. A couple might have jazzed up the basic design, sorted out a couple of minor counterbalancing errors and no doubt added various pretty shapes and geometric tunnel entrances, but the basic creation of Micawber's World was still impressive.

Originally it had been a tiny lump of useless rock drifting through space – possibly having drifted away from the asteroid belt. It was seized by one of Carrington Corp's many scavenger ships and immediately claimed. A quick Claim of Ownership was registered with both the Earth Government and the Galactic Federation, and Chase Carrington had somewhere to achieve his life's ambition.

Creating a Utopia took time. And money. Carrington lacked neither, nor did he find himself short of designers, engineers and architects, all keen to make their mark on history by contributing to his great dream.

And so, thirteen years before, Carrington had formally laid the foundation stone of Micawber's World (Micawber was his mother's maiden name) on the surface of the asteroid. Mind you, the necessity of having to wear a spacesuit, and the fact that Carrington's new world was tethered to forty-three geostationary space shuttles to stop it drifting, didn't exactly ensure that the holovid press call was that well attended. But when his engineers announced their revolutionary new power source, the galaxy took notice. Cynics awaited the announcement that it had all gone wrong, while supporters held their breath to await the start of construction.

A massive metallic skeletal sphere, five thousand kilometres in diameter, was constructed and gradually filled in, working inward like the creation of a Dyson sphere. Fifteen hundred kilometres in, the solid base began to be threaded through with a series of tunnels, with a number of links to the surface. These also provided access to the centre of the planetoid, where several specks of a neutron star were held in a specially positioned magnetic-field generator, supplying the planetoid with artificial gravity. Surrounding that was the pulsator, duplicating the power of a small sun, using harmless solar radiation to power and heat the surface via a network of microscopic cables threaded back up through the tunnels. The technology used to create these previously theoretical but apparently impracticable devices came from three or four different sources, pooling their resources in Carrington's famous laboratories.

And thus, a few years later, Micawber's World opened its spaceport to tourists, who flocked there in their thousands from all over the galaxy. Carrington had indeed created a leisure paradise and, as if to indicate just how satisfied he was, he moved his entire business empire from Mars to Micawber's World. Both the Galactic Federation and the Space Security Service opened bureaux there as well. As more and more shops, hotels, restaurants and bars bought out franchises and licences, everyone, even the sceptics, had to acknowledge that in just a small space of time, Carrington Corp had achieved the impossible. Micawber's World was a success. It came as no surprise when Carrington announced his plans to buy up the

Grecian Corp and secure the rights to the famous Olympic Games, building a stadium to host them on his new pleasure planet.

And now the planet was gradually filling up with dignitaries, sportsmen, ambassadors, royalty and holovid crews ready to take part in the biggest, brightest and best Olympics ever. Carrington intended that it should be a Games no one would be allowed to forget.

Whether the Wirrrn which had settled on the asteroid hundreds of years previously intended him to be right remained to be seen. After all, the Queen was used to being patient.

And what better breeding stock could they ask for?

SSS Agent Jean-Paul Cartwright was not entirely sure how he came to know all this.

To be honest, there was quite a lot SSS Agent Jean-Paul Cartwright could not explain right now. He understood about Andromeda, about the Great Swarming, about the urge to survive, to spread the Seed and to dominate. He understood the entire histories of planets he couldn't remember ever hearing of. He understood so many of the secrets of the galaxies, what they were like millions of years ago, how they had evolved, and about some of the astonishing species that occupied them.

Where did this information come from? He had images of Jill, his sister. Except that he was an only child.

He was certain that Agent Morris had a sister, though. He seemed to recall his referring to a 'Jill' now and again. So how come he could remember watching her growing up? Could still see images of Acquilian pleasure ponds, holodolls and scraped knees? Come to think of it, he could remember growing up among the smells of spicy kitchens, glorious food and Roman Catholic masses. Yet he was sure he grew up in New Lyon, not with a Nouveau Romaine background... So how come the aroma of freshly made wholemeal pasta was so prominent in his mind. Wasn't that Marco Pirroni's life?

Why was he remembering everyone else's experiences, jumbled together, crashing in and out of fleeting moments, half-seen friends and families just out of reach, just on the edge of his vision? Why did the word 'mother' conjure up a dumpy brunette as well as a sad-looking, grey-haired woman standing outside a grey stone cottage, dressed in black, shivering in the harsh Irish winds? Irish? He wasn't Irish!

Or was he?

And why did the image that dominated his mind coalesce into a massive insectoid creature, two bulbous amber eyes, powerful mandibles, a sprouting of antennae, a proboscis and a sectioned body. The same size as he was, but so much more powerful... And that sting on the tail...

Why? What was happening to him?

And where was he?

Jean-Paul Cartwright forced his eyes wide open, panting – almost hyperventilating – in the darkness.

Slowly his eyes grew accustomed. He couldn't move. His arms were pinned to his sides but he was upright – seemingly some way off the ground. A flash of recognition – these were the tunnel walls he and... and... Ed Salt, that was right: he and Ed Salt had been working in.

Something had been there... rearing up, chittering... insects of some sort... blocking everything out. He'd been aware that his tracer, connecting him to Pete Clarke's PMD, had suddenly gone dead. The creatures were shielded from it and so were he and Eddie. They had touched him...

There was a pain in his... his side and back. He'd pulled a muscle. There it was again...

Focus on the tunnels. Think, man, think. What had Dallion drilled into them? Think. Observe. Absorb info– infor–

Absorb. Yes, he was absorbing information from the others in the troop. Bailey, McGeoch, McKay... Ed Salt...

They were there, surrounding him. Hanging off the walls around. They were in a circular area, where the tunnels met, a kind of crossroads under Micawber's World. But why were they here? What was supporting them?

'Ed? Marco? John?'

The others were all unconscious, slumped slightly in their...

The pain... it was causing his head to ache... to *really* ache...

'I am Jean-Paul Cartwright,' he said, determined to stop whatever was hurting him. 'I am... Jean-Paul... I am Edward Salt. And I am Steve Bailey. And I am Robbie Smith. Yes, we're all here. All together.'

A dull light seem to blur around SSS Agent Cartwright's eyes, giving the room an orange but fractured look. Ten, twenty, fifty, a hundred... countless images of the area he was in, all from slightly different angles, burst into his brain, washing over him. He could see the others, he could see himself, he could see their friends, families, lovers, his past, their pasts, his home, their homes, he could see different lives, different worlds, different races, he could understand books, plays, songs in a thousand different languages and cultures. He was... he was... something new.

A huge wave of euphoria overtook his mind, erasing everything and nothing simultaneously. It was all still there but now it was compartmentalised, it made sense. It was neatly filed away, like his own original memories. Stored and stacked, ready to be delved into when necessary. But now he possessed the accumulated knowledge of thousands upon thousands of individuals. Individuals who were, quite rightly, no longer individual. Of course, the other species had been weak. Ineffectual. But now they were together, they were strong. They were perfect.

They were no longer Jean-Paul Cartwright, or Marco Pirroni, or John McGeoch or G'res'lx or Jis Tok Nannarn or... or...

They were Wirrrn, now.

And that was good.

The room was in pitch blackness except the thin beam of very harsh light that surrounded him like a pillar. He could not see how many other people were in the room, but by listening to the breathing he had ascertained there were at least two others as well as Commandant Ritchie.

Neither of them was Sam Jones.

Good.

He took a deep breath. Any second now, Ritchie would restart his pointless questions and he would stand there, answering them truthfully - admittedly most of them were 'I don't know' - and know that Ritchie was getting more uptight. He clearly either did not like conducting interrogations, or else wasn't used to them. After all, Micawber's World was a little out of the way and the Doctor suspected that most SSS prisoners ended up back on Earth, where the interrogators were far better at their jobs.

The Doctor's mind began to wander. He found few things more boring than interrogations. He'd been abused, tortured, had the good-cop/bad-cop routine, and been examined by more mind probes or mind analysis machines than he could remember.

And still he stuck by his best tactic - never stating anything other than the truth. And, as a result, more often than not, the machines or the interrogators - or both - had had nervous breakdowns and given up. Ritchie was no different, except that as he wasn't an expert at this, he wouldn't know when to give up defeated. So the Doctor just smiled unhelpfully in the general direction of Ritchie's last position and hoped this would be over soon.

Truth was, of course, that he had learned far more about the SSS operation here on Micawber's World than they had intended, simply by listening and carefully manipulating the questions

Ritchie asked him, ensuring he got more than he gave.

The SSS were here at the request of someone in Carrington Corp to act as security for the Olympiad. This heavily overcrowded building – usually just an administrative outpost – was making tempers fray. On top of that, a troop of agents had vanished while setting up lighting to help the engineers power the Stadium; a rogue Foamasi had been brutally murdered; and an incident had occurred in the lab where he had seen the Foamasi corpse. To top it all off, he couldn't help but feel that everything was being watched by someone elsewhere – probably the SSS were so paranoid they needed to monitor each other – and he had no idea where Sam was now.

They'd brought her in, spitting fire pretty much as expected.

'How did they know where to find me?' she had asked him.

'Because I told them,' he had replied, hoping she would take the hint. He wanted her here, with him. She obviously did, because she relaxed immediately and started being her usual ebullient, cheerful-to-the-point-of-aggravating and talkative self to Commandant Ritchie. It was a routine they'd had plenty of opportunities to perfect over their time and adventures together, and by now Sam took to it like a duck to water. Ritchie had given away quite a bit without realising they were manipulating him and –

The Doctor's reminiscences broke when the voice from the darkness barked.

'So, Doctor. Why are you here?' Ritchie had restarted his pointless questions.

'I came to be best man at a wedding.'

'Did you know the dead Foamasi?'

'No.'

'Are you with a Foamasi Lodge?'

'No.'

'Did you kill the medics in Sterile Room Four?'

'No. I didn't know they were dead. All three of them were doing the xenoautopsy when I left.'

'Why did you steal the remote?'

'I thought I could reprogram it to work for me.'

'Why?'

'To find out who killed the Foamasi.'

'Most humans don't give a damn about dead Foamasi. If you weren't working with it, why were you so interested in its death?'

'I'm not acquainted with any Foamasi, really. I'm just curious. That Foamasi was beaten particularly viciously, and even given the typical human xenophobic attitude prevalent nowadays, despite the Federation, I thought it alarming that a murder had taken place this close to the Olympic Games.' The Doctor paused, then added, 'Oh, and your security around this building is a shambles. I just walked in. No one challenged me. Maybe that's how the person who killed the medics in Sterile Room Four got in. Through the back door...'

There was silence, then the Doctor could pick out whispers. Suddenly the photon beam cut off and he staggered slightly, free of its grip, just as the room was flooded with light. The Doctor shielded his eyes, wincing at the momentary twinge of a headache that followed. Slowly he moved his arm and looked ahead.

The room was bare apart from Ritchie seated at a glass desk, a smallish-looking panel of coloured switches built into it. Standing beside him was a female SSS agent and, behind her, a medic.

The Doctor smiled. 'How interesting.'

'Please be quiet,' said Ritchie.

There was a silence, so the Doctor sat down. He slowly dug into an inside pocket of his coat and produced a pack of cards, then began playing Clock Patience on the floor.

'Stop doing that,' the woman said.

The Doctor ignored her. 'You're not very comfortable about this, are you, Commandant Ritchie? I mean, you've probed me, questioned me and shouted at me, and, having got the truth, you don't know what to do with me.' The Doctor paused, then flipped another card over. King of Hearts. He moved it to the twelve o'clock position.

'Who are you?'

'The Doctor. Your prisoner.' He flipped a Three of Spades and moved it to its rightful place.

Ritchie glanced back at the medic. 'Is he telling the truth?'

The response was a nod.

'You need my help, don't you, Commandant? With the Games so close, you can't be seen to get your hands dirty.'

Ritchie waved his agent and the medic out of the room. They obeyed without question. After a few moments, he got up from his desk and crossed over to the Doctor.

'And if I did, would you give it?'

The Doctor stared hard at Ritchie. 'Why should I? I've been accused and abused by your people from the moment I arrived here.'

Ritchie sighed. 'Some of my agents have gone missing in the tunnels beneath the Stadium. I've given their leader, Quartermaster-Sergeant Dallion and her remaining troops until the opening of the Games to discover what happened – but I think someone wants them dead. You see there are... other parties with a stake in this, and my hands are, as you point out, tied. Now some of my science and medical team are either dead or missing.'

Ritchie placed a small plastic card in front of the Doctor, who reached forward and slowly pushed it back. 'I can't be bought, Commandant. If you want my help, you have to take it on my terms.'

'Which are?'

'Wait, watch, and see. Give me free rein here, access to your computers – are you still using the Compuvac system? Oh, and a man in your position must have contacts in... shall we say, other areas?'

'Green Fingers.'

'I'm sorry?' The Doctor cocked his head to one side.

'Try the Foamasi Temple. I understand it's a very pretty building.' Ritchie turned towards the door. 'I have to go.'

'Think about what I've said,' the Doctor called out without actually watching him leave.

He scooped up the cards and put them back in his pocket – and felt the comforting sphere of the stolen remote. Some people never learned how to do a decent search. Although with *his* pockets... well, he couldn't blame them.

For a few moments nothing happened. Then the doors at the far end of the room slid open, revealing Sam and two SSS agents, guns holstered.

The Doctor walked over to her put an arm protectively around her shoulder. 'And what can we do for you two gentlemen?'

The SSS agents didn't answer.

'And the odds on an explanation that makes some kind of sense are...?' Sam looked up at him, a wry smile on her face.

The Doctor grinned. 'Too high right now.'

'So what happens next?'

The Doctor looked at the guards. 'I think we've been asked to help in one of those no-one-can-actually-pinpoint-exactly-when-we-asked-the-Doctor-to-help-and-so-will deny-it-all-if-it-goes-wrong sort of ways.'

'Nothing new there, then.'

He smiled at her. 'Ready for action?'

'What do *you* think?'

Then an agent leaned over, passing a strange ID badge to each of them. Both had holo-images of their wearers and claimed they were citizens of The Federation.

'Great. More military nonsense. One day I'd like to meet up with someone serene and nice who doesn't carry guns.' Sam turned to walk away, but the Doctor stopped.

'I might be able to help you there. Remember the Church of the Way Forward?'

'Like I'm going to forget them. They ruined Stacy's wedding.'

The Doctor nodded. 'Sadly, that's unimportant right now. I want you to go and make peace with them. Find out exactly why they're here. And whether or not they have a grudge against the Foamasi as a race.'

'Can't you do that?'

'No.' The Doctor smiled. 'I need to go and see a man about a murder.'

The medic and his two killer friends, all still wearing their tight white gloves, sat in a circle at the centre of the tunnels. Above them, white Wirrrn cocoons were split open, their occupants having successfully hatched.

And standing in the centre of the circle they formed was one of the fully grown Wirrrn, a Swarm Leader.

The medic could hear its voice inside his head, communicating through the special bond they possessed. He tugged at the base of one of his gloves, to scratch at an irritation. The irritation was caused by his human flesh bubbling slightly where it was transmuting into the green, blistering skin of a Wirrrn pupa. He replaced the white glove, apparently completely unconcerned by this physiological change.

The Wirrrn was asking to see the pills.

He produced the container from his pocket and opened the lid, tipping a couple of them into his gloved palm. 'They successfully inhibit the full external conversion process without altering the mind in any way,' he explained. 'We are currently working on a slightly different strain that will enable the athletes to carry on without exhibiting any signs of Seeding. The plan is to use three per planet as carriers. That gives us a more than acceptable risk of failure.'

The Swarm Leader acknowledged this, and asked how they were to be distributed.

'The Foamasi. Once the Lodges here learn that there is a new drug to enhance the athletic prowess of the sportspeople, they will do anything to discover the source. We suspect that the Dark Peaks Lodge are already investigating these tunnels as they appear to be aware of the missing human troopers. The Twin Suns Lodge are also on the planet – one has been brought in dead to the Space Security Service already. The South Lodge will no doubt be here soon. One of them will try to obtain the exclusive rights to distribute the drugs, charge a lot of credits and make a killing.'

The Wirrrn asked how long was left before the Olympic Games would commence. How long did they have before the pills needed to be distributed?

'I'll have them ready this evening. The Games open in twenty-four hours, so we will let the Foamasi have them then.

The Wirrrn began easing itself across the ground, towards one of the tunnels that went lower, towards the solar generator.

The four humans stood up, but one of them arched back and fell to the floor. Two others ran to him, but it was too late. His white smock was already splitting open and from every tear, every gap, green pupal fluids oozed and then gathered together into a single bubbling mound. Of the human body, nothing was left bar the destroyed clothing. The green mass gradually took a new shape, about a metre long, like a giant green slug. It reared up briefly, displaying a cluster of newly formed suckers and at one end, a large single eye stared out from under the canopy of a deep slit. The human was no more, and a new Wirrrn had been created in his place.

The medic knelt down at the pupa, observing it with cold

detachment. It was irrelevant that it had been human just moments before. What mattered was that the pill it had taken to stop this final mutation had failed. Both he and his surviving compatriots were similarly Wirrrn-infected, but the pills he had developed held back the initial change. Within a few hours, this pupa would be a fully grown Wirrrn. And if the pill had failed to work, then how long before he himself was fully absorbed by the wonderful, astonishing new cells that swam through his pathetic mammalian body?

Once upon a time, Dr Miles Mason would have been revolted by his work, by his transformation. But now, he just saw it as a thing of sheer beauty. One day, when his work was done, he could drop the pretence of working as a xenobiologist for the SSS and allow the repressed Wirrrn genes to take over and he, too, would know the true freedom of being part of the Swarm.

But until then, he had work to do.

'Tell me about the work in Sterile Room Four.'

The Doctor and Professor Jeol, the scientist, he had met earlier, were seated in the latter's office.

'The medics were xenobiologists, brought in by the SSS much as I was. With the Games going on, as many medical and scientific experts as possible were required.'

The Doctor nodded. 'Now, two of your team died. The other? The one I spoke to?'

'Dr Mason, a highly talented award-winning pharmacologist we brought up from Earth. Perhaps they took the body with them.'

'Or perhaps he wasn't there? Could he have gone back to his hotel or wherever?'

Jeol shrugged. 'Some agents investigated, but he certainly didn't seem to be there.'

The Doctor stood up and began walking around the office, lifting odd boxes and datapads abstractly.

'I don't think you'll find him in here, Doctor,' snapped Jeol.

The Doctor ignored him and continued his bizarre examinations. He began scratching at the walls and ceiling, then crouched down and looked under the desk. 'Tell me, Professor, why do you think your medics were killed, hmm?'

Jeol paused. Then sighed. 'I've been trying to work that out myself. I mean, if another Lodge of Foamasi were responsible, why not remove the corpse? Ditto if it was his Lodge.'

'The Church of the Way Forward?'

'No. You mentioned them before. Why do they interest you?'

The Doctor stopped. 'I don't know really. I've never had a faith, as such. I had a House. And a birthsign. And a Chapter to be loyal to, but never really any kind of god. But I know plenty who have, and very few of them are still peddling such bigoted doctrines.'

Jeol carefully replaced a datapad the Doctor had knocked over. 'Not been to Earth recently then?'

'No. Why?'

'Religious fervour. Every week it seems as if some new Church of This or Path of That springs up. When so many of the old religions died out through war or boredom, new fashionable ones sprang up. Most were cultish, or faddish, but some stuck around. The Way Forward lot have been around for about thirty years, devoted to their Goddess. No one knows exactly who she is, but she clearly doesn't approve of multiculturalism.'

'Are they against the Federation, then?' The Doctor lifted one end of the desk, shook his head, and replaced it, but away from its former indentations in the carpet by a couple of centimetres.

'I don't believe so, no,' Jeol said. 'They're not racist or xenophobic as such – they just don't agree with different species breeding. Ironically, I think it's more to do with keeping each race pure rather than trying to suggest any race is better than another. They have non-human members scattered around.' Jeol eased his desk back into position with his foot, hoping the Doctor wouldn't notice.

The Doctor ran his hand along the side of the door, then checked his fingers. 'How often do you have the cleaners in here, Professor?'

Jeol was surprised by this question. 'Er... About once a week, I suppose. I don't really see them come in. We use Tees.'

'Tees?'

'Robots. Invented by some old professor, MacTaggart or somesuch, who went off his rocker, lost his job and ended up creating the Tees. He let them set up their own civilisation, but they failed and the Federation bought them lock, stock and barrel.'

The Doctor sat on the floor looking at his fingers. 'I'm very surprised that in an environment like this, devoid of paper and powder-based products, and with efficient servo-robots to do the cleaning, you'd have quite this amount of dust around your door.'

'And your point is?'

'It's not dust. Someone is bugging your office, Professor Jeol, using microscopic particle recorders.' He waved his fingers at Jeol. 'Look, Ma, we're on *Candid Camera*.'

Jeol frowned. 'I'm sorry, I simply don't know what you're talking about.'

The Doctor sighed, and Jeol felt unpleasantly as if he were being treated like a child by a teacher who was having problems explaining rudimentary mathematics. The Doctor was up again, shoving his hand in the direction of Jeol's face. 'Look. This is not dust. It is a form of surveillance equipment that is placed here to record simple things such as who is using this office, what electronic transactions take place and such like. It's heat-sensitive and will have recorded every conversation that has taken place in here, both vocally and over the networks. You, Professor, are being spied upon.'

'Who by?' This was, of course, ridiculous, but Ritchie had

insisted that everyone play along with the Doctor.

'By whom. Someone high up, I should imagine. Someone with access to the knowledge that you are the sort of person they'd want to spy upon in the first place.' The Doctor walked out of the office. 'Let's go and see how sterile Sterile Room Four actually is, shall we?'

Jeol shook his head and followed the Doctor out. The man was mad. A sterile room was... well, sterile. No amount of dirt-pretending-to-be-surveillance-equipment could get in there.

Ritchie needed his own head examined for foisting this moron upon them at this time.

Sam stood and watched the water cascading down the side of the sculpture, catching the glow of the multicoloured lights behind it and making different shapes and patterns all the time.

The statue was Prometheus, the life-bringer. It also had the words © *Grecian Corp* stencilled at the bottom of the plaque.

She quite liked fountains – there was one outside the swimming pool at Bethnal Green, but that just dribbled a green slime most of the time. During school holidays, when she was a kid, Sam and her mum would stop and look at it on their way to Mum's DSS office. 'Once, it was really pretty,' her mum said. 'Then the vandals got to it and buggered it up. Shame really.'

But as her mother dismissed it, so Sam got indignant. She didn't know why exactly, but she took an instant dislike to vandals. Her mother had said something was beautiful but wasn't any longer – and they were responsible. Looking back, maybe that was something to do with where her efforts at campaigning, joining demos and marches came from – a desire to see things that were once beautiful put right again. Of course, that path took a few twists and turns that neither of her parents entirely approved of, but Sam knew her own heart was in the right place.

'God, was I ever that young,' she muttered, smiling at the naivety of youth that believed the world's wrongs could be so easily put right. Preaching to the converted, that was the trouble with demos.

The Prometheus statue glistened as the water splashed across it, the multicoloured lights exposing dents, scratches and tiny imperfections that the daylight would never have shown up. Sam liked that – unlike most things on Micawber's World, the statue wasn't perfect. Come to think of it, if she looked closer at Carrington City late at night, she'd probably find a few dents and scratches in that as well. She hoped so – perfection was very pretty but became dull after a while.

She sat on the side of the fountain, letting the occasional water spray soak her neck and shoulder as she looked back at the business district. She had passed a Menards all-purpose store a while back and bought a datapad, a ball of string, three balloons and couple of local delicacies (well, actually, they could have come from anywhere – she just knew they weren't from Earth) called gwampa fruit, according to the somewhat chatty and kindly grey-haired old man who worked there and insisted on telling her his name was Szmanda and that his family had originally come from Earth. Exactly what she needed the odds and sods for, she had no idea, but he had been very persuasive and it had passed a few minutes harmlessly.

Relaxing beside the fountain, she tugged at the little string bag the gwampa fruits were in, took one out and bit into it. Sweet but a bit stiff, a bit like an unripe pear, but not unpleasant.

God, when was the last time she'd had a pear?

'I wonder what Mum's doing right now.' She smiled a little sadly at that. She had really wanted to ask the Doctor to take her back for a visit just once, after all these years – just to let them know she was fine. Seeing Stacy with her parents rubbed salt in that little wound a bit more – although she was very happy for Stacy to get the chance to be with her parents again.

And Sam had no doubt that he would take her if asked. But did she have the right?

She had been seventeen when the Doctor met her (well, give or take a few months). Now she was twenty-one. All that time on Ha'olam meant she must have missed a couple of good parties back home.

So, to Mum and Dad she had been away perhaps four years. Did they think she was still alive? She could imagine the *Crimewatch* programmes, the newspaper reports and announcements on GLR or Kiss FM. Missing girl. Samantha A. Jones. Last seen wearing jeans and a white T-shirt with SHORTLIST across it and dates from a club tour on the back. Blonde hair, slim, five foot sixish.

By now they'd have opted to accept, if not quite believe, she was dead. The joky postcards from far-flung galactic locations had seemed funny at the time; now they just seemed a bit cruel. Another mis-per on the Sun Hill nick list. To return home after four years without warning, healthy and unhurt would be something rather difficult to explain. And she couldn't just arrive the minute she left, not looking like this, not with everything she'd seen and done and... *lived* through. So what should she do for the best? A flying visit in person? Get a message to them? Or just leave well alone?

And she couldn't even get that tatty old Shortlist T-shirt on now if she tried. God, what did she ever see in that type of music anyway? She only fancied the lead singer because he reminded her of Stevie at school.

Sam finished off the gwampa fruit, threw the core into a nearby waste bin and set off for the Mirage hotel, where that religious group had said they were staying.

She had moved away from the well-lit fountain and into a thin walkway between two buildings. Halogen street lamps lit the path well, but some instinctive feeling made her move a bit faster. Thinking of home reminded her of the alleys down by Barton Street and how unsafe they could be – Baz and his stupid gang doing their Charlie deals, trying to feel important and never quite realising how unimportant he was when there were bigger, organised gangs who'd slit his throat without hesitation rather than let some seventeen-year-old big-mouth on their patch and attract the attention of the police.

Behind her, one of the street lamps flickered and died.

Carrington Corp must have backups to override that or some little nanites that would repair it before morning.

Two more went out, in sequence. Then another. And another.

Sam found herself quickening her step instinctively, breaking into a light jog.

The first boy that appeared in front of her caused her to slow down, but another two behind him made her decide to stop. She glanced around, and five or six more were emerging from behind the bushes behind her, cutting off her retreat. They seemed to be quite broad but very small, about three feet high.

They watched her, some standing, some crouched. Expertly. Wherever she could think of moving, she was covered.

She couldn't see any weapons, but again, that meant nothing.

The darkness meant that she was unable to distinguish faces, even on the nearest. Were they masked?

'Evening, lads,' she said. 'Can I help?'

They didn't answer, but one towards the rear of the group directly in front took something from his pocket. It seemed to resemble a bolas and the others parted as he walked forward. As he got nearer, Sam became transfixed by the bolas – each of the tiny balls had barbs on it, as did the tiny threads of metallic filament that connected them. If they wrapped themselves around her, she'd be sliced apart in a moment. These boys were not playing.

As the leader got closer, she could see his face. No, they weren't human – or at least this one wasn't. It was a dark face, possibly a sort of muddy green or brown colour, with a small rubbery snout and huge finlike ears pinned back by a series of bejewelled studs – clearly some kind of fashion accessory, because his snout had some as well. Apart from the snorkelish nose, there were tiny gills rising and falling on his neck. Amphibians of some sort?

Two of the others walked closer, wearing different jewels on different parts of their faces. They had manga eyes, white with tiny black pupils, and the snouts were of varying length. The leader had a tiny scar on his cheek, although Sam had no way of telling whether this was a battle scar or another fashion statement. 'Ya, waya do'adis bass, Thainch'k?'

It took Sam a second to realise it was asking her a question.

'Did you turn the lights off?' she countered.

The creature nodded. 'Da, out tabeamers. A'bass, ya view, Thainch'k?'

Sam shook her head. 'I'm sorry, guys, but you're losing me.'

'She's not a Thain,' came a human voice from the far end of the walkway. The creatures looked over Sam's shoulder, so she turned as well, but kept one eye of the swinging bolas. 'Leave her alone, please.'

The leading alien just gurgled, a sound like very sludgy water going down a blocked drain. He raised the bolas, and Sam took her chance. She dropped to the floor, scooping up the mud and grit – at least, she hoped it was mud, but she'd wash her hands carefully later, just in case – and chucked them at the leader, catching him full in the face. He went down spluttering, the bolas dropping and bouncing on to the grass.

Two of the others went for Sam, the rest concentrating on the man, believing a human male was more dangerous than a human female. Fortieth-century chauvinism had its place then, Sam decided, as she dived aside and landed on the grass, rolling back on to her feet. The two creatures promptly collided with their leader, who was still wiping dirt from his large eyes, and the three of them went down in a tumble of arms, legs and vitriolic curses.

The others, however, were overpowering her knight in shining armour.

She saw an opportunity and grabbed at the stunned leader.

A second later, she yelled at the attackers. They turned to look.

Sam was gingerly holding the bolas – how were they to know she'd never use it? Like all bullies, Sam noted, the leader was bricking it and the others were confused.

The walkway lights went back on in rapid succession and four SSS agents ran over, one carrying what was presumably a portable gadget-for-turning-lights-back-on. The creatures surrendered immediately and the agents dragged them off.

'Sorry,' said the sergeant. 'We thought we had this area flushed weeks ago but this lot must have laid claim to the turf of the previous gang.'

Assuming that was all the explanation required, he followed his men as they got into a silently hovering vehicle Sam took to be this century's equivalent of a Black Maria. Within moments they were gone.

The man who had saved her passed Sam her dropped bag with its single remaining gwampa fruit.

In the light, she could see the familiar vestments of the Church of the Way Forward – the young man who had saved her was the same one she'd accidentally thumped at the wedding. He even had a small bruise on the side of his head.

'I hit you hard, didn't I?'

He nodded. 'Still,' he smiled at her, 'they say pain is good for the soul.'

'Well, thank you.' Sam wanted to give him a piece of her mind about the way he and his mates had ruined Stacy's wedding, but remembered the Doctor's mission. And this was as good a lead into the enemy camp as she was going to get. 'The name's Sam. Sam Jones.'

The man shook her hand. 'Kyle Dale. One day, it'd be nice to meet under pleasant circumstances, Sam Jones. Luckily for you I saw the lights out and guessed what the Kleptons were up to.'

'Kleptons?'

'Those little parasites are Kleptons. They dislike humans because they remind them of their old enemies, the Thains. The irony is of course that the Thains died out ten thousand years ago and so generation after generation has never actually met a Thain. It's more a mantra to them.'

'Or a religion?'

Kyle paused and thought about this. 'In a way, perhaps, yes. I shall put that point of view to Reverend Lukas.'

Sam saw her chance. 'Maybe *I* could. It'd give us a chance to sort out this morning's fracas.'

Kyle smiled. 'He'd like that.'

'How about right now?' suggested Sam, brightly.

Kyle's smile grew broader. 'Please, let me take you there.'

As he led her off, Sam just hoped that religious orders were still polite, respectful of others and not a lion's den of lecherous old men with seedy pasts and dubious moral hypocrisies who'd jump a girl's bones before she could say three Hail Marys.

Feeling that she might be wise to rename herself Daniel, Sam followed Kyle along the quiet streets.

'It's nearly midnight,' whined Jeol. 'How on Earth do you expect me to track down all my staff now? Most of them are at home. With their wives and children. And their holos. And their datapads. And their sleep.'

'So? I need to speak with as many people as possible.'

'Now?'

The Doctor stared at Jeol. Why did humans never understand that every so often, urgency was quite a positive thing? Or was it a quirk of this new personality of his that he regarded humans a little less tolerantly since becoming acquainted with his own –

how could he put it? – genetic heritage?

He grabbed Jeol's shoulders. 'Don't you see it, Professor? This is an adventure. Some excitement to add novelty to your ludicrously humdrum existence.'

No, that hadn't come out quite right. Still, press the advantage...

'Together, you and I can solve this mystery. It's like a jigsaw – we're just missing a few pieces. And the overall picture. And especially all the nice, flat edge bits.'

No, still Jeol didn't seem inspired.

'Think about how proud Mrs Jeol will be when she hears how you made a major contribution to stopping the Foamasi disrupting the Olympic Games.'

'My mother is dead.'

'Ahh.' The Doctor released his shoulders. 'I meant your wife, actually.'

'I'm not married. Any more.'

'Why not?'

'Because I was forever being called into work at midnight. Receb didn't like it.'

The Doctor sighed heavily and began to wander off. He could see he wasn't going to get anywhere with Professor Jeol. 'Useless oaf,' he muttered ungraciously.

'What was that?'

'Goodnight, Professor,' he called. 'Thank you so much for your help.'

'Well, er... Goodnight then, Doctor. What are you going to do?'

The Doctor turned and flashed him a smile. 'Oh potter about a bit, see what I can find.'

As Professor Jeol shuffled off, the Doctor decided he didn't particularly want to stay in the SSS building any longer. It was high time he paid a visit to the mysterious Green Fingers. Whoever he might be.

* * *

Sam was sitting in a large room, comfortable enough, if a little too Spartan for her tastes.

It was rectangular, about thirty foot by fifteen, a series of camp beds lining the walls, each bearing a small rucksack. Obviously the Church of the Way Forward travelled light.

The hotel itself seemed plush enough so perhaps the Reverend Lukas had stripped it himself of any luxuries. Well, he did run this bizarre sect, cult or whatever. And what a weirdo *he* was.

Still wearing his wide-brimmed hat, Reverend Lukas was positioned in the centre, his followers and Sam (seated next to Kyle Dale) in a circle looking in on him. He was smiling, but there was something wrong with him, Sam was sure of that. It was the eyes: they didn't smile – they just stared. Probingly. Perhaps it was the shadow cast by the hat.

God, travelling with you, Doctor, is making me paranoid, she decided, relieved no one could hear her thoughts. Unless Reverend Lukas was telepathic...

More paranoia, Samantha. Stop it now.

Kyle tipped his head towards her. 'Reverend Lukas asked me earlier if you would care to stay for the night. He thinks it might be a bit dangerous to try to retrace your steps at this time of night. If there are other Klepton groups out there they might be looking for revenge.'

Sam nodded. 'That'd be great,' she lied. 'I really appreciate it.'

Oh Doctor, you are going to pay for this.

One of the young men – Jolyon, Sam remembered – brought some trays of fruit into the circle and they all began handing them to one another. It was strange. Every person took one fruit but passed it to the person on their left. A curious ritual, Sam decided, and tried to remember if any of the tedious scripture lessons at school made mention of it...

'Do you believe, Miss Jones?'

The Reverend Lukas's question caught Sam off guard. She

noticed he was not eating, either. Weird guy. Before she could answer, he asked another question, again with a smile betrayed by the lack of humour in his eyes.

'I assume that is your real name. It's a bit archaic and you don't dress like one of the retro-movement brigade.'

Like Lukas and Jolyon weren't positively medieval names?

'No, it's mine. The Doctor once suggested we called ourselves Kid Curry and Hannibal Hayes, but I realised no one would get the joke.' Sam noted with some satisfaction no one here did, either. She'd remind him of that later. 'I think he spent too long in America, watching bad TV.'

Reverend Lukas just nodded, as if he, and only he, understood exactly what she was saying.

'You are nervous, Miss Jones. Deflecting my questions with flippancy. I apologise if the Church unsettles you. Our belief is very important to us and my questions are out of genuine curiosity, not malice.'

'Unlike your adventures at Stacy's wedding,' snapped Sam.

She expected everyone to 'oooh' at that, or at least look warningly at her. But no one seemed to notice apart from Kyle and Reverend Lukas.

Reverend Lukas smiled again. 'As I say, you are not obliged to understand our motives. I will not force them upon you.'

Sly git wants me to ask. That way he can spout off legitimately, like the Jehovah's did every Sunday morning on the doorstep back home. God, were they flummoxed when Sam had countered one of their house calls by discussing her latest copy of *Humanist News*. And they ended up paying her fifty pence for it before skulking away. They never came back.

God, I hope Mum didn't turn to them when I vanished...

'No. No, I don't believe, I'm afraid. Of course, I respect your desire to believe, but for me God's just not, well... well, I don't really know him, I suppose, but I have a job seeing where he's coming from at times.'

Reverend Lukas nodded slowly.

Still smiling. Weirdo.

'We follow the Goddess, not the traditional Earth God you are familiar with.'

Sam decided to try to look interested. It was only polite – after all, these guys were feeding her. And the Doctor *had* asked her to find out what they were doing on Micawber's World...

'So, who is the Goddess? If that's not too impolite.'

Reverend Lukas laughed, and a couple of the others joined in. 'You have been in seclusion for a long time, Miss Jones.'

'Sam.'

Reverend Lukas ignored that. 'You see, the Goddess is the beauty that is the Universe. She is the one true power of creation.'

Sam thought about this. 'Are we talking some kind of Gaia hypothesis here? Mother Earth, God is a woman? Or are we talking someone totally... different?' Sam almost said 'totally new' but realised that might further complicate her time of origin if it came up. Which it just might if she showed any further ignorance about religious cultures in the fortieth century.

Jolyon interrupted. 'You see, Miss Jones –'

'Sam.'

'The Goddess is far more than just a deity. She is a total way of life. We are out here, amongst the stars, seeking her divinity, and spreading the word as we do so. Older religions on Earth have become embroiled in a sociopolitical rut, bound by the whims and wishes of whichever government has control of the planet. The Church of the Way Forward is exactly that.'

'Seeking out new paths, new angles,' Phillipa added. 'And if people join our campaign en route, then that is all the better.'

'As I did,' put in Kyle.

Reverend Lukas just stared hard at Sam.

And everything else in the room seemed to melt away. All Sam could see were his eyes, blinking suddenly, filling her entire range of vision. Tiny, bloodshot eyes that seemed to be boring into her... her soul? Looking for something.

Sam was suddenly somewhere else. In a windswept desert – Sansom Plains on Ha'olam – and around her she could feel, without seeing, the presence of the I.

A flash of white.

She was on the Mu Camelopides moon, with Anton.

A flash of white.

Seeing the Doctor through the eyes of a Jax...

A flash of white.

A jumble of images – cracks in a wall forming letters; a military woman trapped; the Doctor; a strange wasplike insect, chittering away, gazing around with bulbous brown eyes; a Spider Dalek, blasting down Thals; the Doctor; an Earth dominated by Tractites; a man blurring, becoming a Zygon; Carolyn; the TARDIS, in Shoreditch; the Doctor...

'Get out of my memories, you thieving bastard!'

Sam was back with the others, in the circle. She was sweating, her clothes sticking to her sodden back. But no one seemed to notice the change. They clearly hadn't heard her outburst either.

She could see Reverend Lukas watching her, but for the first time the smile had gone. His face was now a picture of astonishment and something else. Something almost predatory...

Sam stood up. 'Look, guys, thanks and everything, though, but I think I ought to try and get back to the TARDIS, you know. The Doctor will be worried.'

'Kindly sit down, Miss Jones.' That was not a request. That was an order. Instinctively, Sam started to sit.

'Hey, I'm not at school nowadays, Reverend.' She straightened up again.

'Oh, please sit down, young lady!'

Sam sat. The others broke the circle, quietly clearing away the food things. Reverend Lukas waved to one of them, who sat down beside Sam. It was Kyle Dale.

Oh, great.

Reverend Lukas leaned forward. 'You seem to be a very interesting and – how can I put it? – well-travelled young woman, Miss Jones.'

'Sam.'

'I think you could make a very valuable contribution to the Church.'

'Is this where I get brainwashed and join a cult? Were you David Koresh in a previous life or something?' Sam eased back a little.

That's it, Sam, keep the one-liners coming. A good defence mechanism. Make out you're cockier than you are. Don't let them know how scared you feel, OK?

She glanced around the essentially bare room. Two doors, one either end. The one she'd come in by and the untried one. Which was nearer.

'You are free to leave, Miss Jones. I would suggest the door by which you came in. The other leads to the toilet area. It's a very long drop through a very small window. You wouldn't survive.' Reverend Lukas smiled once again. 'It is not my intention to brainwash you, intimidate you or frighten you. I am merely… curious. I sense an aura around you, an emission of general goodness that the Goddess would appreciate.'

'You read my mind, my memories.'

'A gift from the Goddess,' Reverend Lukas said. 'It's more a psychic impression. I imagine you saw far more of your actual memories than I did. I just received an impression, a feeling if you will. An intuitiveness that you have travelled a very long way to be here on Micawber's World. Have you?'

Sam shrugged. 'We came for a wedding, which you buggered up, frankly.'

'The Goddess does not approve of interracial marriages,' said

Kyle. 'The resultant offspring cannot be of an entirely whole soul.' He was obviously speaking some kind of Church doctrine from memory. Or at least Sam hoped so, because otherwise it meant he most likely genuinely believed in that.

'Stacy and Ssard can't have kids,' Sam said. 'Not that it's any business of yours, frankly. But besides which, what you're spouting is tantamount to racism.'

'How so?'

Sam just stared at him. 'You really don't see it, do you? Like so many religious hypocrites, you hide your own personal philosophy and bigotry under some great meaningful crusade.' She leaned forward, feeling Reverend Lukas's breath on her face. 'Throughout history, more people have died, been persecuted or hounded simply because of religion. In the name of God, Yahweh, Allah or whoever, everyone who doesn't fit some nice, neat, tidy ideal of perfection has been abused and denigrated. You ask me why I don't believe in anything, Reverend Lukas. Well, I cannot follow or believe in any so-called supreme being who so wantonly allows people to be persecuted that much.'

Reverend Lukas nodded, and then looked across to Kyle.

The younger man took Sam's hand, but she snatched it back. Undaunted, he began to talk quietly. 'Throughout history, you are quite correct. From the Roman violations against the Christians through the Spanish Inquisition, witch hunts, right up to the Second American Civil War when the Christian Right-Wing Fundamentalist movement attempted its coup, people have used their religion as an excuse to dominate.'

Sam nodded. 'And let's not forget the Muslims, the Hindus – I mean, it seems to me they're all as bad as each other. God, Buddha, Mohammed…'

'Mohammed and Buddha are not, strictly speaking, the same as God,' interrupted Reverend Lukas. 'They were good people who ascended to Divinity. But I'm splitting hairs. Do go on.'

Sam wondered if he was taking the piss. But so what? She was on a roll. It was like being back home again, arguing with her parents. 'My point is that God, in a variety of forms and denominations, causes more war and suffering than anyone could think possible.'

Kyle shook his head. 'People use religion not as a reason for war but as a weapon in war. Just as many people stay at home, praying that the fighting will end. And you are rather forgetting all the positive things that religion can do.'

Sam raised an eyebrow. 'Oh yeah? Like what?'

Kyle shrugged and began counting off on his fingers. 'The abolitionist movement which ultimately resulted in the formation of the Galactic Federation was started by church leaders back in the mid-twentieth century. Hospitals were started by the Church. Look at the mission work that various saints did on a variety of worlds. The whole of the G'narlan civilisation was saved due to the interference of missionaries, despite the wishes of the military junta that ruled Earth at the time. All the charities that have been run by a variety of faiths and denominations all over the cosmos. Religion has done a lot of positive things as well. I think that may be something you have chosen not to think about.'

Sam was about to reply when she realised she couldn't actually think what to say. Sure, all those things were great, and no doubt run by well-meaning individuals and organisations, but there were equally a number of things destroyed by people's insistence on slavishly adhering to a religion, no matter how it affected other peoples' rights and basic dignities. She said so, once she'd got her thoughts unjumbled.

And was then surprised to find Reverend Lukas agreeing with her. 'And that is the important distinction, Miss Jones,' he said, waving a finger just like Dad always did. Does. Whatever. 'It is always a handful of people who use religion as their pennant, because it attracts people. It is convenient and easy. Torquemada was the greatest exponent of faith in God and used this to influence the court of Queen Isabella. He tortured and murdered hundreds in God's name – according to him. But had he been a real follower of his God, he could never have done the things he did. The same with Hitler's obsession with religious artefacts, the Knights Templar in medieval France and the Islamic Ayatollahs of the thirty-second century. They did what they wanted and abused the name of God. By telling people you are doing God's will, people quickly come to accept that indeed you are.'

Kyle shrugged at Sam, clearly hoping she was getting Reverend Lukas's meaning. 'But saying you are doing what God wants and actually following his lessons have very rarely gone hand in hand,' he said quietly. 'Few people understand the words of the Bible.'

'Few people consider the Bible to be much cop,' countered Sam. 'After all, it's just a series of notes written and rewritten over the centuries based on a load of second-hand oral information. It wasn't written down at the time in any great detail, and what was has been interpreted in a number of different ways by whoever was doing the writing and translating. They all had the chance to add their own opinions, bigotries and adaptations. No one can truly say what the Bible really is any more.' She looked at Kyle, daring him to argue. 'Besides, what if I say God doesn't exist? What proof do you have that he does?'

'What proof do you have that he doesn't?' countered Kyle. 'I mean, you could point at the book of Genesis and say the whole Adam and Eve story is rubbish. You could point at the dinosaurs and Darwinism and say science has proven that evolution created mankind, not God and his magic clay or a reshaping of Adam's rib. But I could go through the whole so-called proof of evolution and punch fist-sized holes in every argument. People often talk about the 'missing link' but there are far more than just one. Evolution is a convenient theory, but relies just as much on supposition, unproven theory and a bunch of scientists telling you it is fact as the Christian Fundamentalists of the twenty-first-century crusades telling you the attempted genocide of homosexuals was God's will.'

'Go on then,' said Sam. 'I'll enjoy this.'

Kyle nodded. 'OK. Let's start with cell structure. Evolutionary theory works on the premise of the simple cell – Darwin's evolutionary theory was started long before cells were being looked at under electron microscopes. In fact, there really is no such thing as the simple cell with the membrane, nucleus, and cytoplasm. There are tons of complex organelles – mitochondria, Golgi apparatus, chloroplasts, et cetera.'

She thought about this. Her grasp on science wasn't as good as the Doctor's (bet he'd give a good refutation of this) and so she didn't fancy butting in yet. Wait until Kyle said something she could trip him up over. 'Do go on,' she said.

Kyle did, throwing a look to Reverend Lukas, who nodded encouragingly. 'Evolutionary theory states that from just a few species, a vast number of subsequent species evolved. However, the fossil records on many planets, including Earth, show that this is not the case. If this were true, there would be huge amounts of species today compared with billions of years ago – one branching off into others. However, the fossil record shows many, many types of past species with much more variety than today. It actually seems that out of many, only a few remained.'

'Maybe we've wiped them all out. I mean, here we are embarking on the fortieth century. How many millions of species have become extinct over the last billion years or so?' Sam realised that this was actually irrelevant to Kyle's argument, but she needed to say something. God, she hated being lectured.

'Evolutionary theory also says that out of the oft-quoted 'primordial soup' and chaotic conditions, mere chance had it that mutations from radiation developed that made certain animals more adept at surviving. These evolved into other things and thus created this ordered ecosystem. Two things counter this theory, I'm afraid. Firstly, all shown mutations are neutral at best, while most mutations are at least detrimental to the organism's chance of survival, if not lethal. Survival of the fittest is a true concept but the idea of these "lucky" mutations is pretty much based on guesswork and wishful thinking. Plus, the Second Law of Thermodynamics – please remember, Miss Jones, that this is one of your Scientific Laws as opposed to just a theory – says that things tend towards chaos and destruction.'

Sam nodded. 'Yeah entropy. As a good friend of mine once said, "the more you put things together the more they keep falling apart." What of it?'

'Basically this – Darwin's evolutionary theory is in direct contradiction to the Second Law of Thermodynamics, saying that out of an unordered mess, order developed.' Kyle smiled. 'Had enough?'

'Yeah.' Then she held up her hands. 'But you can't deny fossils. I mean, hey, they found that bird thing that linked reptiles to avians, didn't they? I don't recall them chancing on a perfectly preserved Garden of Eden.' Sam then crossed her fingers – who knew what had been uncovered by archaeologists since she left Earth in 1997?

'Oh, I agree,' said Kyle. 'For a while, archaeopteryx was indeed supposed to be a link between reptiles and birds. However, once they found true birds in lower rock strata than archaeopteryx, the idea of archaeopteryx being a forerunner of birds simply didn't ring true. Darwin himself said that the greatest threat to his theories would be the fossils record and so far, instead of showing transient species, fossils tend to reveal whole new groups of species that would flourish out of nowhere and then suddenly disappear, such as the dinosaurs. All examples of "evolution" that are offered are microevolution – where traits of a species change but the species doesn't become a new species. You know the pepper moth?'

Sam shook her head. She couldn't quite see how this proved the book of Genesis, but Kyle was a good speaker. And she could always ask the Doctor to take her back to prehistory later. They'd meet either an amoeba or Adam. Maybe take him in a ride in the TARDIS and bring him to Kyle's time.

Hey, that'd shake up the establishment.

'Pollution made the trees black, so to camouflage, the moths apparently became black and when the trees got cleaned, they went grey again. The problem with that theory was that there were always black pepper moths, and just when the trees turned black, they had a better chance of surviving so they flourished. This is not evolution - the pepper moths didn't become something new, they were still pepper moths. Just look at the different races of mankind back on Earth. Caucasians are essentially just the same as Negroids. One has not evolved to be superior to another. No, Sam, despite the evolutionists' theories - and they've had the best publicity, often simply because it can be used to discredit the Bible - there has never been a proven example of macroevolution.'

Sam was not convinced. 'I'm sure I could argue all of those points if I thought about it, you know. I mean, you dismiss evolution so easily, but I simply don't believe that millions of scientists have been wrong all this time, you know?'

Reverend Lukas joined in. 'Ah, but there you see the crux of it all, Miss Jones. None of this is about proof. Or science. Or even religion, God and the Bible. It's about faith. About standing up for what you believe in. I think it takes an extraordinary amount of faith to believe that all this evolution business happened just by chance - the chance of random energy sparking off life or whatever. It seems to me almost easier to believe in a supreme power. And, to paraphrase the great detective, when you've disproved the probable, surely the improbable must be the answer. You choose to use your faith in science to believe the circumstances were right, that the transient species' fossils are still waiting to be discovered, and that, for just this once, the Second Law of Thermodynamics didn't apply. That requires a lot of faith, Miss Jones. And to me, well, that is essentially a religion.'

'OK, I think I see where you're coming from, Reverend.' Sam wanted to sit and think about this. All her life, people had told her what to think about issues like these. Her father was a doctor. A scientist, in effect. She had been brought up to accept science as the ultimate truth. But what if Reverend Lukas had a point?

'But it sounds as if you're discarding scientific research in favour of a – frankly – badly written old book.'

'No, Miss Jones – Sam,' said Kyle. 'The Church isn't discarding or slavishly agreeing with either. Maybe truth isn't in the hands of some grey-bearded man. Nor is it in fossils beneath the Earth. Truth, Miss Jones, is a universal act of faith. Truth, absolute truth, can only be found in here.' He pointed at Sam's heart. 'Everything else is just hearsay.'

Sam glanced over and saw Reverend Lukas's reaction to this. She expected a smile from a proud teacher, pleased his student had conveyed the intended message. Or, at worst, a supercilious patronising glance that would attempt to make her feel two inches tall. Instead, he was frowning at Kyle, as if the boy had done something wrong. The moment he saw that Sam had seen this, he tried to smile, but the spell was broken. This could get very interesting. What was Reverend Lukas's problem now?

'I need time to consider this,' she said. 'Although it doesn't shake my belief, my faith if you like, that far more suffering has occurred in this galaxy because of organised religion. If it wasn't there, there would be fewer wars.'

Kyle shook his head. 'Man, Martian, Klepton or Cantryan – everything will find a reason to make war, Sam. For every person who claims that God has been responsible for more death, more destruction and more evil than anything else overlooks the fact that it is not God, but one or more mortals abusing God's name to suit their own purposes. Every war is different. And every invocation of God's will – no matter what religion practised – varies from year to year, century to century.'

Sam raised an eyebrow. 'You mean, you don't actually believe that there is a Goddess? You're chasing rainbows?'

Reverend Lukas smiled, broadly. 'I didn't say that, Miss Jones. I have an open mind on the subject. As with all things, there are degrees of belief and reason and proof. I hope to one day meet the Goddess, but if I don't, I am still proud that my life is devoted to following a set of ideals I perceive as being her wishes. I am content to believe without requiring solid proof.'

'But without proof, how can you hold any convictions? That's like me saying I'm a scientist and believe in, oh, I don't know, warp-drive engines that go faster than light, but when I'm asked to show someone such things, I can't. My credibility goes. Surely your credibility must suffer when you try to tell people that your Goddess wants this, that and the other but cannot offer any solid facts or proof to back up your claim.' Sam smiled. Gotcha. 'Then you have to admit that you could be wrong? That you are potentially kidding yourself, chasing a pipedream?'

Reverend Lukas nodded. 'That possibility exists. I am not a fool, Miss Jones. I have to consider that, but having done so, I still believe that without hope, without a goal, mankind, or indeed any race out amongst the stars, will wilt and fall away. My mission in life is to guide the souls of my flock towards a degree of enlightenment. I don't require scientific proof of a divine being, I require only my faith.'

'And that of Kyle here, and the rest of your "flock". Right?'

Reverend Lukas nodded in agreement.

'So defend the wedding fiasco!' Sam said suddenly. 'Go on. Defend that, if you can.'

'The Goddess is not against other life-forms, Miss Jones. Merely the belief that each race can only find the absolution and peace it deserves – as all do – through the purity of the soul. And the purity of the soul can only come through the purity of the body.'

Sam paused, then smiled at him. 'OK, I grant you this, Reverend. You've given me much to think about. Thank you. I cannot honestly say I agree with you, but what the hell! I certainly acknowledge your right to think as you do, however I may disagree with it.'

Reverend Lukas stood up for the first time and held out his hand. 'Even if our motivations and beliefs may not meet each other's standards, let us at least be friends.' He pointed to Kyle. 'Kyle here is taking part in the Games, you know.'

Sam was taken aback by this.

'Oh yes,' said Kyle. 'That's why we're here really.'

'So tomorrow,' Reverend Lukas continued, 'I thought maybe Kyle could take you to the Stadium. Give you the backstage tour before his daily training session.'

'I'd like that,' said Sam, and Reverend Lukas suggested they meet briefly before breakfast the next morning.

'Kyle will find you somewhere to sleep tonight,' he said, and Sam allowed herself to be led to one of the camp beds, a little apart from the others.

'Thank you, Miss Jones... Sam, for listening.' Kyle began smoothing out the blankets and pillow.

Sam glanced back to where Reverend Lukas was talking to Jolyon and Phillipa, then gave Kyle a big grin. 'This is going to be fun.'

Kyle smiled his appreciation and wandered off to his own bed, leaving Sam to lie down. At last.

She looked again at Reverend Lukas, and did not know exactly how she felt about him, or his 'mission'. She certainly didn't trust him, but his words had at least got her thinking.

Was there more to this? Was she going to turn agnostic? Sam knew she could never truly believe in a god herself, but was there something else? Some part of her that actually wanted to find something to believe in? Since she was separated from her parents – hell, she'd spent three years on Ha'olam with little more than a slight consideration of their feelings, their fears or worries – was she now searching for something new?

In a way, the Doctor had been that something new for a while. But that was back then – *that* Sam Jones had been a rather idealistic and frankly embarrassing seventeen-year-old, focusing all her frustrations into the Doctor, believing he could solve everything. What happened in the moonbase on Hirath's satellite showed her back then how badly she'd coped with her Doctor-as-the-be-all-and-end-all-to-life. Since hooking up with him again... well, she'd felt there was something missing. She wasn't about to jump in with Reverend Weirdo Lukas and his band of merry monks – at least she trusted the Doctor – but the evening had genuinely given her food for thought.

And what would the Doctor say about all this? What were his convictions? There he was, probably safe and tucked up in the Carlton. Or the TARDIS, or somewhere. Meanwhile, she was stuck here, at his request, trying to 'find out' about the Church and why they were here. To stop Stacey's wedding, and play rounders in the Olympics or something? And now it was dark, late, and she could imagine a very belligerent group of Kleptons, probably bailed and slapped on the wrist, who would delight in bumping into her again. Whether she was safe here with Lukas, Sam wasn't sure. But she was definitely safer.

It felt, in a way, a little like being back at the Mission on Ha'olam... Lying back, tugging the rough blanket around her and hoping to make a swift getaway in the morning, she yawned and, within minutes, was fast asleep.

Chapter Seven
Green Fingers

'Ms Sox, could you come in please?'

Ms Sox frowned at the voice on the intercom. Mr Carrington very rarely used the intercom, in case everyone else heard it. The operations at Carrington Corp were supposed to run so efficiently that it should always look to others as if she and Carrington had a bizarre, almost telepathic relationship.

Truth was, of course, that Ms Sox carried a tiny vibrating pager in her back pocket which buzzed when he wanted her. But to prying eyes, it just looked liked a well-oiled office machine working perfectly.

Of course, today, no one had heard the intercom because they were down watching the athletes train. But even so, Chase Carrington shouldn't have done that.

She entered his office and was immediately surprised to see another woman in there. A young lemon-skinned Doradan, her typically snow-white hair cut into a neat bob, was tapping away at a datapad.

Carrington seemed tense, Ms Sox could see that straight away. 'Where is everyone today?'

'At the Stadium, Mr Carrington, as per your instructions.'

Ms Sox was not entirely sure, but she could have sworn there was a momentary look between Chase Carrington and the new woman.

'Yes, right. Of course. Ms Sox, I want you to meet our new Executive Secretary, Ms Raymond. She's transferred here from Ganymede.'

Ms Sox looked Ms Raymond up and down, noting that the traditional Doradan red tunic had been replaced with a fashionable human trouser suit. 'I wasn't aware we needed a new secretary, Mr Carrington. I'll have Ms Raymond added to the payroll at once.'

Carrington stood up. 'No, Ms Sox. No thank you. Ms Raymond is on my personal staff, as you are. As such, she receives the same payment schemes and benefits as yourself.'

'Indeed,' Ms Sox was immediately intrigued. This one had completely passed her by when she'd been going through Chase Carrington's personal financial projection last week. Why was he playing this so close to his chest? 'In that case, sir, I shall issue an e-memo alerting everyone to Ms Raymond's placement and status. Will that be all, sir?'

'Yes,' he said, then clicked his fingers. Or tried to. Instead, they just slapped against each other pointlessly. Chase Carrington wasn't known for his infirmities, but perhaps he was just tired.

Ms Sox was very puzzled now. This was so unlike him…

'Ms Sox, on no account will anyone enter this office at any time of day or night without alerting Ms Raymond to their arrival first.'

'I understand sir.'

'That includes you, Ms Sox.'

'Oh, absolutely, sir. I understand.'

Ms Sox left the office, furious. Something was going on, something that Carrington was not revealing to her. The man had always displayed the occasional eccentricity, but reducing her status and banning her from his office was a new one.

As no one else was around, Ms Sox once again activated her independent holocomputer screen but, instead of checking up on the Doctor, this time she began researching any Doradans, living on Ganymede, calling themselves Raymond.

Not the most common of Doradan names.

Within moments she had found one. Suki Raymond – the holo

showed the woman she had just met – and her biog suggested she had a preference for human males.

'Married... twice. Firstly to one Andrew Raymond, a software designer from Mars Colony 1, then J. Garth Wilcox, CEO of...'

Ms Sox shut the computer off, and swung around. No one was there, yet she felt sure she had been watched by someone.

She glanced at Carrington's closed office door.

'Married to the CEO of a Carrington subsidiary for two hours before his reported suicide. Call me old-fashioned, Ms Raymond, but I didn't notice a black veil or an armband on you just now.'

Ms Sox decided this needed further investigation.

The Foamasi Temple was a stark contrast to the hi-tech sterility the Doctor was used to in the SSS Building.

Painted granite walls, lush creams and purples, dado rails, picture rails, concrete pillars and ornately carved architraves around the doors, beautiful ceiling roses and thick carpets and curtains. If it wasn't for the fact that logic insisted it could only be as old as everything else on Micawber's World (fifteen years, the Doctor guessed, or thereabouts), the Time Lord would have sworn he was standing in something built on Earth, around 1924.

Leading off from the carpeted hallway was a large stairway that split into two directions against the far wall and under those junctions, on the same level as he was, were small corridors, with mosaic flooring. A similar corridor reached away to the right, the more decorative arch that announced it suggesting that this was the way into the Temple proper. The other two were probably service corridors for the staff, and upstairs was probably out of bounds.

Which was a pretty good reason to go up, but he needed the Foamasi Lodges' help right now, so it was best not to offend them.

He paused to look at the paintings (interesting – paintings, genuine oils and watercolours, not holograms or CGIs) which were clearly of important Foamasi Lodge members.

'Can I help you, sir?'

The newcomer was that great universal constant, a butler; there was no getting away from that. He spoke imperiously, wore a black suit with white shirt and black tie and carried a silver salver. The fact that he was a Foamasi, and the salver was held up by his tail, and that he looked faintly ridiculous in the get-up was irrelevant. He clearly took his role seriously, so the Doctor decided to as well.

He placed a calling card on the salver – white with a black stripe and a ? symbol across it.

'I see, sir. And you wish to see?'

The Doctor smiled. 'Gielgud!'

'Me, sir?'

'No, I meant your voice synthesiser... It's John Gielgud! From *Arthur*?'

'No, sir. From *Arthur 2: On the Rocks*, actually. Now, who did you wish to see?'

The Doctor flung his arm around what were presumably the Foamasi's shoulders. 'Tell me, Gielgud, do all Foamasi steal voice synthesisers from twentieth-century human film stars?'

Gielgud stepped away a bit, clearly offended. 'Heavens, no, sir. Whatever gave you that idea? Each Lodge, sir, takes its synthesised voices from a different cultural element of a different planet. Only the Twin Suns Lodge does that.'

'Twin Suns Lodge?'

'Yes, sir. You do not understand the workings of the Foamasi, do you, sir?'

The Doctor shook his head. 'I'm awfully sorry, but no. You see, I have come across the West Lodge once or twice, so I assumed they were compass-coded.'

Gielgud snorted derisively. 'Humans. No concept of anything outside their own rather mundane sphere of influence.'

'For a man who's stolen the voice of one of Earth's finest actors, I think that's a bit rich, actually. And, anyway, I'm not human.'

Gielgud looked him up and down, his feelers on his face twitching more, his eyes emerging slightly from their sockets and rolling about a bit, taking in the view of the Doctor as much as possible. 'My apologies, I'm not terribly good at aliens. Now, who did you want to see, sir? I have duties to perform.'

'Of course you have.' The Doctor gave him a winning smile. At least, Sam always said it was a 'winning smile'. Not that it often won her over, but it worked on other people. Sometimes.

Gielgud wasn't one of them.

The Doctor shrugged. 'I was told to ask for "Green Fingers". Personally I don't remember an actor called that. Sydney Greenstreet. Hughie Greene. And a pop star called Johnny Fingers who played the piano. But not a Green –'

Gielgud walked away, so the Doctor opted to follow. 'Nice building.'

'Again, sir, based on Earth during the twentieth century.'

'Naturally.'

Gielgud stopped at another hallway, identical to the last except that the staircase off this one only split one way, to the right, and thus had only the one service corridor. Gielgud pointed to it. 'Down there sir. Third corridor on the right, fifth on the left, second the left and then I believe it is the eighth on the right. Down past some doors until you see a green one, Room 101. Knock three times.'

The Doctor nodded. 'OK, third right, fifth left then... ahh...' but Gielgud was merely looking at him with a kind of bored expectancy.

With a sigh, the Doctor wandered down the corridor, having of course memorised the instructions perfectly. He just wanted to make Gielgud think he was a bit more stupid, but Gielgud had either guessed otherwise or couldn't care less.

Within moments, the Doctor was outside Room 101. If Sam had been here, he could have bet her a bag of toffees that Green Fingers would sound like a Chicago gangster. Had to be Sydney Greenstreet.

He knocked.

'Do come in,' said a very deep, Welsh accented voice.

Room 101. *1984*. He owed Sam a bag of toffees.

'Richard Burton, of course,' said the Doctor as he went in.

The room was very dark and rather dingy. The curtains were frayed at the edges, the paint was peeling and various stains of dubious origin littered the uncarpeted floor and even the ceiling. A number of wooden benches were arranged haphazardly around, brimming with rather old laptops, monitor screens and a holographic projector that flickered rather badly, displaying three naked female Jadeans and a Pakhar frolicking in mud. Amid all this were welding irons, bits of broken circuitry, and smashed communications equipment from a variety of different cultures.

Standing over an inoperative holocamera, probably stolen from one of the broadcast companies covering the Olympics, was the thinnest Foamasi the Doctor had ever seen, with skin more a sickly greeny-yellow than the bright vibrant colour of the other Foamasi on Micawber's World.

He wore a simple white gown just like the human scientists back at the SSS Building, and a strange ocular device was clamped around his left eye. The Doctor could see himself reflected in it, upside down and bloated, rather like the image seen through a fish-eye lens.

'Hello, I'm the Doctor.'

'Really?'

That was it? The Doctor harrumphed. '"Really" as in "Oh, are you really the Doctor, how nice"? Or "Really" as in "Are you really here or just a holographic projection?" or "Really" as in "So what?" I wonder?'

Green Fingers removed the ocular device slowly and plopped it into a pocket of his gown. 'As I've never heard of you and I can see you're not flickering at the edges, have no thick blue line around you – and my alarms would have alerted me to any unwarranted carrier waves anyway – I presume I mean the latter. What do you want, human?'

Before the Doctor could answer, Green Fingers put up a hand, displaying his... well, green fingers. 'No, wait.' He dug out his ocular device, refitted it and stared at the Doctor.

'My apologies. Not a human at all. Two hearts, very odd arrangement of haemoglobin and some other internal organs whose origin or purpose I wouldn't like to guess at.' Green Fingers nodded. 'Bit of a mongrel, aren't you, Doctor?'

The Doctor smiled, not so much winningly this time as disarmingly. 'I hope so, Mr Fingers. Keeps everyone on their toes, anyway.'

There was a sudden sound, like that of a tiny generator breaking down, and from behind his bench, Green Fingers moved towards the Doctor. His lower body was missing from just below his thighs, his legs and feet replaced by a square box on tiny elongated wheels covered with caterpillar tracks.

'Indeed,' said Green Fingers, apparently without a trace of irony. 'Now, what do you want?'

The Doctor carried on, ignoring his faux pas. 'I actually don't know. I was undertaking the autopsy of a Foamasi from, I believe, the Twin Suns Lodge who may have been known as Sanders.'

'Ah, George. Yes. We call him Typtpwtyp.' This came out as a series of chirps and twitters, the traditional Foamasi language – hence the vocal synthesisers. 'Is he dead, then?'

'Most people undergoing an autopsy tend to be, I believe.'

Green Fingers laughed suddenly. 'Oh, not at all, Doctor. Not in my line of work. Who sent you?'

'Commandant Ritchie of the –'

'Yes, yes, yes. I know who Ritchie is. Blasted SSS. Dreadful types, always prying into Foamasi business, trying to stop us running our Lodges our way.'

The Doctor eased some useless-looking equipment away from the corner of the nearest bench, and sat on it. 'The way the Foamasi conduct business is a little... different from most members of the Federation.'

'Ah yes, those nice little people sitting in nice big skyscrapers, making awfully nice deals, handing over vast amounts of capital, acquiring and losing stocks and shares. And then, when it suits them, turning to my Lodge for help. Do you know, Doctor, most of my customers these days aren't from the Lodges. They're from other planets, other races across the Federation and a few outside – although I draw the line at Daleks. Won't work with biomechanoids, because they never live up to their side of bargains, claiming that to do so would be 'illogical' or some such rubbish. But on the whole I work for Martians, Pakhars, humans, Cantryans, Chelonians, the Tzun, Lurmans, Vegans –'

The Doctor coughed. He could sense this list going on for hours. Foamasi were so verbose. 'And what exactly is your service? The Commandant omitted to fill that part in.'

'Me?' Green Fingers trundled back noisily behind his bench and tapped his jumble of tatty equipment. 'I'm an assassin, Doctor. Appointed by anyone anywhere to kill anyone else.'

'A sort of court poisoner, then. Don't you fear that someone will kill *you* one day?'

'Me? Why ever would they want to do that? I'm a professional, Doctor. I work for whoever pays me. I have no grudges, no axe to grind. I rarely know the victims and make it policy not to meet my employers. No, I provide a service – and a very good one at that, at very reasonable rates – which everyone needs at some point or other. No *point* in getting rid of me. Or asking questions. As I said, I never meet my employers, deliberately to avoid the possibility of being asked by aggrieved relatives or friends to name their dearly departed's unloved ones.'

The Doctor looked straight at him, frowning. 'And does the Foamasi Ambassador know you do this?'

Green Fingers laughed in his deep, faked, Welsh accent. 'Oh yes, *he's* well aware of it. He wouldn't dare argue. After all, he might have to poison himself if he did.'

'I'm sorry?'

Green Fingers trundled back to the Doctor, throwing his stubby three-clawed hands out in a conciliatory gesture. 'I *am* the Foamasi Ambassador, Doctor. I'm the only person not affiliated with a Lodge, therefore, I act as the independent adviser to all of the leaders of each one. Simple really. No one argues with the court poisoner, do they?'

The Doctor digested this. If Green Fingers was the Ambassador (and by the typically convoluted Foamasi logic of honour, mistrust and deceit – in that order – he must be the only possible candidate) then that was why Commandant Ritchie had sent him here. The Doctor suspected that someone else was pulling Ritchie's strings, apart from the SSS Headquarters here and on Earth. The Foamasi made sense. They would easily find a use for the military power on any world and infiltrate it.

Was Ritchie a disguised Foamasi? Unlikely, otherwise why send him here? Foamasi were good strategists, but it was a pointless double-bluff. Which meant the Foamasi Lodge he had contact with were blackmailing him. Why? And why, if he didn't want them to know the Doctor was being employed, was he sent to Green Fingers?

After the Doctor provided a précis of these thoughts to the Ambassador, Green Fingers scratched at the apparatus covering his left eye. 'I imagine your Commandant does not have enough support to get rid of whoever is blackmailing him. And I suspect, as you do, it *is* blackmail. Which narrows the Lodges down. The

West Lodge infiltrate. The South Lodge extort. The Twin Suns Lodge, hmm, they're not opposed to blackmail. And if it were the Dark Peaks Lodge, then they're breaking the rules. This world is off limits to them.' He looked straight at the Doctor's face and, if the Doctor was learning to read Foamasi body language correctly (never easy with reptilian species), then he was frowning. 'They're banned from Micawber's World.'

'Why?'

'Because they do a mixture of everything and cause havoc for everyone here. Strictly speaking, the Dark Peaks Lodge don't exist. They're new, only been around for a couple of centuries. No official standing, you see, in Foamasi criminal society.'

'There's another kind of Foamasi society?'

Green Fingers thought about this. 'Good point, Doctor, but actually irrelevant to our discussion. I shall call a meeting of the Patriarch of each Lodge and find out more.'

'They'll tell you? Just like that?'

'Of course. I am the Ambassador. And the Foamasi Government. And the Foamasi Bureau of Investigation. And, of course, the official poisoner and assassin, as well. *No one* argues with me. Give me twenty-four hours, Doctor, then return. I'll let Gielgud know he is to expect you.'

The Doctor nodded. 'Thank you. I shall try to find something to do until then.'

'Talk to Ms Sox, Doctor.'

'Who?'

Green Fingers trundled back to a monitor and flicked it on. After a few seconds, it focused on the Jadean woman he had seen with Carrington at the wedding.

'I'm sure she will have been monitoring all your conversations with Commandant Ritchie.'

'That's a bit adventurous for a Jadean,' the Doctor said, thankfully. 'I mean, I thought they were genetically engineered to be quite submissive, almost drone-like.'

Green Fingers nodded. 'That's how they were when the Federation first found them, Doctor. But whoever did that initial engineering left plenty of scope for further refinement. The Federation has spent some time and effort working out how to augment them, and Ms Sox is a prime example. Taking the instinctive Jadean intellect and adding a healthy dose of... oh, I don't know really. Guile. Cunning.'

'Sophistication?'

'And elegance. Ms Sox is perhaps the first of a new breed.'

'Why? Who sent her here?'

'That I don't know. Possibly the Federation? Perhaps they don't trust Chase Carrington. Perhaps they think he's going to blow up the Olympic Stadium and start a galactic war.'

'Or perhaps that's what whichever Lodge is controlling Commandant Ritchie is planning to do,' offered the Doctor. 'After all, with Space Security in their pockets plus whatever it was your friend –' the Doctor attempted to imitate the Foamasi chirping to create 'Typtpwtyp' but it came out only as 'thweepipeep' – 'was up to, there'll be enough confusion out there to start a very good battle, with the Foamasi arising from the ashes as controllers of the Federation.'

'I hadn't thought of that,' said Green Fingers.

'I'm sure you hadn't,' replied the Doctor. 'That's why you haven't told me any of this.' He offered his hand. 'A pleasure meeting the Foamasi Ambassador,' he said.

Hesitantly the Foamasi returned the gesture and tried not to wince as the Doctor squeezed his clawed hand. 'A pleasure to make your acquaintance Doctor. I'm sure that between us, we can avoid any unpleasantness in the days to come.'

The Doctor smiled and left.

Today, Kyle Dale decided, was going to be a good day.

Sam was so engrossed in the view of the Stadium that she completely forgot she was holding on to Kyle's hand. Seeing a new variety of alien she hadn't spotted before, she lurched sideways to get a better look, dragging the startled young man with her. 'Sorry,' she whispered. 'Forgot you were here.'

'Gee, thanks, Sam,' he grunted. 'So nice to be thought about.'

'What's that, then?'

Kyle had been showing her around the athletes' enclosure of the Stadium, giving her a unique insider's view of what went on behind the scenes of the games. 'Who needs Des Lynham when you've got this lot?' she had said, but Kyle hadn't the foggiest notion what she was talking about. Come to think of it, Kyle realised he very rarely understood more than one in three of Sam's phrases, statements or questions. There was more to her than just being "a young woman from London", he was sure of that. Something about her manner, her phraseology and her moments of thoughtfulness combined to make her the single most interesting person Kyle had encountered since... Well, since Reverend Lukas, really. Or maybe before that. A comment of Reverend Lukas's rang in his memory, something about not letting a single individual get in the way of his life's work, his mission, for the Goddess. But Samantha Jones didn't really fit into any of his preconceived categories of the type of person he felt sure Reverend Lukas had meant. Sam was, in her own way, as diverse and captivating as an entire species.

'The Goddess be praised,' he muttered. 'You are beautiful.'

If Sam heard, she did not reply, which was probably a good thing after their talk the night before. Sam didn't seem to like discussing belief systems. Which was sad, because she had a reasonable mind, if a little closed to some things. He looked forward to trying to prise it open. She didn't have to agree, or believe. But listening would be nice. He might not be able to alter her views, or shape them in any way, but just knowing she had at least listened –

understood his point of view – well, that would be something.

Kyle found himself smiling. She was certainly a different kind of woman from those he surrounded himself with normally. They tended to be either members of the Church like Phillipa or aggressive athletic types. Sam had a clear mind, opinionated, certainly, but at least she had ideas. She understood the need to see new things, and observe new people. Kyle occasionally wondered if Reverend Lukas had really liked her or was being pleasant for his sake.

Kyle reached out and rested his hand on Sam's shoulder. She was eyeing a frankly bizarre spherical creature made, it seemed, entirely of silky white fur, tiny pink feet poking out from its lower regions. Two spindly pink hands fiddled nervously with a big red ball, and it had a smaller spherical head, with long ears, a snubbed nose and huge almond eyes.

'It's a Meep. They're not as innocent or gullible as they seem,' he told her. Kyle smiled – when he had been a young boy, he'd had a cuddly Meep to sleep with each night, but when the Meeps found out that some cultures saw them as little more than toys, a diplomatic request was made to the Federation and subsequent lines of the stuffed toys were discontinued. Kyle wondered if his Meep was still in his mother's attic back home on Mars.

'For many years,' he said, 'they used their ability to make people see them as little more than a soft toy to cheat in negotiations and such like. They're actually very cunning and have an unpleasant past based around conquest and colonisation. Thankfully they are now one of the more peaceful Federation members, but are still very competitive in the Games. I'm up against one in the Discus.'

'That one?'

Kyle shrugged. 'I've honestly no idea. They all look alike to me.'

Sam didn't return his chuckle. Instead, he realised she was giving him a strange look. 'What?'

'Sorry,' she said. 'But back home, a comment like that would have got my back up.'

'Oh.'

Sam looked away. 'I don't know what's worse. The fact you said it without thinking or caring, or the fact that I'm not jumping up and down screaming at you for it.'

Kyle didn't quite understand this and said so.

Sam sighed and looked at him, her blue eyes clearly hurt by something – but he had no idea what he had done.

'When I was a few years younger, before I met the Doctor, I used to join up on what my mum called "Crusades". At the time I thought she was just being Mum, typically sarcastic. But looking back now, I can begin to see where she was coming from. Every time I saw an advert for some campaign to save whales, stop animal experiments, go on gay-liberation marches or demonstrate against racism, I was there. Building banners, decorating floats, whatever. I used to go and join people sitting in trees, stopping motorways, bypasses and airport runways being built. I did everything. Now I do it on other planets in different centuries... it's a struggle, you know? And it's a decent struggle. Sure, the bailiffs dragged you out of the tunnels eventually, or chopped the trees down and you fell out, but we'd say, "OK, we lost this one; but the bad publicity will make them think twice next time." But how many times do you have to go through it? Yeah, breakthroughs were made for gay people in laws and equality. Yeah, peoples' consciousness was raised and fewer Pakistani shopkeepers in Stafford Row got their front windows smashed in. But for every victory we had, others lost somewhere else. The Dreamstone Moon was mined out, people died... it's just like a never-ending merry-go-round.' She laughed hollowly. 'My last protest was in the twenty-third century. It's ludicrous, isn't it?'

Kyle said nothing.

'And here I am,' she continued, looking at the Meep. 'It's 3999, twenty thousand years since I started trying to make a difference in my own time, and still some guy looks at a Meep and says "they all look the same to me". And I just wonder what the point of it all was. Is. Whatever.'

Kyle was lost. He didn't have a clue what to say. Should he say something to justify what was, after all just a quip, that would make her feel better? Should he ignore it? Should he apologise?

His mouth opened and replied before his brain could stop it. 'Well, maybe Meeps think *we* all look alike.'

Her hand was pulled away from his before he'd finished and by the time he realised what that meant, Sam was running back towards the exit, away from the enclosure. He called after her but if she heard him – and he suspected that she did – she ignored him.

All around him, jostling athletes of many races, shapes and sizes blocked his view of her diminishing form until finally he lost track of her.

Frustrated, he wanted to yell. To shout. But he knew that would be wrong – Reverend Lukas had instilled that in him from Day One. He had to keep his mind in check, and began slow-breathing exercises to help him. He closed his eyes, shutting out the visual stimuli, and gradually his mind drifted, allowing him to ignore the noise and the clamour of the outside world. He concentrated on that tiny spot of light, the Eye of the Goddess, and let himself drift towards it, knowing he would never actually catch it up, but feeling his mind just float along.

Serenity.

Sanctuary.

Absolution.

He opened his eyes and smiled. Sam was gone still, but she would return. He would find her. More important to him right now was the start of his training.

He looked around and saw one of the hovering droids, a cap perched on its head, the word COACH stencilled across it.

He tapped on its head and it swivelled around, looking at him. The faintest sound of a camera zooming could be heard as he let it read his features.

'Oh, hi,' it said. 'You're Kyle Dale. Training Ground Four.'

Kyle thanked it and looked for the signs to the training grounds. Today was going to be such a good day.

Professor Jeol sat at his desk, twisting a pen around aimlessly. The Doctor had vanished and Commandant Ritchie upstairs seemed to be going through some sort of denial about the man's very existence.

His thoughts were interrupted when a Teknix walked in, without knocking.

Jeol was about to reprimand him when he saw the name tag (well, it was the only way to tell the wretched things apart) and realised it was Krassix, Ritchie's PA.

'Can I help you, Krassix?'

Krassix dropped a datapad on his desk. 'Commandant Ritchie considered your questions... inappropriate. However, he asked me to prepare some answers for you.'

Without waiting for a reply, Krassix turned and left.

Jeol shuddered – Teknix gave him the creeps. What on Earth provoked Ritchie to employ one he could not imagine. And what would the powers that be on Micawber's World do if they found out? Oh well, so long as Krassix kept his head down...

He activated the datapad and began reading about the Doctor, why Ritchie had employed him and a few pertinent facts gleaned from the Federation database about his activities in the past.

Jeol assumed that Krassix had downloaded some corrupted information as the dates were way off (unless the Doctor was more than two hundred years old) and shook his head. Given even the simplest tasks, administrators couldn't get them right.

After a few moments, Jeol was aware that he was being

watched. Expecting it to be the Doctor, the scientist looked up and prepared to challenge him on a few things.

Instead, he was facing his missing colleague, Dr Miles Mason, his arm in a sling.

'Dr Mason, how are you?' Jeol was at his side in an instant. 'We thought you were... well, anyway, I'm very glad to see you. The Doctor and I were very concerned.' He guided Mason to his seat. 'Can I get you a drink?'

Mason shook his head. 'Doctor? Doctor who?'

Jeol shrugged. 'Some weirdo brought in by the SSS Administration. Odd, but has a knack for observation frankly lacking in most of our interns these days. If he wasn't so damned strange, I'd ask him to do some lectures.'

Mason tilted his head slightly and Jeol wondered if he'd hurt his neck. 'You all right, Mason?'

'We're fine, thank you, Professor Jeol.'

'We?'

'I. We. We're all the same.'

Jeol decided Mason had clearly had a rough time. 'Hurt your head, did you? Where have you been?'

Mason stood up and took the datapad from Jeol's hand, scanning it very quickly.

Jeol assumed he was looking for something, because he couldn't possibly read it that fast. 'Can I help?'

Mason stopped reading and slowly looked back at Jeol. 'You know this person well?'

'The Doctor? Not really, but yes, we were working together last night. Trying to find you in fact.'

Mason suddenly crushed the datapad in his hand, ignoring the bits of plastic and plexiglass that splintered into his palm. 'We are perfectly healthy, thank you, Professor. We need you to see something. It's terribly important.'

Jeol was staring at the destroyed datapad which Mason let fall to the carpet. 'What the hell…'

Mason suddenly tugged his injured arm out of the sling. In place of his hand and most of his lower arm was a green pulsating mass of mucus-like skin. His shirtsleeve was somehow melded into it and the arm was constantly changing shape, as if it was moving of its own accord, growing then subsiding.

'My God, Mason, what happened to your arm?'

'Perfection,' hissed Mason. He swiped the thrashing limb at Jeol's face.

The professor gasped as some of the mucus came away from Mason and coated his cheek.

He wanted to cry out, in surprise and alarm, let alone the sudden burning pain.

But then a voice in his head told him not to panic. Everything was going to be fine.

It was his own voice. And Miles Mason's voice. And Jean-Paul Cartwright's voice. And Steven Bailey's voice. And Jis Tok Nannarn's voice And…

And everything really was perfect now.

Ms Sox regarded the Doctor pretty much as she regarded most people – with suspicion and a healthy dose of scepticism.

'So Commandant Ritchie asked you to work, undercover, for the SSS, to discover something his own agents couldn't?'

The Doctor grinned with delight. 'That's *exactly* right, yes…!'

Ms Sox glanced back towards the office door, behind which Chase Carrington was at work.

'And why should I believe you?'

The Doctor seemed to just look at her, his head cocked slightly. Ms Sox felt almost… uncomfortable at this. Certainly surprised. It was as if he was seeing past her… no, *through* her. Trying to read her mind. Instinctively, she took a step back.

'You may be right, Ms Sox,' he said quietly. 'But, if I am on the level, you have an ally, not an enemy.'

Ms Sox reasserted her cool. He was just a good manipulator. It wasn't as if he could really read her mind. Jadeans were blank to telepaths (that was why they so often found employment in business offices – no one could unwittingly scan them for the opposition), so she shouldn't be affected by his prying. So why *was* she?

'What do you mean, Doctor?'

But the Doctor just smiled, his greyish eyes impenetrable pools of liquid platinum. Ms Sox felt she could almost drown in them...

She turned away suddenly. 'You're very good, Doctor. I'm tempted to believe that Ritchie did employ you – you can be... persuasive.'

The Doctor was suddenly beside her (when exactly did he get out of the chair and cross the room?) and taking her left hand in his. She looked down, astonished at his physical touch, but surprised herself by not pulling away.

'You know as well as I do that something is not right around here, Ms Sox. The Foamasi are gathering their different Lodges together. SSS troopers are disappearing. Commandant Ritchie is caught up in something so big, he suddenly entrusts himself to me, whom he doesn't know from Adam, and you... You think something is very wrong here at Carrington Corp, don't you? And all these things might be taken as odd coincidences if the Olympics weren't about to happen.'

'And if the Duchess of Auckland wasn't here... and...'

'Yes.' The Doctor squeezed her hand, encouragingly. So few humans knew how Jadeans like to be touched...

She frowned. 'Mr Carrington seems unusually... preoccupied today. He seems to have forgotten the simplest of things.'

'Go on.'

'Well, a group from the pool were going over to see the Stadium today, watch the athletes training before the Games begin.

Yesterday, he was all for it. Today, he was angry that they were there.'

'He changed his mind perhaps? Wanted his staff here?'

Ms Sox shrugged. 'No, it wasn't that so much as… so much as they were going to the Stadium. I mean, it's a project we've been working on for months. Everyone is very excited. But today, he's annoyed that anyone has gone near the place.'

'Has he now? I wonder…'

Ms Sox jolted out of her reverie and snatched her hand back. 'Anyway, Doctor. What were you doing at the Foamasi Temple? They don't normally let non-Foamasi into their embassy like that.'

The Doctor had sat in his seat again (again, she must have been momentarily distracted for him to move that fast). 'Oh, a tip-off. I went to see the Ambassador.'

'Green Fingers? You must be well connected.'

'Interesting…'

Ms Sox sighed. The Doctor seemed to find everything "interesting". 'What now?'

'You knew he was Green Fingers. I didn't. Not until he told me. I didn't think many people knew that. Certainly Commandant Ritchie didn't.'

Ms Sox was herself "interested" to note this. 'I'm very surprised at that, Doctor. I fear he may have misled you. I really doubt that the security chief of the SSS didn't know that.'

'And how did you know?'

Ms Sox shrugged. 'Because apart from my duties as Mr Carrington's PA, I'm also head of security for Carrington Corp.'

The Doctor clapped his hands together. 'Delicious. I imagine Commandant Ritchie is unaware of *that*.'

'Of course. I would not be a very good head of security if people knew it.'

The Doctor shot out of his chair. 'Delightful! Absolutely delightful.'

Ms Sox stepped back. 'What is, Doctor?'

'What? Oh, this. This painting. A delightful example of pre-republican Dolmite artwork. Quinaposki, if I'm not mistaken.'

'You're not. Third Dynasty, Eighth Lineage, actually. Quinaposki's finest century, some believe.'

'You don't?'

'I work with figures and lists, Doctor. I acknowledge art, I have no opinions on it one way or another.'

The Doctor nodded. 'Tell me, Ms Sox. A casual stereotype, I know, but as I remember, Jadeans are well versed in numeracy and literacy. The Federation employs them throughout the administration as... well, administrators. Your reputation is both formidable and accurate. Why did you sidestep into the murky world of politics and security?'

Ms Sox glanced back at the door to Carrington's office, hoping her employer was not listening. Before she could reply, the Doctor interrupted.

'All right, I'm aware you feel a great deal of affection for Mr Carrington, I can sense that. But even so, I imagine you must have come up with the idea prior to meeting him... five years ago, wasn't it? On Sirius 4?'

Ms Sox gazed open-mouthed at the Doctor. Eventually she spoke. 'How did you know that? You haven't accessed anything here or –'

'Or you would have been notified. Because nothing goes on in this corporation without your knowing who is doing what, where and when. And frequently why and how.' The Doctor turned away from her, tracing his finger across the painting he so admired, touching the outline of the rolling hills and soft trees it showed. 'But you see, Ms Sox, I know far more. That's my job. My mission. I came here for nothing more than a wedding. I ended up investigating the savage death of a Foamasi called George, and becoming embroiled in Commandant Ritchie's dangerous games. He, you see, is working for two separate masters. One of which I know, the other I can only guess at. You, on the other hand, are a bit of an enigma. When we met after the wedding fiasco, you allowed your guard to fall.' He turned and looked straight at her. In place of the relaxed, almost whimsical young man she had seen before, she suddenly saw a new Doctor. Beneath that casual exterior, she realised, was a sharp, incisive man. She felt she was being not so much spoken to, or looked at even, but examined, as a scientist might look to see if a white mouse had done its job of spinning a wheel or eaten its food – something mundane and simple. For a moment, Ms Sox had a glimpse of something else via his eyes. A darkness, an agelessness. He might look like a human male in his late thirties, but Ms Sox suddenly knew here was someone who measured his experiences in hundreds, possibly thousands, of years.

'Who... What are you?' she breathed.

He stepped towards her. 'Irrelevant, Ms Sox. All you need to know, need to understand, is that somewhere on this planet is a danger we haven't foreseen. On Earth they have a saying about cows. Do you know what a cow is Ms Sox?'

She nodded. 'A bovine Earth mammal, and a source of nourishment. Cows have been exported all over the galaxy, even to Jadea. They are about the only creatures on the planet that aren't green.'

The Doctor smiled. 'Indeed. And cows, unlike most humans, know when it is going to rain.'

'Nonsense. Earth has a fully functional weather-control system, and has done for thousands of years.'

The Doctor didn't miss a beat. 'Ms Sox, I was on Earth when they set those devices up. I was on Earth when they only dreamt of such things. I was on Earth when mankind settled in various parts of their world simply because of the weather. I have seen the very birth of mankind, from a single-celled amoeba mutated by neutronic radiation. I have witnessed the birth and destruction of entire solar systems. And, above all, I have watched cows sense when it is going to rain and watched as they settle down on a dry area of grass, ensuring that after the weather has passed, they will have dry grazing to munch on. Cows and I share a common aptitude, Ms Sox. We know when it is going to rain and we know when something is wrong. And unless I find out exactly what is going to happen round here, I fear that a great many people may die.' He suddenly threw his arms out. 'And I absolutely *love* the decor of this room.'

Ms Sox turned away from him, taking in the decor, despite the fact that she knew it inside out. She had designed it, selected the colours, the paintings, the furnishings and the carpets. Shaking her head, she turned back to the Doctor.

He was gone. The room was empty apart from herself.

She just looked at where he had been. There were some holographic words floating in the air, a small pad lying on the floor beneath, projecting them.

SEE YOU IN TEN. WHERE WE FIRST MET

'Oh. And by the way, Doctor,' she muttered. 'I *loathe* cows.'

Jesus, Sam, what the hell is wrong with you? Running away from a boy who'd pissed you off was something you did when you were sixteen, not nowadays.

OK, so Kyle had said a jerkish thing, but he was from 3999, not her era, and just as she found it sometimes difficult to adjust to the different times and places the Doctor took her, why the hell couldn't she understand that people in those times and places might have to adjust to her. 3999? Huh, that's not a year, she decided. It's a shirt from *Gap*.

No doubt she'd spent too long on Ha'olam, too long in just one place. She'd become settled, too confident. Too easy to spook again.

Oh, where was the Doctor when you needed him? Where were his words of comfort and reassurance right now?

And why did she still need them, anyway?

Sam took in her surroundings and tried to get some bearings. She was outside the Stadium now, but not where she had come in. No, that must be around to the… yes, to the right. Yes, they'd passed some stores on the way, and that had to back towards the main city. Which meant she could either go straight, or cut back around to the city road.

She went straight ahead.

'No contest. Been there, done that. This is new.' Simple philosophy and one that far too frequently got her into trouble. But this was Carrington City. This was Micawber's World. And, Kleptons notwithstanding, she'd had a fairly easy time of it so far.

The road ahead was lined with trees, palm trees of some sort, and went off to the horizon. Between her and that horizon seemed to be nothing, but she would surely hit one end of the city before too long, so yes, this was still the way to go.

After about fifteen minutes of walking, she could see some kind of building ahead, quite large by the look of it.

Ten minutes later, she could still see it, but it still seemed to be far away. Then it hit her – it was a building but it was also rather large. While she was indeed closing in on it, it was so tall that her distance ratio was confused.

'You're very big,' she told the building when she finally got to it. 'I mean, *very* big.'

Standing by the flight of steps that led up to the glass frontage, she tilted her head back but could not quite see where it ended. At least forty storeys high then, probably more.

She climbed the steps and the doors slid silently open to let her in.

CARRINGTON GRANDE, said a large sign above a reception area.

'You must be a hotel and I claim my five pounds,' she murmured.

There was a chime and an elevator door opened, expelling two men. One was rather ordinary-looking, late fifties, balding, and gave off waves of fussiness, without actually doing anything concrete to reinforce that opinion. The other man was glam, to say the least. Looking like something out of a play, he was in full Regency get-up, including a voluminous white wig, beautiful jacket and humbug waistcoat, his stockinged legs thinning into knee-high boots. He had an expression on his face that told the whole story. The less extravagant man was clearly a nuisance and the Regency man looked like he wanted to murder him.

'Oh, miss,' the Regency man said, 'would you mind getting someone to sort out Her Highness's room? I am her Consort, Ethelredd. She will be back shortly and I couldn't find one of the maids. Terribly sorry.'

Sam was about to point out that she didn't actually work at the Grande, but then smiled. This could be a fun distraction.

'I'll see to it immediately, sir. How long before Her Highness returns, exactly?'

Consort Ethelredd glanced at the clock on the wall. 'Twenty minutes, I should think.'

'Oh, no problem,' Sam lied, not having the foggiest notion what to do. 'I'll get it sorted.'

'Thank you.' Ethelredd almost shoved the other man away, but did it gracefully enough to make it look like steering rather than pushing. 'Now, Mr Chalfont, I understand you have a story to post?'

Chalfont clearly knew he was being side railed but, Sam guessed, knew there was little he could do because he nodded and went into one of the rooms off the reception area.

Checking he had gone, Ethelredd looked at Sam, darkly. 'If there's any justice in this world, the Duchess of Auckland will have broken a nail while out shopping and I will have to spend many hours trying every manicurist on this godforsaken planet to repair it. Meantime, Torin bloody Chalfont will have licked his fingers and shoved them into an electricity point, frying his stupid brains out.' Ethelredd shook his head. 'But no, there is no justice after all, is there?'

Sam realised the source of his new irritation. A hovercar had pulled up and some people were flocking around it, grovelling. Ethelredd straightened his waistcoat and put on a beatific smile as he walked out of the building, his greeting of 'Welcome Back, Your Highness' cut off by the closing doors.

The Duchess's room was not going to get cleaned any time soon, Sam realised, and it might be a good idea if she scarpered before they blamed her. Trouble was, she didn't know how to get out, so her only option was the elevator. All she had to do was select a floor about halfway up. The odds of that being the Duchess's (royalty were always near the top anyway) were rather slim at least.

As the traditionally plummy tones of the Duchess wafted back in through the opening doors, Sam jumped into the elevator that the Regency man and Chalfont had emerged from. The doors closed on her and she looked for a floor selection.

'Penthouse only,' said a computerised voice. 'Non-stop.'

Oh great, thought Sam, someone today really, really must hate me.

Quartermaster-Sergeant Dallion froze as the knock on the door alerted her. She waved to the others to stop what they were doing, and slid her blaster rifle from its scabbard across her back.

Carruthers immediately took up a position behind the door, while the others slowly stood up behind their sergeant. She nodded to Fenton, who walked forward and opened the door slowly.

Facing him was a human male, quite tall, with wavy brown hair flowing to his shoulders. He had a well-chiselled face, a wide smile and grey eyes. He was wearing a strange velvet long coat that seemed to be green or grey or tan, depending how the light from the sun outside caught it as he moved.

He raised his hands welcomingly. 'Please put your gun down, Dallion,' he said quietly. 'I'm not here to cause trouble. And if Mr Carruthers could move away from behind the door... Well, I'm sure we could all do with a less tense atmosphere.'

No one moved.

'Oh.' The man put his hands behind his back. 'All right, then. I am the Doctor. I'm working for Commandant Ritchie. Oh, and he thinks someone is going to try to kill you, so he sent me here to warn you.'

'Who is going to kill us?' Dallion asked slowly.

'He is. Unfortunately.' The Doctor shrugged. 'That's executive stress for you, I'm afraid.' He stepped forward, crossing into their room. He looked about, taking in the peeling walls, the damp patch in the far corner, the overturned crate that doubled as a card table, and the carefully positioned sleeping bags, ensuring that every conceivable entrance was covered. Just in case.

'No guns lying around,' he muttered. 'All concealed no doubt. Probably right in front of me. Very efficient. The Commandant trained you well.'

'Forget the compliments,' said Dallion sourly. 'Who are you?'

'I told you. I'm the Doctor. Here to ensure Ritchie doesn't kill you.'

Carruthers stepped from behind the door, covering the Doctor with a handgun held firmly in both hands. He trained it confidently on the back of the Doctor's head, while McCarrick stepped over and began patting the newcomer down. 'Why should the Commandant want to kill us?' Carruthers asked.

The Doctor shrugged. 'He doesn't want to, I suppose, but he feels he may have to. He's in trouble of some sort, but won't say what. I have my suspicions, but nothing grounded in evidence, I'm afraid. It's all to do with whatever happened to your colleagues in the tunnels, deep under the surface. He asked me to save you from him.'

The others all looked to Dallion, who lowered her blaster. 'Sit,' she said, indicating another crate. 'You have ten minutes.'

'Five, actually. We have to meet another ally in ten minutes and it'll take five minutes or so to get there.'

'I don't like this, Sarge,' said Clarke.

'Nor me,' agreed Klein.

Dallion shook her head at them, a slight movement, but one they understood. The Doctor seemed to understand it, too.

'If I may explain?'

'Four minutes left,' said Carruthers.

The Doctor nodded. 'All right, as I see it, something is here on Micawber's World. The Olympic Games are about to start, bringing millions to the planet. Whatever is here, whatever killed or kidnapped your fellow agents, is here for that very reason. Your Commandant is involved in this in some way. Maybe someone's blackmailing him. This is either the someone who dealt with your fellow agents or someone else who is interested in their whereabouts. Ritchie is answerable to the SSS. He is also answerable to this other force. I think he's answerable to something else as well, which is why he brought me in. He needed an independent outsider whom he could deny any knowledge of or use as a scapegoat to cover himself. He saved you lot from regulations. Why? Because he's a nice man? Possibly. Because to discipline you would bring attention to whatever happened? Most probably. I don't think anyone outside his office and this room is aware that your friends have vanished. I *do* however believe that whoever Ritchie is frightened of knows, and he wants you to find out the truth before they do. If they get there first, then he'll have to kill you to cover his back. It's a shield he's rather adept at. My only question is, do you trust him? In fact, do *I* trust him? If you trust him, you'll have to trust me. And if you trust me, I, logically, have to trust him, because you trust him, and therefore trust me. Are you following this?'

Everyone except Dallion shook their head. She just began polishing the butt of her blaster with spit and her finger. 'Two minutes, Doctor,' she said.

The Doctor took a deep breath. 'Also on Micawber's World is a rather unusual Jadean, a Ms Sox.'

'Carrington's PA,' interjected McCarrick. The Doctor nodded.

'That's her. She's also his head of security. She arranged for the SSS to be brought in right at the start. She feels that Micawber's World is being compromised. Her involvement is strictly personal. She's in love with Carrington and wants to protect him. Only problem is, I'm rather afraid she's failed. It's my guess that Carrington is dead. The man in his office is probably a Foamasi spy, possibly from the Dark Peaks Lodge. Which makes me wonder if the Dark Peaks are in fact Ritchie's unseen allies-cum-foes.' The Doctor paused. 'Now, that's an interesting possibility. If the Dark Peaks want control of the Games, that will cause severe ructions within the other Lodges as, strictly speaking, the Twin Suns have this planet. If the Foamasi killed at the Stadium was a Twin Suns, killed on the orders of the Dark Peaks, then on top of everything else, we're in the middle of an escalating struggle for power.' He looked at Dallion. 'I hadn't thought of that, you know. Thank you.'

'For what?'

'Making me consider that possibility.'

McCarrick tapped his watch and Dallion nodded.

'We're not convinced.'

'Odd that,' added Carruthers. 'Because I'm sure it sounded convincing to someone.'

'Just not us,' added Klein.

Dallion replaced her blaster in its holster. 'However, I'm intrigued.' She looked at the others. 'Keep him here. I'll meet up with Ms Sox and make my own mind up.'

The Doctor tried to stand up, but four pairs of hands clamped on his shoulder, and even if that had not been enough, Carruthers's blaster suddenly pressed against his temple made his mind up fully. 'You don't know where, Sergeant Dallion.'

Dallion smiled. 'I'm a soldier, Doctor. While you were gabbling away, Ms Sox came out of Carrington Corp and got into her flyer. I'm tracing it now.'

She pulled the PMD out of the shadows, and the Doctor could see it was jury-rigged to a few datapads and a computer.

'Ingenious,' he said. 'Are you monitoring everything that's going on?'

Dallion nodded. 'Just about. Had my eye on you since you left SSS Admin last night. Oh, and I don't trust you a millimetre.'

The Doctor's face fell. 'Why?'

'Going to the Foamasi Temple to see Green Fingers. The Ambassador only sees people he knows.'

'Am I the only person who didn't know Green Fingers was the Ambassador?' The Doctor shook his head. 'Once upon a time, in another lifetime, I saw everything. Nowadays, I keep missing the important bits. It's really not fair.'

Dallion shrugged. 'More fun for the rest of us, Doctor. Knowing you're not perfect.' She glanced down at the PMD readout. 'The Earth Church.' She looked at Carruthers. 'You're in charge. If I'm not back in fifteen minutes, blow off his head and then get off this planet. If it *is* a set-up, we're dead. If nothing else, he's right about Ritchie covering his ass. We'll be an embarrassment before too long.' She looked back down at the datapad, preoccupied. 'Good luck.'

The others muttered their agreement and farewells and Dallion left.

The Doctor looked up at his captors cheerily. They looked down at him impassively.

'Well,' he said. 'Isn't this jolly.'

* * *

Torin Chalfont was bored now and was beginning to feel that today was just one big waste of his time. The Duchess of Auckland had returned ages ago – tomorrow she was due to open the Olympiad and so far he hadn't managed to get that contract to publish her Olympic memoirs.

Every time he tried to talk to her, that blasted Consort, Ethelredd, interrupted them. Or Counsellor De'Ath. Worse still, that pathetic little fussbudget from Carrington Corp – what was his name... oh yes, Co-ordinator Sumner – was getting more attention than *he* was! And Torin Chalfont was adored by his public, accredited by the news servers and applauded by his peers.

Thank God none of them were here to see how he had been relegated to the lower divisions on Micawber's World.

He was seated in his rooms at the Carrington Grande, which, according to the sign floating outside the door, was the Colby Suite. The trappings were tasteless, the chairs uncomfortable and the two bedrooms positively filthy.

'I have to get away,' he declared to no one in particular.

The door from the lobby opened, and Secretary Aigburth slipped his head around.

'Ah, there you are, Chalfont. The Duchess has a message for you.'

Oh, at bloody last.

'Marvellous, my dear Aigburth, quite marvellous. I assume she is ready to receive me after her shopping and sightseeing expedition. No doubt full of tales of exquisite purchases, sweet-smelling perfumery and taste-searing chocolates. I simply cannot wait. And yet –' he held up a hand to stop Aigburth interrupting – 'I fear I must, as I need to bathe. To greet Her Highness in such a manner as this –' he waved a hand towards his morning suit – 'would be disrespectful.'

'Actually, Chalfont,' said Aigburth with ill-concealed glee, 'the Duchess regrets that she cannot entertain you until after the opening ceremony. She says she will meet you in her chamber tomorrow afternoon. Après luncheon, bien sûr.'

Before Chalfont could reply, Aigburth had vanished.

Chalfont was livid. 'That two-faced bitch. I'll give her blue blood – I'll pump it out of her veins and into the gutter by the time I've finished with her.'

He threw himself into an armchair, ignoring its protesting creaks.

After a few moments' fuming, he grabbed at his laptop and began tapping the keys. Unlike so many of his contemporaries, he despised modern technology, refusing to use voice-activated systems, feeling that to convey accurately the journalists' true feelings, one simply *had* to type it all up longhand oneself.

His laptop did, however, have another use. He long ago understood how the thing actually worked, and how similar machinery worked, and, best of all, how to hack into other systems by creating echo files and fake passwords.

'If Torin Chalfont is here on Micawber's World, he is going to find and write a story that will make Her Royal Highness and her wretched Court completely unimportant.'

After only about ten minutes' hacking, he found the kind of thing he was looking for. A secret SSS carrier wave, giving details of eight missing, presumed dead – SSS agents. Further research showed that they vanished investigating some tunnels beneath the Olympic Stadium.

Already, Torin Chalfont could see the newscasts, the server headlines and the Pulitzer (Offworld and Interstellar Division) Prize.

He closed down his laptop, shoved a datapad into his pocket, straightened his collar and left his room.

Crossing the lobby, he had to duck aside slightly, nipping behind an ornate pillar, as one of the hotel maids came out of the elevator carrying a bag, presumably of wastepaper from Her High and Mightiness's bedchambers. Probably planned to sell it to one of the low-taste holochannels that were overrunning Micawber's World right now. After a few seconds he peeked back from behind the pillar and she was gone. He quickly left the hotel and consulted his datapad for a map – the Stadium was off to the left, but the entrance to the underground passages was nearer to the industrial area, where the power feeds would come from. That made sense – the tunnels were presumably hosting all the electrical cabling, so getting in should be quite easy.

All he had to do was find eight dead bodies and he'd have a story. Gracious, if he could find them alive, he'd have a far better one.

This was going to be such a good day after all.

Sam Jones was trying not to be intimidated, but no matter how foppish the Consort to the Duchess looked in his Regency gear, she had to admit he had a certain air of authority about him that reminded her of the Doctor.

Matters hadn't been helped when, on suggesting that he was a reject from one of those *Blackadder* episodes, and beginning to quote from one of her favourite scenes involving turnips and Mrs Miggins's pies, a less than masculine man referred to as the Counsellor had looked the reference up in his datapad and started to give a fairly good description of what that series was actually about before losing all interest.

Everything had gone wrong earlier, when she had gone up in the elevator and realised that the Duchess's suite was the only place that particular one went. She had not been able to get back to the lobby because the elevator had been called straight down again and returned a few moments later with the entire royal entourage – minus the funny little man she had seen the Consort being rude to in the reception area earlier.

'I thought I told you to make the beds,' he had hissed at her when exiting the elevator.

Sam had glanced into the various bedchambers and seen what a mess they were in. Dishevelled silk sheets, books on the floor (mostly, she later noted, with very large print, few words and lots of colourful pictures), half-empty glasses (in a situation like this, no way were they half full), and clothes thrown everywhere. A couple of fluffy teddy bears and something that looked curiously like an outlawed cuddly toy Meep were thrown around the floor.

'Actually, I don't work –' Sam had started to say, but the Consort had interrupted her wearily.

'Obviously. No one on this planet seems to. But if you could sort it out as quickly as possible, I'd be very grateful.'

'How grateful?' Sam had smiled, but the Consort had not smiled back. The rather camp Counsellor, who was steering the Duchess towards the living room, shot Sam some fairly venomous looks – probably the butchest thing he'd ever done – and then closed the door behind him.

The Consort and a big tall alien who looked more ferocious than anything else she'd seen on Micawber's World so far stared at her, as if daring her to argue.

With a sigh, she said it would take ten minutes, which seemed to satisfy the Consort, and he followed the others into the living room.

Only the white-furred chap in the military uniform stayed, to ensure she actually did it.

'Hi, I'm Sam,' she said as she began picking up the books.

'Gar.'

'Hi, Gar. What d'you do for the Duchess.'

'Gar.'

Sam decided to try again. 'Nice uniform, but not Regency like the others I noticed. Where do you work normally?'

'Gar.'

'Thought you might say that,' Sam replied, deciding to give up before it got too surreal.

'Gar,' he said again, pointing at a book she'd missed, poking out from under a pile of rejected dresses.

'Oh, absolutely. I agree totally. Hideous mess.'

'Gar.'

Sam shook her head slightly. 'I'm from the twentieth century, by the way. Came in a space-and-time craft called the TARDIS. My friend is called the Doctor. He's probably wondering where I am right now.' She started to sort the bed out. 'I'm wondering where he is, too, as I'd like to get the hell off Micawber's World and go somewhere else.' She started rearranging the stuffed toys neatly on the now plumped-up pillows. 'Do you know where he is?' She suddenly pointed at him, warningly. 'And if you say "Gar" again, I'll chuck this Meep thing at you, OK?'

'Oh, all right. Spoilsport.'

Sam dropped the Meep. 'You can *talk*?'

Gar smiled, displaying a full set of blunted, large, white teeth which matched his fur. 'Be a bit pointless working for Her Highness's main transport ship if I didn't.'

He held out a furry paw in a very human handshake gesture. 'The name's Gar. Really. I'm the Petty Officer aboard the *Space Pioneer*. You're not really an employee here at all, are you?'

Sam returned the handshake, giving her name. 'No.'

'So, why are you here, making the beds?'

'Because the Consort guy told me to, frankly.'

Gar nodded. 'Consort Ethelredd. Nice guy, really, but has to deal with Her Highness, which isn't always easy. Between him and Counsellor De'Ath, they keep things going quite well.'

Sam shrugged. 'Aren't you going to give me away? I could be a terrorist or something.'

Gar seemed to screw his eyes up for a moment, then relaxed again. 'Nope. No guns or bombs on you.'

'How can you tell?'

Gar smiled again. 'The V'orrn can see over three hundred and eighty alternate spectrums of light.'

'Infrared?'

'Absolutely.'

'Ultraviolet?'

'No problem.'

Sam frowned. She had a bad feeling about this. 'And you could tell I'm not carrying a gun because...?'

'Yup, because I can see on a submolecular level as well, stripping away what I don't want to see.'

'X-ray vision then. You're seeing me naked.'

Gar paused, then nodded like Dave Wilson used to in biology class, trying to look like an innocent three-year-old because he'd just looked the word 'vagina' up in the dictionary for the fifth time that afternoon. It never worked for Sam when Dave did it, and it didn't work when Gar did it.

But as Gar didn't start shouting 'vagina' in a variety of silly voices and giggling and pointing at all the girls in the room – which at this moment consisted of just Sam, of course – she didn't chuck a heavy biology book at him as she used to do at Dave all those years ago. Instead she suggested that if he did so again, she'd forget Royal protocol and offer to insert a blunt object somewhere painful.

Gar nodded that he'd got the hint just as Ethelredd and De'Ath came in. Behind them another Regency-clad man whom Ethelredd referred to as 'Secretary' disappeared into the elevator, laughing.

'He looks happy,' Sam muttered.

'He is,' said De'Ath. 'He's got a message for the delightful Torin Chalfont.'

'Who's he?'

De'Ath looked at Ethelredd, beaming. 'I don't know where you found this one, Consort, but I insist we keep her around. Someone to tell Chalfont that he's not as famous as he believes. How delightful.'

Gar put a paw up and Ethelredd indicated for him to speak.

'She's not actually on the staff of the hotel,' he said.

'I guessed that,' Ethelredd muttered. 'The room is tidy, the bed well made and she's not looking under the bed for used underwear to sell to souvenir merchants.' He turned to Sam. 'So, who are you?'

'A traveller. I accidentally got into your elevator after you told me to get up here. I thought I could go to another floor and then get out of the Grande.'

'There are no other floors,' De'Ath pointed out, unhelpfully.

'Yes, thank you, I had noticed that,' Sam said. It was at this point that she had remarked on the Regency attire and her favourite TV show of the 1980s.

And now here she was, wondering what they were going to do with her.

'I just do not know what are we going to do with her,' De'Ath muttered, showing a remarkable gift for stating the obvious.

'She's not armed,' interceded Gar.

'Had a damned good look to make sure, too,' Sam sniffed.

There was a call from the living room and all three men looked at one another. Eventually the deadlock was broken when, with a heartfelt sigh, De'Ath wandered away.

Ethelredd could not help but smile. Then he regarded Sam again. 'I suppose we can't keep you here. You've not done anything wrong and it was I who assumed you worked here in the first place.'

'And I did make the bed well,' said Sam with a sarcastic flutter of the eyelids.

'That too. Go on then, you'd better get going.'

Sam bent down to the floor and picked up the toy Meep. 'Mind if I take a souvenir?'

Ethelredd was about to object when Sam pointed out that on this planet, at least, they were illegal and if the Duchess was found to possess one while the real Meeps took part in the Games, it could make for bad publicity.

Ethelredd grunted something about needing people like Sam around the Duchess now and again, then disappeared into a side room, returning with a large brown paper bag. Sam stuffed the Meep toy into it and promised to make sure it was destroyed.

After Ethelredd said another thanks, she patted Gar's shoulder and got into the elevator that would take her back to the lobby.

As the doors opened, she saw Torin Chalfont somewhat obviously hide behind a pillar.

This could be fun.

Sam hid behind another pillar but far more successfully. There was no accounting for experience, and life with the Doctor provided plenty of opportunities for behind-the-pillar eavesdropping.

Chalfont then emerged, seemingly believed he was safe from prying eyes and ran out of the Grande.

Having sod all else to do, Sam decided to follow, still clutching the brown paper bag.

Chapter Eight
Paradise Place

The man who had been Jean-Paul Cartwright was gone. For ever.

Now in his place were three hundred million other personalities, memories and experiences all combined into one being.

Beside its bloated body was all that remained of Cartwright's seven former compatriots, encased in the mucus-encrusted rolls of Wirrrn pupae, crawling around the floor, preparing to spread their seed on to whatever flesh they encountered. But, as a Swarm Leader, that which had been Jean-Paul Cartwright was entrusted with the command of the batch and sent them their orders telepathically.

In response, the twenty or so pupae grouped there reared up, acknowledging their leader's commands.

Then they crawled off into the tunnels, on their mission: to find new Wirrrn host bodies among the races on the surface of Micawber's World and transform them into Wirrrn drones like themselves.

The Swarm Leader knew this was good.

It turned to the hybrids standing beside it, twitching its mandibles and antennae, sending questions into the brain of the less-dominated one – the one that could still work among the alien creatures above.

Mason, that was the designation it used with the aliens. Mason nodded slightly, horrible alien eyes with their limited vision and easily damaged parts staring pointlessly at the Swarm Leader. It pointed to the four forms beside it. Two of them were almost full pupae now, the last bits of their humanoid appendages retracting beneath the pupal chitin. The most recent conversion still wore shreds of its ridiculous outer clothing. The Swarm Leader looked into this new mind, sensing the time was right to absorb it.

'Leave… me alone…' it was thinking. 'I am… an individual…'

The Swarm Leader considered the futility of this. Of all the races the Wirrrn absorbed, humanoid ones were always the most aggressively independent ones, but even they surrendered in the end, adding their information and memory to the hive mind.

This one was no different. The Swarm Leader began to draw the consciousness into itself, automatically transferring it to every other Wirrrn everywhere. This was once a human male from Earth, like Mason. It had been Dev Jeol, a scientist among its people.

And the creature once called Mason had alerted the Swarm Leader to one particular item of information it possessed. There was a strange humanoid on Micawber's World helping the humans – the intellect and physical strength it possessed would help the Wirrrn greatly.

It was known as the Doctor.

Despite Dev Jeol's attempts at resistance, the Swarm Leader took little effort to finally absorb it completely, dominating its thoughts, making them Wirrrn thoughts and memories.

There was a brief flash of euphoria felt throughout the hive mind as Dev Jeol finally became a Wirrrn, and all his/its memories became shared and known.

And instantly the Swarm Leader knew it needed the Doctor.

The other Swarm Leaders on the planet knew they needed the Doctor.

The Queen, protected near the solar generator at the heart of the planet, also sent its message.

Absorption of this Doctor was to take immediate priority. It was time to attack the surface, to propagate and further the race existence.

But the Wirrrn were not combatants. They were not a race who walked into a battlefield, guns blasting pointlessly, as so many of the Wirrrn's foes did.

No, the Wirrrn used more intelligent, more subliminal means.

Mason unfurled his hand. In his palm were a series of tiny red and blue capsules. 'They are perfected,' he said slowly.

The Swarm Leader sent an extra boost of independence back into Mason's neural circuits, returning a degree of apparent freedom that would make him capable of mixing with the aliens above.

'I will distribute the pills among some of the alien athletes. The rest will seek them out. Our work will have begun.'

Ignoring the other three scientists he used to work alongside, all of whom no longer resembled anything vaguely human, Mason began his trek back to the surface.

And the Swarm Leader sent his last new pupa to follow the others to the surface.

And if it had wanted to recall which one had once been Dev Jeol, it would have been impossible. Now it was just a Wirrrn.

For ever.

Kyle Dale was wandering away from the Stadium, having packed in his exercise for the day. His kit was in a bag floating beside him, and he was studying a small red book as he walked.

The Way Forward was embossed on the cover.

He was looking up the passages on romance. And what the Goddess said about his feelings.

Kyle had never been one for the girls really. Or the boys. Or anything. A bit of a loner back on his colony world, he had studied hard at school, and after a few years of being beaten up by the school bullies who saw him as overtly studious, he had decided to start building his body up. Getting involved in physical activities such as water-skiing, rock-climbing, gravity-well free-falling, those sorts of things. After a couple of years of that, he'd become involved with a soccer team and then moved over into the more independent world of athletics. With no team to be responsible to, or for, he was far happier succeeding or failing on his own terms.

When his father had died in a submersible accident on Kandalinga, Kyle had opted to travel.

He'd made friends with a couple on the cruiser and they'd disembarked together on Shem. There, one of the Simian travel agents had introduced him to the local night life and over the next few weeks, Kyle had been offered a variety of opportunities to experience, well, just about anything he could imagine – and few things he'd never have imagined in his wildest dreams.

But Kyle had been frightened by this – his inexperience coupled with an unwillingness to become experienced gradually tried the patience of his hosts and friends. In the end Kyle had joined up with a local team of long-distance runners who seemed far more interested in taking care of their bodies than the inner-city types had been.

He had met Reverend Lukas one afternoon when Jolyon and Phillipa had literally bumped into Kyle during a rainstorm. Reverend Lukas said he could immediately sense that Kyle was directionless – needing some kind of pattern in his life.

He left *The Way Forward* for Kyle to read and, when he did so, he saw himself, his own personal struggles and questions and fears and...

Everything he believed he needed was there. No distractions, no pressure to eat, drink, take drugs, have sex. Nothing but a dedication to his soul, to what the Goddess told him was part of his nature. *The Way Forward* made him feel special, to realise that his nonconformity was not an aberration but a gift, a way to celebrate his differences.

And Reverend Lukas had coached him on the Goddess's path,

the methods and structures of his mobile caravan of gospel spreading. As they moved from world to world, they gained followers and – although Reverend Lukas never said anything cruel or spiteful about them – lost a few.

'They have their own paths, Kyle,' he would say. 'Some people are with us for ever. Some just need a little variation, a little enlightenment, and are then ready to face the universe on their own terms rather than everyone else's. One day, you too may decide to do that.'

'No,' Kyle had said. 'No, I will never leave you. I love the Goddess, I believe in what the Goddess offers us.'

And Reverend Lukas had put his hand on Kyle's shoulder and squeezed. 'You cannot know how pleased I am to know that, Kyle. Together, the Church will go forward and prepare the people of this galaxy for the return of the Goddess, for she will come soon. Be sure of that.'

Five years on, Kyle still awaited the Goddess's arrival, but with no less patience. It was possible that she would not come before Kyle's life had passed, but no matter. The faith kept him strong, kept him alive. Faith in the Goddess and faith in Reverend Lukas's convictions.

So why, right now, was he so... aware of this girl, Samantha Jones? Why did it bother him so much to think how she had run away from him earlier in the day?

And why was he looking for her, here, as if she was just going to be walking along the road? Or sitting there, waiting? The coincidence would have to be huge.

To see her laughing in his mind's eye made his heart beat faster. He shook his head, trying to clear it.

The Way Forward wasn't helping him – he wasn't concentrating.

Besides which, Samantha Jones *was* on the road ahead.

Following someone.

Surely that couldn't be her – she ought to be back in Carrington City with her Doctor friend by now.

But it certainly looked like her. Walked like her.

He clenched his fists. Something inside him found her presence exciting. Motivating.

He had to take a deep breath. This was silly.

And if it was *that* silly, why was he following her?

Ms Sox was not used to being kept waiting. The Doctor was late and she was still worried not only about the ease with which he seemed to have been able to talk to Commandant Ritchie and Green Fingers, but also Chase Carrington's bizarre attitude earlier.

What was going on?

'Ms Sox?'

Ms Sox turned. The voice had been female, so she had assumed it would be the Doctor's fiery young woman friend from the Church fracas. Instead it was an SSS sergeant, aiming a gun at her.

Ms Sox tried to bring to mind her researches over the last few months since she had called the SSS in to divert people from her own security work.

'Quartermaster-Sergeant Susan Dallion isn't it? I thought you had gone AWOL?'

Dallion smiled. 'That was what we wanted everyone to think.'

Ms Sox laughed. 'Commandant Ritchie is no fool. He knew someone would be watching him. You should have been decommissioned after the deaths of your team. But he keeps you around, like a private army, right?'

'Maybe.'

Ms Sox stretched her arms out, to show she was not armed. 'He's a far better officer than I expected. He's also using the Doctor. You to be his army, him to be his scientist. Our good Commandant knows far more about what is going on than I – indeed, *we* – thought.'

'You know the Doctor?' Dallion was still pointing her blaster at Ms Sox.

Ms Sox nodded. 'I'm tempted to trust him, Sergeant Dallion. I suspect you are too, or else you wouldn't have come in his place. Do you have somewhere we can all talk?'

Dallion paused, as if sizing up Ms Sox and the potential threat she might be. Then lowered her blaster. 'Follow me.'

Ms Sox followed, smiling. This was getting better and better.

Torin Chalfont stood outside the entrance to the tunnels. Someone was following him, he felt sure of it, but they were very good at hiding.

Or he was getting paranoid. Still, according to all the reports he'd seen and read over the years, when someone tries to attack you, they come from behind. A second person behind him would be easier fodder for the big chomping monsters that probably lived in the tunnels.

He went into the darkness, surprised that the lights dotting the walls did not offer more illumination.

'Typical SSS, never do their jobs properly. One day I'll write an exposé of their shoddiness and close 'em down.' He was talking out loud not just because he liked the sound of his own voice, but it did dispel a few of the fears... no, not fears but healthy anticipation, he felt, going into an area where eight men had met their deaths.

Grisly deaths.

Torn apart by the Olympic Monster. Micawber's Beast.

'Oh, I can hear the headlines now – Torin Chalfont solves the Olympic riddle. Eight men die before our top prize-winning writer exposes the dreadful terrorist group responsible for trying to stop the Games.' Then he stopped and clapped his hands together. 'And better still, Duchess of Auckland's life saved by our man Chalfont. Candidate for next year's Honours? Sir Torin

Chalfont. Lord Chalfont of –'

Something was slithering towards him.

While behind came a female voice. 'Go on,' it said. 'This is getting interesting. Lord Chalfont of where?'

Torin Chalfont didn't turn around to face whoever it was, however. Because he had made a slight miscalculation.

'Are you here to kill me?' he whispered.

'No,' said the girl behind.

'I wasn't talking to you,' he hissed back.

'Who then?' The girl adopted a whisper as well.

'That!' screamed Chalfont as a huge mass of browny-green mucus reared up in front of him, one huge yellow eye staring unblinkingly at him.

'Oh God,' breathed the girl, and Chalfont felt himself yanked backwards as she grabbed his collar – just in time, as the creature slammed its back down exactly where he had been standing.

He was then bundled into a cavern, the girl wrapping her hand around his mouth.

Chalfont tried to glance around. It was a small cavern, bits of abandoned equipment scattered all over. Behind them was a sheer drop, and a series of walkways going deeper into the bowels of Micawber's World, all unlit.

'Quiet,' the girl hissed. He nodded.

They watched as the creature slithered past, followed by another, even longer... no, it was loads of small ones. Their bodies were astonishing. If they came to a lump in the floor, rather than go over or around it, their bodies split and rejoined as each segment encountered the lump.

The two humans jumped in surprise. Amid the mass of larvae-like creatures was a man. A human, dressed in white. Chalfont immediately recognised the uniform of the SSS science section. The man (Chalfont vaguely recognised him – could he be famous?) had his left arm in a rough sling, but apart from that he seemed oblivious to the things at his feet. Indeed, he seemed oblivious to everything except –

The man stopped and stared briefly into the cavern. Chalfont hoped it was too dark to see either him or the girl who held him.

Chalfont couldn't say whether the scientist had seen them, but he didn't enter the chamber. He did smile, however. A smile that sent a very uncomfortable shiver down Chalfont's back. The smile of someone who knows something you don't...

The man restarted his slow march amid the larvae creatures and was quickly out of sight.

Across the way was an alcove, cut off from the tunnel by an SSS wire-mesh fence, a small sign saying KEEP OUT on it. One of the creatures turned against this mesh, its body turning into tiny globules of mucus, each one oozing through the grid and re-forming on the other side. After a few moments of exploration, the creature again divided its body, emerged back into the tunnel and again became one before shuffling after its fellows.

After a few moments more, the girl released Chalfont's mouth and he gasped in air. Whoever she was, she was clearly more friendly than they had been, but he was still cautious.

'Who are you?'

'Sam Jones. Your hero. You're Torin Chalfont, right?'

'Yes. How did you –'

'Oh, where I come from, you're famous. I mean, everyone adores your work.'

Bless her little cotton socks. 'Why, thank you, Miss Jones.'

'Sam.'

'Sam. I never realised people thought highly of the little insignificant work I do. Just a public service, really.'

'Yeah, whatever.' Sam seemed suddenly distracted. 'Fact is, whatever those were, they were going to do us harm if we got in their way.'

'But you rescued us both.'

'Nah,' said Sam. 'If they'd actually wanted to eat us or whatever, they'd have found us in here easily. And the guy in the white suit saw us easily enough. He stared right at me and smiled.'

'I noticed that. Why didn't he do anything? Do you think he was their prisoner? He thought we would rescue him?'

Sam shook her head. 'He wasn't in any danger. I imagine we simply weren't important enough for them to worry about.' She pushed past him and knelt down in the tunnel, looking at the floor.

She was a young woman, early twenties perhaps. Nice blonde hair hanging to her shoulders, a longish fringe parted in the middle. She was wearing a rather short dress which, he realised, staring closer, had been a lot longer until she had either ripped off the bottom, or hacked it away with a pair of blunt scissors.

She was also wearing a pair of dark shorts and Chalfont suddenly realised he'd seen her earlier – the dress tucked into the shorts. The maid from the hotel who that oaf Ethelredd had spoken to. Now, dress hanging out, he could see she looked more like some kind of street urchin, but as she turned back to face him, he realised he was looking at a young woman of formidable experience. She might be young, but her eyes indicated she'd been through enough trouble and danger to last a lifetime.

He immediately felt a new respect for her. He also knew that she would see through his normal bluster, his fake charm and high-society attitudes. And if she could see through that, maybe it was time to put the old Torin Chalfont into gear. The journalist who had reported from the front line on the first Galaxy 5 war. Or the reporter who had kept sending his reports to the holovid crews on Blakkis Moon 3 when Blakkis itself was declared a plague zone and quarantined and he was tapped in the middle of it, hated by the locals because the plague had been brought to their previously isolated world by space travellers.

'You aren't a fan of mine at all, are you, Sam?' he said quietly.

'Truth? Nah, never heard of you till today. But back at the Duchess's rooms, they seemed to think you're a bit of a bore and a joke, so I thought I'd better humour you.'

That hurt. Obviously, he knew what they thought of him, but having it said so bluntly by someone who wasn't even born (probably) when he decided to give up serious reporting for a cosy life with the toffs and wannabes of high society, that really hurt.

Trouble was, she was right and it seemed rather pointless arguing with her. Instead he just said 'Oh well', and asked her what she was doing.

She was using a thin metal object of some sort to scrape some kind of hardening slime trail off the ground.

'Like a snail,' she said. 'When it reared up to attack, did you see a mouth?'

'Can't say I was really looking,' Chalfont replied. 'But thinking back, no.'

Sam nodded. 'Doctor's lessons are paying off, I think.' He did not know what she meant by that, but before he could ask, she carried on. 'I'll bet that they just ingest food – you know, without having to chew. Probably something in this sludge dissolves things.' She looked back at him again, with a thin smile. 'Dissolves people. You.'

Chalfont shuddered. 'Not a particularly pleasant thought, thank you.'

He stopped suddenly and Sam looked first at him and then back towards the tunnel entrance.

Someone was standing there.

'Oh, great,' Chalfont muttered. 'Now the SSS agents have come to arrest us for trespassing.'

Kyle watched with horror from behind a rock as the slug creatures emerged from the tunnel entrance. He closed his eyes, fearfully, and when he opened them, the creatures were gone. Kyle stared down the road where he had come from, but there was no sign of them.

He crawled around from behind his rock and noticed the pools of slime on the roadway. They coalesced into one large pool and then the trail led to the edge of the road, where it stopped. If they had crawled on to the sandy surface of the roadside, maybe the slime had dried out instantly or been absorbed.

Sam and the man she had been following had gone into the tunnels. Maybe they'd seen those creatures...

Or been attacked!

Kyle ran full pelt towards the tunnel entrance and then stopped. Kneeling some way down, just visible in the rather useless low light, was Sam.

'Sam!' he called.

Another figure, probably the man, emerged from the right. 'Who are you?' he called.

'It's OK, Torin,' Sam said. 'That's Kyle. He's all right, as they go on this planet. Come on down, Kyle. The weather's lovely.'

Once again, he didn't actually understand what she was talking about, but he strode purposefully inside – and stepped into the sticky substance. 'Ugh,' he muttered and lifted his foot up.

'Don't touch it!' yelled Sam. 'It may be dangerous.'

She ran up to him, carefully avoiding the slime. 'Hiya,' she smiled. 'Good of you to join us. Did you see –'

'Yeah,' said Kyle. 'But they just went on to the sand rather than stay on the road and I lost track of them. What were they?'

'No idea.' Sam started walking back towards the other man, Torin. (Surely not that boring newshound Torin Chalfont? Why wasn't he interviewing the Duchess or whatever it was he did?) 'But I'm sure the Doctor would know.'

Sam suddenly stopped and pointed at the hovering bag beside Kyle. 'Hey,' she said, 'you got a container in there of any sort?'

'Lunch box?'

'Cool. Let's have it.'

Kyle opened his bag and removed his lunch box. It was a small red plastic cube and contained one small piece of fruit. Sam took it from him, removed the lid and popped the fruit in her mouth. 'Great. Starving. Thanks.' She then scooped a bit of the hardening slime up with her 'sonic screwdriver which I half-inched from the Doctor' – whatever a 'sonic screwdriver' was, but she'd shown it to him earlier that morning – and flopped it into the box, resealing the lid. 'Keep that in your floating friend, will you?' she said. Kyle resealed his bag.

Torin Chalfont (yes, it was him – as his eyes adjusted to the light Kyle recognised him from the holos) offered a hand, which Kyle took and they introduced themselves.

'C'mon, guys, I want to get that sample back to the Doctor.'

They began to go back to the tunnel entrance.

Torin Chalfont relaxed. These seemed to be intelligent young people – Sam especially.

As she passed him, he bent over to look at the slime again. To think, it could have enveloped him. If Sam was right, it might have killed him.

Tentatively he reached to it with his right hand, and poked at it a bit, but it was rock hard now.

All it did was make the tip of his finger tingle. As he drew his hand back, there was a minute resistance, bit like tacky paint or glue. But that was all.

'C'mon, Torin,' called Sam. 'What are you doing?'

'I hurt my ankle,' Chalfont lied, pretending to rub it, then stood up. 'It's OK now, though.'

As he went to catch up with the other two, he froze. There was a voice. Whispering.

He opened his mouth to ask Sam and Kyle if they had heard it but decided not to. No. It was his discovery.

He tapped his finger with his thumb, checking to see if it was still tacky. It was – a bit of the slime had attached to his finger. But it wasn't eating his flesh – so Sam had been wrong about that.

It just itched a bit.

Some way beneath the surface of the planet was the solar generator that powered everything on Micawber's World.

However, right now, a small but significant amount of energy was being bled off and serving another cause.

Attached to the generator was a vast ball of the Wirrrn larval mucus, with more spread over the walls and floor and cavernous ceiling. It covered everything bar the generator itself – about twelve centimetres thick.

Organic tubes had been burrowed into the generator and were attached at the other end to this wall of mucus. This gave the mucus a permanent orange glow, which pulsated as if it were breathing.

A metre or so above the generator, hanging but supported by numerous mucus membranes, was the Wirrrn Queen. Amber eyes gazed down at the Swarm Leaders scurrying beneath her, carrying out her mental commands, broken occasionally by spoken chirps of anger or demands for extra attention.

She had travelled a long way – having been the Queen for many centuries, she had been there when the Wirrrn embarked upon their journey from Andromeda. She had colonised many planets along the way, leaving behind spawn, Swarm Leaders and the occasional Secondary Queen. She had placed her eggs inside more alien species than she could have imagined existed within the confines of just one small galaxy.

And here she was, taking the opportunity to spread even more by impregnating members of hundreds of different species gathered together.

She had used the intelligence of some of the species she had encountered previously to add to her consciousness knowledge of this Federation. Of its people, planets, politics and history. This way, she had settled on the human Mason who understood the varying different species and used his memories, his knowledge, to create their new, subtle weapon.

And now, clinging to the last vestiges of his humanity, Mason would spread the seed of the Wirrrn anew.

Only then could he be given the reward he so desperately craved – to finally join with the Wirrrn, to become whole and complete. To lose the trappings of individualism and ego and to enter the pool of intelligence that was the Wirrrn race.

To become superior.

In her mind, she could see events throughout the planet from the various Wirrrn grubs, Swarm Leaders and agents she directed.

In her mind, she opened a piece of the consciousness she had absorbed from a human named Jean-Paul Cartwright. There was a species on Micawber's World that would object to her plan more vociferously than the others.

Foamasi they were called.

They would fight. But they would lose. They would be absorbed, their minds, their plans, their civilisation would be absorbed.

They, too, would become superior.

Nothing could go wrong.

Co-ordinator Sumner was flicking rolled-up paper balls off his desk and at a rubbish bin (and missing) when Madox walked into his office. Madox caught one as it zoomed towards an area of wall nowhere near its target. 'Paper is very rare, Coordinator. I really don't think the Federation would approve of you wasting their resources this way.'

'Who are you, Madox? My mother? My wife?'

'So, how *did* your meeting with the Royal Family go, Co-ordinator?'

Sumner sighed. 'She took me shopping, Madox. I mean, I can go shopping with my wife, should I ever want to. Indeed, I *do* go shopping with my wife. And I hate it then. Imagine going shopping with someone who not only has the same tastes as my wife, but has the money to squander on those tastes. And therefore can afford to spend ten times longer in every shop than my wife. And, worst of all, I cannot even suggest however slightly that they might be overspending. Or buying crap.' Sumner threw himself back against the rear of his chair and swung his feet on to his desk. 'Can you imagine how many planets' economies she could single-handedly have saved this morning? I can think of six or seven. Hell, she spent enough money to refloat the Liasici Bank! The Foamasi would have no bankruptcy problems!' He paused, reflectively. 'Have you ever been to Liasici, Madox?'

Madox said he hadn't.

'It's a lovely world, you know. Destroyed by nuclear war years ago by some thugs called the Argolin. All gone now, of course, thankfully. The Foamasi, for all their vices such as organised crime and insider dealings, have actually rebuilt Liasici beautifully. Right now, it needs a massive cash injection to make it bankable again and, perhaps understandably, no one actually wants to refloat them. And there's this Duchess of Auckland - ever been to Auckland, Madox?'

Madox had no idea where Auckland was, so Sumner told him.

'Anyway, she spent more on new dresses and fur coats - *fur coats*, I ask you, in *this* weather! - than I have ever seen.'

'You didn't enjoy yourself, then?'

Sumner sighed. 'No, Madox. I did not enjoy myself.' He saw that Madox was carrying a datapad. 'What's that for?'

'A report, Co-ordinator. It seems there may be a little problem growing that could threaten the safety of the Duchess of

Auckland. And, indeed, the Games.'

'Give it to the SSS then. Commandant Ritchie is in charge of security, I seem to recall.'

Madox passed Sumner the datapad and, with an exaggerated sigh, Sumner read the message. After a moment he licked his lips, which had suddenly dried. 'I see. Uh-huh. Right. Well, I suppose it is up to me – *us* – to do something about this after all.'

He got out of his chair and grabbed his jacket. 'Madox, get me the Federation Rules Database will you. I'd so hate to get my facts wrong.'

Sam kicked at the blockade, but it didn't give.

'How did they do this so quickly?' Kyle reached out to touch the solid wall of mucus that blocked the tunnel entrance. It was blended into the tunnel walls – they would never get it down from inside. 'And why did they want to keep us in?'

Sam tugged Kyle's arm back. 'Survival Rule Number One: never touch weird, alien gunk. You never know how lethal it might be.'

'Do you really think it could be lethal?' asked Torin, standing, slightly out of breath, behind them.

Sam shrugged. 'Dunno. But the Doctor says it's better to be careful.'

Kyle suddenly gave her an odd look. 'This Doctor. You're always talking about him. Is he important to you?'

Sam considered this. Not so much the question, but the odd way Kyle asked it, and the inappropriateness of his timing. 'Yeah, he's my friend, OK? Now, can we try to find another way out? I don't want to be trapped here for ever.'

Sam produced the sonic screwdriver and aimed it at the blockage, then shook her head. 'Damn, he never showed me how to use it as a laser cutter. I only know how to make it work as a, well... sonic screwdriver.'

Kyle took it from her, fascinated by the device, while Torin wandered closer to the tunnel entrance, peering at the solid wall.

'We could shout. Maybe someone outside could find a way to lever that stuff off.'

Sam shook her head. 'I'll bet that no one would hear us through it. And anyway, anyone near enough to hear us would have been got at by those creatures.' She looked further into the tunnel that she and Torin had started exploring. 'Shall we go?'

'Let's not go back the way those... things came,' muttered the journalist.

Sam agreed, suggesting they explore the cavern she and Torin had hidden in. 'There were loads of small tracks and tunnels leading away from that.'

'They were dark.'

'We'll have to be careful then, won't we?' Why did it always fall to her to become leader? Since when did she get voted Brown Owl? Sam nevertheless led the way. She threw a quick glance back at Kyle, and he was staring at his feet as he walked. Was it her imagination or was he avoiding her gaze? Surely he wasn't sulking about their tiff earlier.

Of course, if he'd had a sheltered upbringing by the likes of Reverend Lukas, he might be taking things a bit too seriously. Perhaps he was sour after their conversation last night about God, evolution and the universe.

She dropped back, letting Torin take the lead.

'You OK, mate?'

Kyle finally looked at her. 'Yes. Yes, I'm fine, Miss Jones. Thank you for asking.'

'Whoa!' She put a hand on his chest. 'What's with the formality? Last night it was "Sam". This morning it was "Sam". Now it's "Miss Jones"? You been talking to Reverend Lukas again?'

Kyle looked at his feet again. 'No. But I'd like to.'

He didn't say anything else, so Sam let it drop. Something was worrying him.

He was OK really, she decided. Probably a year, maybe two younger than she was. His straw-coloured hair was brushed back and up, and his blue eyes seemed more watery than usual. She could just about make out the bruise on his cheek from where she had clobbered him in the churchyard. But there was something that made him remarkable amid the already remarkable cluster of aliens she had seen on Micawber's World.

As she tried to put her finger on it, he suddenly reached out his hand and touched her cheek. Then he went bright red (or at least, in the gloom of the cavern, Sam guessed he went red – his skin darkened anyway) and whipped his hand back.

'You're very sweet,' she said. And then it hit her. Kyle possessed something she had never seen in a late teenager before. Innocence. A complete sexual naivety she found suddenly attractive. She wanted to hug him, tell him that it was all right. But it also occurred to her that she was most likely the target for these new feelings. Hence the hand-on-cheek moment.

Poor sod – doesn't realise he's wasting his time. No way am I going to get involved with a screwed-up religious maniac who thinks that the dinosaurs are some great conspiracy theory.

No, that's unfair, Sam. You promised to keep an open mind. Give him a break.

Torin gasped, breaking Sam's concentration.

'What's up?'

Torin was hunched over, fighting for breath. 'I... I don't know...' he said quietly. 'Maybe it's these caves. I'm feeling a little bit claustrophobic.'

He shoved his right hand inside his jacket. 'I think I've left my pills at the hotel. Sorry.'

Sam was instantly sympathetic. She knew enough medicine from her dad to know how bad it could be for people with heart problems or breathing troubles if they didn't have their medication at the right moment. She forced him to sit down, and he let her lean him against a lump of rock.

He was still rummaging around inside his jacket, but Sam ignored that. She loosened his shirt collar and waved some air at him.

Kyle asked if there was anything he could do, and seizing an opportunity to keep both her charges busy – 'her charges'! God, was she playing the Doctor now? – she told Kyle to keep Torin cool.

As she wandered further into the ever-darkening tunnel ahead, she gave up hoping for natural light. She checked two or three others but no: they all seemed to go downward rather than upward. No escape that way then.

'Maybe we should go down,' muttered Torin.

'Why?'

'Because the solar generator is nearby, and maybe there are service shafts leading to that,' said Torin, wheezing badly now.

'You a bit of a tour guide on the sly, then?' asked Sam, raising an eyebrow.

'I've done my research, Miss Jones.'

'Sam! For the last time, "Miss Jones" makes me sound like a bad sit-com character.' She paused. 'Research into what?'

'I was sent here to investigate those vanishing SSS agents,' Torin muttered.

'What agents? What vanishing?' This was news to Sam.

Torin fleshed out the story, and by the time he'd finished, Sam was none too sure about going on. But what choice did they have?

Kyle and Torin looked at her expectantly.

'We keep going,' she said simply.

Torin shrugged off Kyle's attempts to help him and so the young man joined Sam, choosing which tunnel to take.

'That one,' he said, pointing at the third one along the cavern.

'Why?'

'I don't know. It draws me.'

'Good enough, I guess,' she said. She looked back to Torin, who had removed his jacket and was wrapping it around his right arm.

'Now what?' she said, a tad more sharply than she intended.

'Nothing,' he said understandably defensively. 'Just hurt my wrist getting up.'

'Well, I did offer...' started Kyle but Torin coughed.

'Not your problem, young man. Your offer was kind. More fool me for rejecting it, eh?' He suddenly lurched on ahead of them, down the tunnel Kyle had selected, suddenly unafraid of the dark or claustrophobia. He turned back just before disappearing into the darkness. 'Well, c'mon you two. No point in waiting.'

Sam decided she would never understand people. What the hell was she doing with this motley duo of social rejects?

She grabbed Kyle's hand and dragged him after her. 'Come on, Mr Way Forward. You're lagging behind.'

They followed Torin Chalfont into the tunnel.

SSS Agent Bobby Franks was about to start his patrol on the perimeter of the Stadium. Tomorrow morning he would be here with the rest of the Agents, ready to watch as the Duchess of Auckland, come all the way from Earth in the *Space Pioneer*, officially stared the Games.

That morning he'd sent a subspace telegram to his mother (she preferred it to electronic pagers – she was one of the old school who believed in traditional interstellar communiqués) explaining his role. She'd be thrilled that he was there. And if he could 'accidentally' walk in front of one of the holocrews, well, she might even see him. He'd try to wave if he could.

No, better not. Sergeant Major Zzano'pt'll would reprimand him for that.

Oh well.

His thoughts were interrupted by his boot suddenly getting stuck in something. It was a trail – it looked as if someone had spilled a mass of adhesive along the side of the road, towards the nearest Power House for the Stadium. He'd better check, he decided.

Reaching the Power House, he saw that the trail went under the door. Odd.

The Power Houses were small buildings, housing nothing more than a bank of electronic switches and a tiny subgenerator. Little room for more than two people (and only then if they breathed in) and were very restricted in terms of who actually had access to them – they took the power up from the central generator and bled it into the Stadium. This provided power for the holocrews, the lights and, of course, the Olympic torch. No one should have gone inside now – all the repair crews were finished days ago.

Agent Franks pushed gently on the door. It started to open – which immediately made him tense up.

The rules were quite clear on this. Anyone inside had to secure the door behind them. So whoever was in there was either remiss (and deserved to be on a charge) or unwelcome (and deserved to get caught and imprisoned).

As he pushed harder, there was resistance, so he quickly unholstered his blaster and primed it.

Taking up the assault stance drilled into him and his fellow recruits by Sergeant Major Zzano'pt'll, Franks prepared to order the intruder(s) out into the open.

Before he could speak, the door opened and one of the SSS scientists came out.

'Dr Mason?' Franks recognised him. 'Why are you –'

Franks stopped. And for a brief moment there was something else standing where Mason had been. It was two metres high or more, insectoid in appearance, with a massively muscular segmented body rearing up from a strong tail, a set of pincer claws on the end. Hundreds of tiny suckers on the underside of the tail pushed it upright and on top of the neck was a horrific head – two amber bulbous eyes, bristling tentacles and antennae and a massive set of mandibles that looked as though they could crush anything.

He raised his blaster…

'Stop!'

Mason was there again.

The monster was gone.

'What on Earth are you doing, Agent Franks?' asked Mason, glancing at the agent's name tag.

'I'm sorry, Dr Mason. For a moment I saw… something terrible…' Franks shuddered.

'You're babbling like a baby, man,' snapped Mason. 'Let me help you.'

He held out his hands and without thinking, Franks allowed his own hands to rise up and meet Mason's, dropping his blaster to the dusty ground in the process.

At the last moment, he caught sight of the hands themselves. Or rather the blunt stumps that had replaced them, covered in some kind of greeny-brown substance.

Franks ceased to care after that as his flesh touched the mucus and his brain was flooded with pain and heat.

'Obey this man,' said a rasping voice inside his head. 'Enjoy the glory that is the Wirrrn.'

Moments later, Dr Miles Mason and SSS Agent Bobby Franks were walking through the security perimeter and into the Stadium, entering through the athletes' entrance, which led straight to the dressing rooms.

And left behind, wallowing in the warmth and power they were siphoning off from the subgenerator, the numerous Wirrrn larvae basked in the anticipation of what was to come.

Chapter Nine
Song From The Edge Of The World

It was time.

The Wirrrn Queen could see through the eyes of her agent that Mason was with the alien athletes.

Some of them were uninterested. Some of them were curious. Some of them were greedy. Some of them were appalled. But it did not matter in the slightest. The moment just one group took the pills on offer, the rest would follow. The Queen had observed these people closely.

For many years the diverse races that formed this coalition called the Galactic Federation had enjoyed the regime. Each opted to believe that what they were partaking in was of immense benefit, both to themselves and to their neighbours.

But the truth was darker. Each planet was still torn by bitter paranoia. A majority of them agreed to join the Federation only because they were poor and wanted riches. Or they were weak and wanted more power. Or, more often than not, they were frightened that if they did not succumb to the Federation, they would forever be wondering what they had missed out on.

All of them made their broadcasts, their speeches and their constitutions claiming to believe in universal harmony, free trade and a vast 'brotherhood' to create peace and co-dependency, and to do away with poverty, weakness and solitude. But the Queen knew better.

Few of the planets actually believed in this – most were looking to get whatever they could out of the Federation before making a new bid for more power, or departing and setting up an alternative Federation.

One race would be seen as particularly inflammatory at Federation council meetings and others would whisper how they wished they weren't there, but democracy meant all opinions could be heard. Others would call for moderation, to allow one race to ensure that none of the others said anything unpleasant, or at least present their views in a less hostile manner.

Other groups sought to create subcommittees and councils, focusing on whichever piece of politicking appealed to them alone.

Before long, the Federation would crumble. All the Queen was doing was speeding that up – and achieving domination for the Wirrrn as part of the result.

The simple truth was – and her distribution of the drugs was proof of this – no one wanted anyone else to have benefits they didn't have themselves. As soon as one race succumbed to Mason's drugs, the rest would have to follow, because they were simply too frightened, or too paranoid, that they might be missing out on something good.

These creatures were pathetic.

But soon they would be all Wirrrn.

The Wirrrn Queen sent out another telepathic message to Mason, urging him to hurry.

Doctor Mason tried to melt into the crowds milling around by the athletes' area. A couple of the cleaning droids gave him a cursory look and in the distance he saw a group of Cogwegs practising for the artificial life-forms' sub-Games.

He glanced across to the huge chronometer, counting down to the start of the Games themselves. Not long now.

There was a tap on his shoulder, and he turned, smiling. A group of aliens was facing him. A couple of humans were at the back. In front of them was a Saurian, a small white scale-covered marsupial, with elephantine ears, black oval eyes and a white curved beak. Beside that were a couple of aliens he didn't recognise, tall, white and thin, with red rooster combs on their heads, silver suits and rough, un-made looking faces. To their right were Morogs, squat humanoids from Pindant, and he tried not to wince at their pungent smell. Not good form for a famed xenobiologist, after all. At the front of the group were the bald, salmon-skinned Hiinds, who, having overthrown the Mufl Empire a few decades back, were now trying to ingratiate themselves with the Federation. If they were alongside these desperate, and pitiful, specimens, they wouldn't keep their newly won empire for long.

'We want the pills,' said a snarling voice to his right.

Mason turned to see a group of less than pleasant-looking athletes. Two of them were four-armed Morrains, their pointed heads cocked, leering smiles on their faces. The speaker was one of three lupine Werelox, bouncing and catching a small medicine ball with one hand.

Mason held out his hand, and the crowd gathered around. 'Call this a free sample,' he said quietly. 'Take whichever colour you prefer. The red ones metabolise slightly faster and are less identifiable on narc-testing, but the blue ones are slightly more powerful. Believe me, after you've taken one of these little gems, you'll feel like a new... a new person.' Mason smiled.

The Werelox leader tossed his ball to one of the Morrains, who caught it perfectly. He picked out a blue one. 'Strong is better, I think.'

Mason shrugged. 'Take what you want, but only these are free. You're the lucky ones, because you're willing to be upfront and ask. All I want is for you to spread the word. I'll be here until about thirty minutes before the opening ceremony, OK?'

The athletes, pills in hand – or, in the case of the Werelox, already swallowed – muttered their appreciation and wandered away.

The Werelox leader stopped and snarled, shoving his furry muzzle right up close to Mason's face. 'What about the Foamasi? They won't like you dealing on their pitch, you know?'

'Don't worry about the Foamasi. I'm not planning to make a habit of this. After today, the Foamasi can distribute these drugs wherever and whenever they want. All I need is this day. I'll sort it out with them.'

The Werelox leader frowned, then bared his canine teeth. 'We'll be back,' he growled and then followed the others.

'Oh yes, you'll be back,' Mason muttered. 'You just might not be quite yourself by then.'

Like the Wirrrn, the Parads were an insectoid race from the Dermaptera sector of Alpha Centauri. To many among the Federation, they were known as the 'earwigs' due to their physical similarity to the tiny creatures of Earth.

But the analogy was reasonably sound, if somewhat Federally incorrect, as the Parads were experts at surveillance and many were employed in the Federation research centres and, particularly at the moment on Micawber's World, among the holovid crews. They were experts in sound. As a highly telepathic and sensitive race, they made for excellent audio technicians.

However, like so many Federation races, they had their secrets. Prime among theirs was that they were open to psychic storms – tiny ripples in the ether that wouldn't be noticed by all but the most powerful human telepaths were like force-twelve hurricanes to their sensitive minds. For the most part, Parads had ensured that they never entered into deals or contracts that exposed them to potentially dangerous situations.

Of course, the Parad leaders had not foreseen the presence of the Wirrrn on Micawber's World so when the Wirrrn Queen sent her command out to Miles Mason, the Parads picked it up too.

And it wiped their minds clean in less than a second. Every Parad on Micawber's World, all those in orbiting satellite holovid relay stations and a large number on neighbouring worlds died instantly, their brains simply shutting down their bodies in a futile effort to weather the psychic storm that invaded their heads.

If the Wirrrn Queen had known about this, she would have greeted the news with indifference – a weak race not worth absorbing.

But to the Pakhars, Lurmans, Shistavanens and others who operated the holocrews, the sudden wave of instant deaths was something of a shock.

Reverend Lukas was on his bed in his room at the Mirage hotel, sitting cross-legged, head bowed, hands tightly clasped together, eyes closed.

He was meditating – a daily occurrence that would have no sinister appearance if it weren't for the fact that Eldritch and Marcus were effectively standing guard, staring dead ahead but clearly prepared to stop anyone from going near their master.

Just outside, in the corridor, Phillipa and Jolyon wanted to talk to him, to tell him some exciting news.

'Don't bother right now,' Max Girard warned them as they greeted each other by the door. Max and Veronique had been getting supplies for the evening meal, and Max was carrying bags of fresh fruit and vegetables. 'He's meditating.'

Phillipa nodded but Jolyon was too excited to care. 'I'm sure he won't mind being interrupted this once. We have such good news.'

'What is it?' asked Veronique, hanging on to Max's arm as she always did.

'We've elected to get married. Officially,' said Jolyon. 'We want Reverend Lukas to join us in matrimony as soon as possible.'

Veronique looked at Max. 'See! I knew they'd decide first.

Typical.' She laughed at Max's astonished face and then moved over to hug Phillipa. 'I'm really happy for you.'

'You won't… you know, leave the Church?' Max was frowning.

'Of course not,' said Jolyon. 'This is our life. But imagine: as a married couple we could start our own caravan. Meet up with you and Reverend Lukas whenever possible but, of course, it will give us two lines of communication to the masses.'

Max nodded, then gripped Jolyon's hand and shook it. 'Well, my blessings to you both. It's good news.'

Without waiting, Jolyon waved his hand over the door sensor and it opened. He began to walk in, but Marcus and Eldritch turned as one and put their hands up to stop him. Neither of them spoke. They rarely did.

And then the unexpected happened.

Reverend Lukas screamed and clutched at his temples, pitching forward on to the floor.

Eldritch and Marcus were beside him in a second. Jolyon stood by the door, feeling useless, while Max, Veronique and Phillipa stared over his shoulder.

Marcus eased Reverend Lukas up, while Eldritch brushed his black robe down.

Reverend Lukas was staring at his flock. A beatific smile on his face. He slowly raised his hands and then his eyes upwards.

'The Goddess has spoken to me,' he shouted. 'She is here. We have come home!'

The group by the door looked at each other in confusion.

Eldritch and Marcus resumed their alert patrol between them and Reverend Lukas.

'She has touched my mind,' he said, quieter now. 'She has called me.' He now looked at the others. 'No, she has called *us*. All of us.'

'Reverend Father? Are you all right?'

'Yes, Max. Yes, I am absolutely fine. Everything we have sought, everything we have hoped and prayed for has come home at last.

The Goddess is here.' Reverend Lukas moved forward, Eldritch and Marcus standing aside as he passed them. He put his hands out to the other four and they all reached forward to touch him. 'If ever there have been doubts in your minds, my children, let them go now. The Goddess is here. Waiting for us. And we shall go to her.'

Without waiting for a reply, he pushed through them and into the corridor.

After a few seconds, Max, Veronique and Phillipa followed him. Jolyon Tuck shot one last look back into the room, where Marcus and Eldritch stood impassively.

'Are you coming?' he asked tentatively. Neither of them responded. 'OK,' he said, then ran after the others.

The news of his impending nuptials would clearly have to wait.

One of the Reverend Lukas's fellow Church members was currently cowering in a dark cavern, terrified for his life. Facing him, seemingly looking straight down on him, was the Wirrrn Queen.

Kyle and Sam had followed Torin around a variety of routes and tunnels until finally the journalist had stopped dead.

'What's up?' Sam had asked, but Torin did not answer.

'You're worse than the Doctor at times, you know. He frequently stands still, says nothing, points a finger at just anything and then assumes I've understood something important.' She clearly thought about this. 'Actually, it is usually pretty unimportant in the grand scheme of things, but the way his attention wanders from one minute to the next, well, it's obviously important to him.'

'The Doctor?' asked Torin.

'Yes. What about the Doctor anyway?'

Chalfont then began scratching at his left hand, still wrapped in his jacket. 'Nothing. I think it's this way.' He'd indicated with his shrouded hand that they should go right, so Kyle and Sam had followed.

Within moments they were in a large cavern that glowed orange as dusky light pulsated through the mucus web covering the walls.

And facing them was Kyle's worst nightmare. 'Goddess, protect me,' he breathed.

Sam reached out grab his hand. They took strength from each other but for Torin there seemed to be no respite.

'She knows the Doctor,' he breathed quietly. At first Kyle assumed Torin was talking to him, but when the head of the creature moved, Kyle knew there was a connection between them.

Torin, his back to Kyle and Sam, let the jacket drop to the floor and Kyle registered the vast amount of mucus surrounding it. His shirt had split and most of the journalist's arm was now pulsating with a greeny-brown light.

'What is it?' breathed Sam.

'The most perfect species in the universe,' muttered Torin hoarsely. 'It… we are life. We are death. We are the beginning and the end, all together. All species will become us.' He turned to the two youngsters and they saw that his face was now oozing the mucus. One eye had already been covered and replaced by a similar protruding amber oval like the one on the monster hanging above. He started to crouch slightly. 'We welcome you into the Hive Mind,' he gasped at them. 'You and all your type. We have travelled far, travelled over millennia to be here. To grow, to absorb, to further ourselves. You will become like us.' Torin's clothing split open revealing an entire body covered in the browny-green larval mutation. As they watched, fascinated, it crept up his neck and down over his hair, completely burying his face as it met across his cheek. The amber eye then moved to the centre of the face, the limbs retracted and Torin Chalfont, or whatever he was now, dropped to the floor, just a misshapen rectangular blob of mucus.

Then it suddenly reared up and displayed hundreds of tiny suckers on what Kyle now took to be its belly, and started shuffling towards them...

The Doctor was sitting on the upturned crate next to the PMD-come-scanner, watching the outside of the building.

Towards the door, Klein and Fenton were playing cards, Carruthers was cooking and McCarrick was cleaning his blaster.

And Clarke was sitting just a few feet away from him, watching him like a hawk.

'Really, Mr Clarke,' he said quietly. 'I'm not going to cause trouble. There's no point. I wanted to be here with you, remember?'

Clarke ignored him.

There was a tapping at the door.

'It's Quartermaster-Sergeant Dallion and Ms Sox,' the Doctor reported, peering at the PMD screen. 'How disappointing, I was expecting more.'

Fenton let the two women in, and Ms Sox immediately crossed to the Doctor.

'Are you all right?'

'Me? Yes, why shouldn't I be? Nice of you to ask, though.' He looked across to Dallion. 'Shortly we should be receiving a few more visitors. I hope you don't mind, but I took the liberty of inviting a council of war here today.'

'This place was supposed to be secret,' muttered Klein.

'It was. Until Commandant Ritchie told me where to find you. And I told everyone else.' He switched off the PMD lash-up.

'Except me,' said Ms Sox. 'Not trusted?'

'Oh no, not that at all,' said the Doctor, as if apologising for not inviting her to a party. 'No, I have suspicions about various people you know, and thought the churchyard would be a better place to discuss such things than your office. A chance to talk in an electronic-device-free zone, as it were. Sadly, Sergeant Dallion didn't trust me enough. We'll have to talk here and hope no one untoward overhears.' He indicated for everyone to gather around in a circle. At a nod from Dallion, they did so, Ms Sox squatting next to McCarrick.

The Doctor took a pocket watch from his waistcoat, held up his hand and then started counting down. 'Five, four, three –'

There was a tapping on the door. The Doctor frowned at the watch.

Dallion moved over and gently eased the door open. If seeing her former Commandant, Ritchie, standing there wasn't surprise enough, the fact that a Foamasi with a set of caterpillar tracks instead of lower legs was with him actually caused an eyebrow to rise noticeably.

'Is there a Doctor in the house?' quipped the Foamasi.

'Do come in, gentlemen.' The Doctor held out his arms welcomingly. 'Everyone, you know Commandant Ritchie, your guardian angel if you like. But you're probably not familiar with the Foamasi Ambassador, representing the Foamasi Government (of which he is the only member), commonly known as Green Fingers.' He looked at Green Fingers. 'Do excuse me for not giving you your formal name, but I'm not sure I could pronounce it, even if I knew it.'

Green Fingers waved a clawed hand courteously. 'Green Fingers will do, Doctor.'

The Doctor crossed back into the circle, letting it re-form around him with its new members. 'All right, let us go over what we know. Firstly, Commandant Ritchie. You were faced with the disappearance of some of your agents. You were also facing pressure from Earth to make sure the Olympic Games went without a hitch. On top of that, someone else was aware of what went on in the tunnels and was blackmailing you for information. I imagine that was members of the Dark Peaks Foamasi Lodge. Correct?'

Ritchie was looking pale. 'Well... I...'

'Correct?' snapped the Doctor.

'Yes,' Ritchie said. 'Yes.'

'So you sent Sergeant Dallion and her gang here undercover to try to sort things out. This meant that if they succeeded, everything was fine. If they died, you were blameless.'

Ritchie clearly wanted to die right now. He was desperately not wanting to look anyone here in the eye. 'Yes,' he muttered quietly.

'Good,' said the Doctor. 'That fits.' He looked at Green Fingers. 'Query One: why were the Dark Peaks Lodge interested in the tunnels?'

Green Fingers waved his hands up. 'I have no idea, Doctor. As I said, the Lodge are not supposed to be operating here at all.'

'But they are, Ambassador. Which gave Mr Ritchie here his problem. But we can sort that out for him later.' The Doctor looked at Ms Sox. 'Query Two: You, Ms Sox, are a dark horse indeed. You and Mr Carrington arranged for the SSS to be brought in, correct?'

'Yes.'

'Why?'

Ms Sox shrugged. 'I needed someone else to do official security work while I did my own. We knew that someone had infiltrated one of our associated pharmaceutical groups. We also knew that one of the scientists the SSS were bringing up from Earth a Dr Mason, was seen meeting someone who had no security clearance whatsoever – being delayed by that someone. And that someone was alien – at least to Dr Mason. You see, for basic surveillance work, freelancers have their uses. I wanted to see if there was a connection between this Dr Mason and the infiltration with our company on Ganymede.'

'Query Three: any idea who the spy was on Ganymede?'

'Not until this morning. Mr Carrington has suddenly brought a Doradan over from there. I can only assume she is blackmailing him in some way.' Ms Sox shrugged. 'Beyond that, I've no involvement with any of Commandant Ritchie's bizarre problems. And fewer still in that of the Foamasi Government over there.'

The Doctor shook his head, speaking quickly and urgently. 'Commandant Ritchie directed me to Green Fingers – clearly to help highlight his problem with the Dark Peaks Lodge. In turn, Ms Sox, it was Green Fingers who directed me to you.'

'He knows what I do. He knows everything that goes on here.'

'Indeed,' agreed Green Fingers – rather cryptically, the Doctor decided.

'I'm afraid there probably *is* a connection,' the Doctor continued. 'You told me Mr Carrington was behaving oddly today, yes?'

Ms Sox agreed, then stopped and looked at Green Fingers. 'Oh no... you don't think...'

'I'm afraid I do, Ms Sox. Now, if we work on the assumption that you are right about the Doradan, I don't think it takes too much of a leap of logic to suppose that rather than being blackmailed, Mr Carrington was not Mr Carrington at all this morning, but more likely, he was Commandant Ritchie's not-so-friendly Dark Peaks agent.'

Ms Sox stood up. 'But the real Chase Carrington...?'

'Dead, I imagine,' said Green Fingers. 'If the Doctor is correct, the Dark Peaks Lodge don't leave loose ends. They kill and supplant rather than kidnap or send on vacation their targets for substitution. Traditional Foamasi Lodge techniques, I regret to say.'

Ms Sox bit her lip, took a deep breath and then carried on. 'OK, where's the link?'

'The link is the tunnels, Ms Sox. The Dark Peaks guessed that something killed Dallion's troopers. Would I be right in guessing that you ascertained that when Dr Mason was spotted on Earth in conversation with your "alien", he was discussing drugs?'

'Yes. That's what made me investigate our pharmaceutical division. I hoped it was nothing to do with Carrington Corp. Drugs are bad publicity. Sadly, I was proven wrong.'

The Doctor looked straight at Green Fingers. 'Your Lodges are not averse to a bit of freelance help, are they, Ambassador?'

The Foamasi laughed. 'No, of course not. And any freelancer worth his price would automatically sell us the same recordings as he sold Ms Sox, and I imagine about ten other groups and corporations.'

'So, Commandant Ritchie's Foamasi chum, having already infiltrated Carrington Corp's Ganymede pharmaceutical operation, also knew that Dr Mason was doing a deal. I suspect at some point they had him under surveillance, and whoever he is working for is based in the tunnels. Sergeant Dallion's people encountered them and were killed. So now we have both this Foamasi Lodge and the Earth SSS investigating the tunnels for different reasons.'

Ritchie put his hand up. 'I have to say that I gave the Foamasi I... dealt with absolutely no indication where my troopers went.'

The Doctor shrugged. 'I doubt they cared, Commandant. They just want whoever is in the tunnels. They will either join forces or wipe them out and take over their business as they seem to have done now with Carrington Corp.' The Doctor reached over and took Ms Sox's hands, easing her back down to sit on a crate. 'And I am truly sorry about Chase Carrington. From our brief meeting, he seemed very... honourable.' He straightened up again, a different person once more. 'So, Query Four is: this leaves us where? I suggest we now pool our resources. We have three main operations. One – the Olympic Games must go ahead safely. That is Commandant Ritchie's responsibility. Two – we must stop the drug suppliers in the tunnels. That will be Sergeant Dallion's task. Thirdly – you need to get your Lodges to pull back, Ambassador. If the Foamasi cause any problems here, you and your planet will most likely be expelled from the Federation, which with Liasici's poor financial state right now, will be most detrimental to your home planet, correct?'

Green Fingers nodded slowly.

'And fourthly, Ms Sox and I need to get some of these drugs and find out just why someone has gone to such trouble to attempt this.'

'But Doctor,' said Dallion, 'drugs are an everyday problem. Why is this lot so special?'

'My point exactly, Sergeant, good thinking. Why? All I can assume is that these drugs must offer something very new, totally unique, and probably insanely destructive to make people go to these lengths. With existing drugs, at least the SSS and other law enforcers know what they are dealing with. If someone has designed a new drug, then we must investigate.'

As soon as the Doctor stopped talking, two unexpected things happened at the same time.

First, the Doctor opened his mouth and screamed. Clutching his head, he fell motionless to the ground.

Secondly, the door burst open and a group of heavily armed Teknix came in, pointing blasters at everyone. Through the middle of them, Events Co-ordinator Sumner marched in.

'By the powers invested in me as the representative of the Federation Council here on Micawber's World, I hereby expel every one of you from the planet under the accusation of plotting to murder various officials, members of the Earth Royal Family, eight hundred galactic athletes and numerous spectators. You will be taken to the planet Desperus to await your trial, which will occur within one to five years of the Games ending.' He turned to the lead Teknix. 'Madox, if anyone argues, shoot them dead.' He looked straight back at the group. 'Oh yes, before you ask, I am empowered to order exactly that. Thank you, and goodnight.'

Chapter Ten
The Rapture

Commandant Ritchie stared at the door, willing it to open. Frankly, he was not used to seeing the inside of the SSS cell block and was beginning to tire of staring at the same four blank walls over and over again.

Twenty-four years in the service, and it had come to this. He remembered the first time he had seen a prisoner in an SSS cell – a criminal who had murdered two other agents and a grocery-store owner. Out of his head on FeelGoodz or Cake or Skar. Whatever.

The prisoner had stared at him from within the cell, coming down off his murderous high, and screaming his innocence. When that was ignored, he started yelling obscenities. And when that failed to provoke even a flicker from the young Agent Ritchie, he started pleading.

But Ritchie had refused to be taken in, no matter how convincing the performance. He had left the prisoner to get everything out of his system and, three days later, sat in on his questioning. Interrogation. Whichever. Truth drugs were useless – the junkie had put so much crap in his system over the previous few years that more drugs would just send him over the top again. So it was down to straightforward questioning. And no matter how hard Marshal Tarrant tried to get the truth out of the junkie, no facts were forthcoming.

Unbidden, and against protocol, Ritchie had suddenly asked the junkie about death, and what it meant to him. How would he cope with death? What did he believe in? Was there a God? As the junkie rambled on, Ritchie pressed home each point that was brought up, leading the junkie through his own psyche. Unlike Tarrant, Ritchie listened to everything that was said. Unlike Tarrant, he avoided the set questions and standard threats and actually had a conversation with the junkie. And during this, the confession came out completely matter-of-factly.

Afterwards, much to the annoyance of Marshal Tarrant, Ritchie was praised. Recordings of his technique were used in training sessions for interrogators as an alternative means of getting at the truth.

Ritchie's own career blossomed and before long, he was a Marshal of his own group. He instigated the enlisting of the first non-human members of the SSS – a couple of Pakhars, a Draconian and a Cantryan – and brought about a few necessary reforms in codes and practices that brought him to the attention of the head of the SSS, Karlton.

He was soon rising through the ranks. Some years were spent on colonies, some on Earth, and when his own son was born, they were at Federation Headquarters on Io. Most recently, the promotion to Commandant – just a couple of rungs below Karlton himself – and the posting to Micawber's World had seemed to be the answer to his prayers.

Then the Foamasi stepped into his purview, and he began to lose it. First the gentle cajoling, the requests to turn a blind eye to odd shipments from Green Fingers. But when the Dark Peaks Lodge entered the scene, Ritchie found himself cut off from the Foamasi Ambassador he had helped and shortly afterwards, the kidnapping of his wife and son took place.

And the rest, as they say, was recent history.

Beside him, Quartermaster-Sergeant Dallion regarded him with the same look he had given that junkie all those years back in an identical cell – a look that said, 'You haven't a hope.' On top of that, however, the sergeant's face also seemed to be saying, 'Not only have you betrayed us, but it didn't do you any good anyway.' And Commandant Ritchie couldn't really argue with those sentiments either.

He turned to look at her apologetically. 'It was my wish that you would solve this problem, Sergeant. Please believe that.'

She glanced over to the far corner, where her five troopers glared at their former Commandant mutinously. 'Yeah, whatever. Sir.' Ritchie winced inwardly at the sarcasm that coated the word 'Sir'.

'Of course, if you'd let us in on the secret right from the word go, it might have been easier.'

Ritchie slowly shook his head. 'And if I had said "Excuse me, Sergeant, I'm being blackmailed by the Foamasi, who are holding my wife and son prisoner," would you have believed me? I wouldn't.'

Dallion gave a snort. 'Either way, you let us believe we were being given an opportunity to find out the truth about Cartwright, Salt and the others. In fact, we were convenient scapegoats. We won't forget that in a hurry, Commandant.'

'No. No, I don't suppose you will. Meanwhile, I propose that we use our SSS training to find a way out of here. I don't intend being left here to rot by Co-ordinator Sumner until after the Games – not when we know that something's going to happen.'

'Why did you ask for the Doctor's help?' murmured Klein. 'I mean, he's not even SSS-trained.'

Ritchie smiled at this. 'That's entirely the point, Agent Klein. As soon as I met him, I realised he was... unusual. Irreverent. Undisciplined. Exactly what I needed as an alternative route to discovering what was going on in the tunnels. We lost a group of scientists working on a dead Foamasi. Bearing in mind my own Foamasi problems, an outside agent doing some nosing around seemed an expedient use of resources. He seems to have been right most of the time as well.'

Dallion nodded in agreement. 'So what now?'

'Now? Now we wait. I'm sure the Doctor has a trick or two up his sleeve.'

The Olympic Games were getting ready to start. In just a couple of hours, millions across the galaxy would see the famous opening ceremony, highlighted by the winner of the Olympic Competition™ on Axiss lighting the Olympic Bowl™ with the Olympic Flame™, having been running with it all the way from Axiss to Micawber's World. As this involved a great deal of running around the interior of luxury space cruisers, the poor Axi was probably very exhausted and this last stretch undoubtedly seemed longer than any other.

On top of which there had been a panic when, while crossing the deserts of the planet Metalupiter, the Olympic Flame™ had actually gone out and he had been forced to borrow a cigar lighter from a Metalupitan trader who was paid handsomely by the entourage of Axiss, not just for his trouble, but to ensure he told no one – least of all any holovid crews.

Consort Ethelredd, Secretary Aigburth and Gar the V'orrn were not enjoying themselves at all. The Royal Party had somehow got itself lost between the Carrington Grande and the Stadium – an astonishing feat of incompetence bearing in mind they were on the same road. It crossed Ethelredd's already cynical mind that maybe the sight of green grass giving way to dusty sandbowl had been too much for the Duchess, who may well have insisted on changing her entire wardrobe in case it clashed with the dust. Then he realised that even Counsellor De'Ath would have reminded her that once inside the Stadium, it would be green again.

Still, you never could tell with the Duchess. Bearing in mind that her official duty would involve her making a one-minute speech after which she could sit quietly watching the opening ceremonies for a while, no doubt thinking the time could be better served in the shopping malls, perhaps she had realised the complete pointlessness of her entire existence and irrelevance of human aristocracy to 99.9 per cent of those on Micawber's World right now and imploded in a brightly coloured puff of self-deprecation. In which case, he could look forward to one final trip in the *Space Pioneer* back to Earth, followed by a long period of unemployment. Still, that had a certain ring of charm about it.

'No sign, then?' he said to Aigburth, who, having not moved for the last hour, would have had the same opportunities to see the arrival of the Royal Party as Ethelredd – but asking made for a break in the monotony, if nothing else.

'Nope.' Aigburth was chewing his nails.

Nope indeed. The monotony had increased.

With Torin Chalfont having become part of the Wirrrn Hive Mind, Miles Mason was now aware of the importance to the events of the Duchess of Auckland. He was also aware who everyone in the Royal Party was and their significance to the opening of the Olympic Games.

So, calmly he sat in one of the trainers' trenches, watching the athletes going through their paces, waiting.

And around him were hundreds of athletes, most of whom had succumbed to his pills, either because they lacked the morals to refuse them, or the self-respect to be seen not to be taking them.

This galaxy, the Hive Mind decided, was full of weak-minded creatures. The Wirrrn Queen had been correct. This galaxy would soon be theirs.

The Doctor awoke with a start, sat bolt upright and took in his surroundings in an instant.

'Why am I in a prison cell? *Again*?'

Ms Sox and Green Fingers were his companions and they both

sighed, then looked at each other, exasperated. 'Something's gone wrong again, hasn't it?'

They nodded.

'Typical.' He jumped up off the hard bed he was lying on. 'Tell me,' he said, grabbing Ms Sox by the shoulders and staring at her. 'Tell me what happened.'

After a few seconds of his staring at the quite uncomfortable-looking Ms Sox, Green Fingers decided to intervene, easing the Doctor away from her. Ms Sox immediately shivered.

The Doctor's eyes opened wide. 'Ah ha!' He smiled at Ms Sox. 'I think you're going to do rather well out of your agency, by the way.'

Ms Sox gasped. 'What agency...?'

But the Doctor just smiled. 'Ah, let the future unravel its own truths, Ms Sox.' But she clearly wasn't going to let that go. 'Oh dear,' he said to her. 'I keep doing this. I must learn to watch my mouth.'

'You can see the future, Doctor?' asked Green Fingers.

'No, not entirely. But it seems I have developed something of a gift in this body for reading the patterns of time as they weave around everything. Spotting links between the now and the... now.' He smiled, hoping that explained everything.

By the looks on their faces, it clearly didn't.

'Each new body offers me something new, something unique. Once I was a master of unarmed combat without any training. Another one could fractionally disrupt the brain's electrons at a touch, changing people's moods and emotions. Another one lacked the innate ability most of my bodies have of discerning praxis gases. Simple, really.'

'How many of these bodies were just simply bloody annoying?' asked Ms Sox.

'All of them,' he retorted. 'Or so I'm told. Can't see it myself.'

Ms Sox threw a look to Green Fingers. 'Whatever happened

must have befuddled him more than we thought. He's raving.'

The Doctor ignored her. 'I received a very powerful psychic wave. Somewhere on this planet is an extremely powerful mind. It sent out a message to all those who could read it.'

'What did it say?' Green Fingers clearly had given up trying to argue with him, and now appeared to be humouring him.

'I don't know. The sheer force of it knocked me senseless. But I caught a quick glimpse of something.' He tried to concentrate, letting his mind flow back. Trying to retrace any of the massive overload of images, thoughts and emotions that had hit him before. 'It came from the tunnels. That I do know. I felt that very distinctly.'

Ms Sox also appeared to have given up. 'According to you, everything can be solved in the tunnels. If it's just a few drug smugglers –'

'Oh no.' The Doctor suddenly slapped the door. 'No, it's far more powerful than that. The drugs are something else. Perhaps a diversion, perhaps a tiny part of a master plan. We need to get out of here.'

'Bravo,' said Ms Sox. 'I mean, we'd have never thought of that. We thought staying in here was a great idea.'

The Doctor sighed. Why was everyone so taciturn these days? It wasn't as if he was deliberately uncommunicative, or talked incoherently. He took great pains to explain everything, in great detail, all the time.

He'd just done so.

Anyway, time to escape. He reached into his jacket for his sonic screwdriver but it was gone.

'Gone! How can my sonic screwdriver have gone! The guards wouldn't be able to locate the pan-dimensional pocket I sewed in here, let alone the sonic screwdriver!' Then he remembered. 'Sam! Sam must have it. But why has Sam got it? What does she need my sonic screwdriver for?' A new thought crossed his mind and he turned back to his fellow prisoners. 'Where exactly *is* Sam and why isn't she rescuing me?'

Miles Mason watched the giant holographic chronometer floating above the Stadium scoreboard. Fifty minutes and the Games would officially start. At which point a diversion would be created, the Games would be cancelled, the athletes would return to their respective planets and the Wirrrn plan would be into its last stage.

An electronic fanfare started up.

The Duchess of Auckland was being led on to the podium just in front of him.

Ethelredd grabbed De'Ath's arm. 'Where in God's name have you been?'

The smaller man squirmed. 'Her Blessed Highness decided the dress she wore didn't match the colour of the stadium!' He was close to tears. 'I tell you, Ethelredd, I can't work with her. I can't cope any longer. I'm going to have to resign the very second we get home.'

Ethelredd patted De'Ath's shoulder. 'There, there, it'll turn out all right. At least she's here.' He looked at Gar, who moved up to take his place next to the Royal Podium.

The Axiss runner came into the Stadium, and the assembled crowd roared their approval.

Standing just behind the Duchess, Mason saw one of her entourage ease her out of her seat and whisper in her ear. At which point she squawked delightedly and began clapping. The rest of the Royal Party politely followed suit.

Mason was aware of someone standing beside him. A Teknix who had removed his name tag. Obviously needing to be incognito.

'I am interested in some samples of your pills,' he said.

Mason frowned. And inside, the Hive Mind probed deeper. There was something different about this Teknix from how he should have been according to the different memories he now possessed.

Then Mason understood. This was perfect. Without a word, he passed a handful of blue and red pills to the Teknix, shook his hand, and turned away to watch the Stadium.

Their deal was completed.

The Teknix's ordeal was just beginning. And he hadn't even flinched at the slight burn he must have felt as Mason's mucus-topped fingers touched the palm of his hand.

The Axiss runner – he hadn't taken any pills yet: an omission that would soon be rectified – ascended the steps towards the Bowl, the fanfare and the cheering getting louder.

Finally, he threw the torch into the bowl, which erupted into flame. The crowd went wild.

After a few moments of cheers, the Duchess stepped forward to a microphone and began speaking. Immediately the crowd hushed and listened to her.

Ethelredd glanced at De'Ath and Aigburth. At least coaching her on the speech hadn't been his job. He noticed De'Ath was whiter than normal, and immediately knew something was bound to go wrong.

'Hello, everyone. My name is Duchess. Duchess of Auckland, actually.' And she giggled.

Ethelredd wanted to strangle her on the spot and noticed that the few titters across the crowd were overshadowed by the deafening silence.

'No really,' she continued. 'Everyone calls me Duchess, so I think that must be my name now.'

The crowd were conspicuously quiet. Ethelredd saw his

pension conspicuously vanishing in his mind's eye.

'Anyway, one is proud to be here, representing not just the people of Auckland but everyone back home on Earth.'

'The Federation,' Ethelredd gasped, as quietly as possible, hoping she would hear and the microphone wouldn't pick him up.

De'Ath was close to fainting, Gar supporting him.

'Oh yes, my Lord Consort is of course correct. I'm here on behalf of all you aliens in the Federation. Everyone in Auckland loves you, too. Anyway, it gives me great pleasure to open these Olympic Games, the last Olympiad of this millennium, I imagine, what with this being 3999 and all that.' She giggled again.

There were no titters. Just astonished stares from the 'aliens'.

'I now formally declare the Olympiad open!'

A pause, then enormous cheers and applause, fanfares started up and the athletes from the various worlds began their ceremonial, pre-competition jog around the circuit, waving their pennants and banners.

The Duchess moved away from the microphone, but not quite far enough.

'Can I please get to the shopping mall now? Before it closes?'

It was a matter of some pride to Ethelredd that, apart from a couple of Carrington Corp officials, ninety per cent of the assembled crowd chose to ignore that one and carried on enjoying the pageantry of the Games. At least they had taste.

Still, at least now nothing else could possibly go wrong.

No one was more surprised when the cell door opened than the Doctor. He had been thumping on it fairly regularly, but to no avail. Then suddenly it had slid back and he just managed to stop himself slapping Co-ordinator Sumner straight in the face. Behind him, a mixture of SSS agents and Teknix stared at him.

'Oops.' The Doctor almost toppled over but one of the Teknix reached forward and eased him back up straight. 'Thank you,

Mr...?'

'Madox.'

'Mr Madox.' The Doctor straightened his cravat and ran and hand through his hair, trying to look dignified. 'So, you finally answered my calls and thumps then?'

Co-ordinator Sumner shrugged. 'The doors are soundproofed, Doctor.'

'Ah. Who are you?'

'I am Events Co-ordinator Sumner, appointed by the Federation to ensure the smooth running of everything on Micawber's World that doesn't involve the Space Security Service or the Carrington Corporation.'

The Doctor digested this. 'Which means you don't actually do very much at all, do you?'

Sumner smiled. 'No. But it keeps me in the office, away from my wife, and in turn employs a lot of Teknix to do all the bureaucracy.'

'What bureaucracy can you need? I mean, unless you create one level of bureaucracy to chase another level to chase the first level... Ah, I see. Very good. Very efficient way of staying away from home.'

'Exactly my point.' Sumner sauntered into the room. 'Madox here tells me that, according to your friends, you weren't asleep when I arrested you, but having a fit, or something. You seem to be all right now.'

'Yes, I am, thank you. I had a psychic moment. A sort of telepathic Mexican wave, lots of information uploading into my conscious mind at once.'

'Ah.' Sumner looked at Madox. 'Do you follow any of this?'

Madox shook his head.

'Nor me. Are you a bureaucrat, Doctor? If not, you ought to be.' Sumner looked at Green Fingers and Ms Sox. 'Now, which of you is going to explain how Chase Carrington's PA, a Federation

Ambassador, and a "psychic" human all happened to be sharing a tête-à-tête with wanted SSS criminals?'

The Doctor frowned. 'According to whom? As far as the SSS were concerned, Sergeant Dallion and her entourage were on their way home in disgrace. And there was nothing to link Commandant Ritchie to them. He saw to that.' The Doctor suggested that Sumner get hold of Ritchie and bring him in.

Sumner was about to protest when he caught sight of Madox's face. He too was frowning, like the Doctor.

'Madox?'

The Teknix turned to two other Teknix and gave them an order.

The Doctor laughed at Sumner's outraged face. 'What?' asked the human.

'I just realised, you think the Teknix work for you, don't you?'

'Of course they do.'

The Doctor shook his head. 'The Teknix are an altogether different stratum within the SSS. Good technicians yes, but supreme strategists. Why do you think the SSS use them? Why do you think Commandant Ritchie employs one?'

'Ritchie? The SSS don't have any Teknix.'

'I have to agree, Doctor,' added Ms Sox. 'The Teknix are limited on Micawber's World to just a handful of Co-ordinator Sumner's administrative staff. They are expensive to clone and maintain, and are only given to private executives who need them. The SSS couldn't afford one here. Even Chase Carrington couldn't swing being allowed to have any on his staff.'

Madox's fellow Teknix returned, along with Commandant Ritchie.

'Doctor! Are you all right?'

'Yes, thank you.' The Doctor threw an arm around Ritchie's shoulder, steering them both out into the corridor, followed by Sumner and his group. 'Tell me, Commandant. How many Teknix are on your staff?'

Ritchie glanced over at Sumner, then sighed. 'One. Krassix. Personally appointed by SSS HQ on Earth.'

Sumner was furious. 'But he can have no official status. I have no records of his presence here. This is intolerable...' He stopped and looked at Madox. 'Of course! Your mysterious ever helpful "source". It was another Teknix, wasn't it? You knew!'

'No. I'm sorry, everyone,' said the Doctor, 'but that's the latest piece of the puzzle. Krassix cannot be a Teknix. They're too loyal. And I assume, Madox, it was Krassix who told you of Commandant Ritchie's "betrayal".'

Madox nodded.

'Krassix must be a Dark Peaks Foamasi as well,' interjected Green Fingers.

Ritchie breathed deeply as the realisation of this sank in. 'Which means that every single plan, every high-level SSS command and instruction has been fed straight back to the Lodge. And, more importantly, every time I believed I had outwitted my blackmailer, I told Krassix. Every confidential word I had with him...' Ritchie shook his head. 'How stupid am I?'

'Pardon my self-congratulation, Commandant,' said Green Fingers, 'but not very stupid at all. With a mixture of pride and embarrassment, I have to point out that Foamasi are superb operatives. Krassix might have been with you for ten years, and still you would never have suspected.'

Sumner gasped. 'Do you mean that there could be long-term Foamasi infiltrators throughout the Federation?'

'Or the SSS?' added Ritchie.

Green Fingers nodded. 'Oh yes. And even if I knew who they all were, I wouldn't tell you. But I will say this. The Foamasi deal with their own. The Dark Peaks were warned away from Micawber's World and have broken that commandment. They have forfeited the right to continue operating here. When I get back to the Temple, I will call a meeting of the Lodge Patriarchs and put an end to their insidious underhand dealings.'

'I thought every Foamasi Lodge did insidious underhand dealings,' said Ms Sox, without any hint of sarcasm.

Equally stoic, Green Fingers nodded. 'But we still do it by the rules, Ms Sox. And, nine times out of ten, we do it with style, panache and a degree of pride.'

The Doctor looked at Sumner. 'The ball is in your court, Co-ordinator. My suggestion is that you let us all go. Commandant Ritchie and his troopers can explore the tunnels, Mr Fingers there can sort his Lodges out and Ms Sox and I can investigate these drugs. Oh, and I don't suppose anyone has seen my young friend, Sam, anywhere?'

But Ritchie ignored him. Instead, he was staring straight at Sumner, a new understanding between them. 'And Krassix?' he asked.

Krassix walked through the empty offices of Carrington Corp, heading for the elevator to the Executive Suite.

If the few odd people scattered around, or any of the cleaning droids, registered its presence, they opted not to make a fuss. Obviously, a Teknix visiting from the Events Co-ordination Sector of Carrington City, with some request for Chase Carrington.

Especially as that was where it seemed to be headed.

Krassix regarded a couple of the humans tapping at the datapads, uploading information from the live broadcast of the opening ceremony. Pathetic creatures. How it hated wearing a human-shaped bodysuit, its hollow bones compressed into such a small form. If they were going to the bother of genetically engineering a race of subservient superbrains, the humans might at least have made the Teknix larger.

No. This was irrelevant now. Now this body, this mind, had a greater purpose. Now it... he... I... we...

Krassix entered the private elevator and seconds later got off outside Carrington's lobby. Walking in, Krassix passed the desks and knocked on Carrington's door.

'Yes?'

Krassix walked in, holding out the handful of pills Miles Mason had supplied.

'Excellent. Whoever is supplying these will soon be out of business. With the advantages Carrington Corp offers the Dark Peaks Lodge, we can mass-produce this and undercut them within days.'

As Carrington reached out for the samples, Krassix whipped the proffered hand back and with the other hand tugged sharply at Carrington.

There was a tearing sound and the fake Carrington arm was pulled away, revealing the Foamasi flesh underneath.

'Whatever are you doing, Chwekitwpt?' The Carrington Foamasi was about to move back when the Krassix Foamasi pulled off its own 'hand'. If the Foamasi replacing Carrington and Suki were expecting the familiar green flesh, they were surprised instead to see it intermingled with bubbling browny-green mucus.

And the Krassix figure – part Foamasi, part Wirrrn – slapped the fake Carrington's green scaly flesh and then advanced on the one that had called itself Suki Raymond.

Sam dived back, tugging the shocked and mute Kyle with her. Bizarrely she realised she was still holding the paper bag with the stuffed Meep toy in it. Like a good-luck charm.

A second later, the formerly Torin Chalfont grub thing flopped on to the cavern floor where they had been standing.

'Come on, Kyle. We need to get the Doctor. Run!'

Kyle seemed to finally break out of his reverie and turned to go.

Blocking the way out was Reverend Lukas and the other Church members.

'Reverend Father, we must get away from here,' he

practically screamed.

But Reverend Lukas just stared at the huge monster before him.

'You called me, Goddess.'

Kyle stopped and stared.

Sam just laughed. 'Jesus Christ, Lukas, you can't seriously believe that's your Goddess?'

While not quite as informal as Sam, Jolyon and the others seemed to be swayed more by her arguments than Reverend Lukas's now they had actually seen the 'Goddess' with their own eyes.

Veronique and Max took a step aside, glancing up at Reverend Lukas, who seemed to be staring at the creature, bemused.

'He's in rapture,' muttered Phillipa, holding Jolyon tightly.

'The most perfect being in creation,' Reverend Lukas said, dropping to his knees and bowing his head. 'There is nothing superior to this divine creature,' he breathed. '*She* called me here. I realise that now. The wedding was just an excuse. She needed me close.' He looked up at his Church members. 'Us. She needs us. Your Goddess needs our love.'

Jolyon turned away, trying to ease Phillipa with him, but Veronique and Max were confused.

They had followed Reverend Lukas for so long...

'C'mon.' Sam tried to tug them away from the cavern. Only Kyle moved with her.

'Please, Reverend. This isn't the Goddess. This is... evil!' Kyle was crying, begging Reverend Lukas and the others to leave. 'Quickly, we have to leave.'

'This is not evil...' Reverend Lukas stared happily at his Goddess.

Sam made one last plea. 'Reverend Lukas, you talked to me about belief. About the flaws in evolutionary theory. About what keeps you going. Look at that thing. How can this be your Goddess? Your Goddess is good. This is just... evil.'

'This is purity, Ms Jones. The Goddess is pure, through and through.'

'Pure evil, Reverend. Please!'

But he would not move. Sam gave a last desperate shout to the Church members but no one except Kyle moved.

She turned and ran, Kyle following just behind.

In the near darkness, without Torin's – as it turned out – alien-inspired sense of direction, Sam realised they could easily get lost.

Or plunge into a chasm. Or –

She was grabbed by a pair of masculine hands. For a brief moment, she thought it was the Doctor.

But then she heard Kyle behind her. 'Brother Marcus! You must save us. Help us save Reverend Lukas!'

And Sam realised she was staring at the always impassive Brother Eldritch.

At the Stadium, the Doctor was rooting through the lockers of the parading athletes.

Ms Sox was outside the changing room, keeping an eye out for any returning sportsmen or coach droids.

'Got some!' The Doctor found a handful of pills in an antigrav bag belonging to a Centauran table-tennis player.

'Red or blue? I wonder which…'

'Doctor!' hissed Ms Sox. 'Someone's coming!' The Doctor was at her side in an instant. 'I recognise him… wait a minute! He was the scientist who disappeared from the SSS place. One of Professor Jeol's team.' Ms Sox stared a moment longer. 'Human. Er, let me think. Yes, Mason! Miles Mason, an expert in xenobiology. We sorted out his entry visa for the SSS, found him quarters. Very popular with the service actually. Chase Carrington even knew a bit about his background.' She swallowed, trying not to think about Carrington. 'Anyway, he's turned up here, and if he finds us, we'll be in real trouble.'

The Doctor nodded. 'Oh yes. And if my suspicions about him are correct, more trouble than you anticipate. Come on, let's go through the toilets!'

Kyle had always thought nothing could ever break Marcus's or Eldritch's concentration, but the sudden terrible screaming from the cavern behind them gave him the break he needed. He shoved at Marcus, who fell straight over. Eldritch turned to look, and Sam knocked him off balance with the toy Meep. Without waiting to see whether he toppled over, she grabbed Kyle's hand and ran, almost dragging the young man with her.

'I just hope I don't miss my footing or we could be in for a long drop,' she shouted.

But Kyle didn't answer – all he could think of was what had prompted the screaming. There was no mistaking Veronique's voice.

With his own SSS clearances plus the expertise of all the SSS agents and a variety of bloodthirsty killers from a dozen worlds all floating in his joined consciousness, Miles Mason had very little difficulty moving freely around the behind-the-scenes areas of the Olympic Stadium.

He had even less difficulty entering the area beneath the stands, adopting the persona of a Carrington worker checking the underseating areas for safety. Were the life-forms above too heavy? Too congested in one area? Were the emergency exits clear and safe and ready to use? That sort of thing.

The real worker sent to check this was curled up in a corner, slowly transforming into a larval Wirrrn grub.

And after a few moments, Mason sat down to relax, with his little portable box of tricks put together with the aid of all the thoughts in his head.

Directly above him, the Duchess of Auckland was being told in no uncertain terms by Consort Ethelredd that her place was at the Games for the rest of the afternoon.

Mason smiled. He twisted a dial on his box and the timer started its countdown. In forty minutes, the distraction the Wirrrn Queen had ordered would be provided.

The laboratories at SSS Administration were almost empty. A majority of the workforce were either working or spectating at the Stadium.

'In here.' The Doctor pushed open a set of double doors to Sterile Room Four and dug into his pocket, retrieving the globular remote recorder he had obtained last time he was there. It floated up and hovered at eye level.

++HELLO DOCTOR++

'Prepare to begin recording. Label it replacement case nine oh three oblique delta red.'

++CONFIRMED++

The Doctor passed some pills to Ms Sox. 'Can you prepare me some slides. The electron microscope should be good enough to tell me what I need.'

'I'm not a scientist,' she snapped.

'No, but you're an exceptional woman, with a strong personality, pretty good in a tight situation, you're intelligent and you care about people.' He smiled at her. 'I believe those are generally the main requirements to help me.'

He wasn't sure if Ms Sox would hit him or start preparing the slides. As he turned back to the recorder, he smiled faintly as he heard her activate the electron microscope.

He broke one of the blue pills open, watching tiny motes of a dusty substance spill on to a glass slide. 'Looks like talcum powder. Recorder, begin recording everything that is said in this room from now on.'

++CONFIRMED++

Ms Sox slapped a few slides down. 'Luckily for you, Doctor, despite what I said, I do have a passing familiarity with the subject due to my augmentation.' She smiled tightly at him.

'Splendid!' The Doctor grinned as he broke open a red pill, this one containing tiny solid capsules. 'What have you got for me?'

Ms Sox regarded the readout for the electron microscope. 'Well, they are combined essentially of acetylsalicylic acid compounds with a metabolite of phenacetin, which appears to be acetophenetidin-based. Add to that trace elements of dichlorobenzyl alcohol, amylmetacresol BP, carmoisine and, just to make it taste better, sucrose.'

The Doctor frowned and slipped her his red pill. She crushed some of the tinier capsules, placed them in the chamber, adjusted the microscope and repeated the description. 'Nothing more than a powerful paracetamol. Effective on a headache or a mild cold, neither of which the athletes were bothered by anyway. They're identical.' The Doctor frowned. 'Identical? Why?' He sat on the edge of the bench. 'Back to our queries again. Query One: why would someone pass out identical pills made to look different? Query Two: why do it anyway? Query Three: are they having any effect?'

'Query Four,' added Ms Sox. 'What are we missing?'

'Missing?'

'Oh come on, Doctor. Why go this effort if they're just pain relievers. Apart from the fact that an overdose could kill certain species, they're pointless. Yet a load of people have died or been kidnapped or substituted by the Foamasi in an attempt to get these. Either we're being taken for a ride by the greatest scam artist in the Federation or –'

'Or we're missing something. Of course!' The Doctor reactivated the electron microscope, reading out the ingredients one by one.

'I think I just said that,' Ms Sox muttered, but any further waspish comments were cut short by the arrival of Co-ordinator Sumner, displaying an SSS security pass, no doubt given to him by Commandant Ritchie.

'How are things going?'

'Badly,' shouted the Doctor. 'I'm missing something.'

'You're telling me.' Ms Sox walked across to the sink. 'Glass of water, Co-ordinator?'

'No, thank you, Ms Sox. Doctor?'

'Uh-huh?' The Doctor was clearly not listening.

'Doctor, I have received a message from the Foamasi Ambassador. Government. Whatever he is.'

'Green Fingers,' filled in Ms Sox, pointlessly.

'Exactly. He would like us to visit his Temple in half an hour.'

'All three of us?'

'Specifically, Ms Sox. He also asked for Commandant Ritchie but he's gone to secure the Stadium with Quartermaster-Sergeant Dallion and her agents.'

The Doctor suddenly moved away from the microscope. 'Got it!'

'What is it?' Ms Sox and Sumner moved closer, anticipating his response.

'My sonic screwdriver. That's why Sam had it – she was working on my car! I remember now.' He beamed at Sumner and Ms Sox. 'That's been worrying me for a while now, you know.'

A look passed between the Jadean PA and the human co-ordinator. It spoke volumes on the subject of a justifiable homicide about to take place in Sterile Room Four.

++IMPORTANT++

'Yes?' The Doctor clicked his fingers to get the remote's attention without looking away from the electron microscope.

++DATA DOWNLOAD FROM THE ELECTRON MICROSCOPE SUGGESTS THAT THE BLUE PILLS HAVE A RETARDING AGENT++

'Aha! So, not quite identical. Take the red pill and whatever it is works quickly. Take the blue and it takes longer, and is therefore probably stronger.' He slapped the table top. 'Of course! If it remains dormant for a period of time, the effects will kick in long after the Games are over and the athletes are back in their own planetary systems. Spreading whatever it is halfway across the galaxy...'

The remote hovered towards the Doctor once more.

++URGENT DATA. THERE IS AN EXTRA INGREDIENT ATTACHED TO EACH MOLECULE. IT HAS NO RELEVANCE TO THE EXISTING PURPOSE OF THE ACETAMINOPHEN. UNABLE TO IDENTIFY EXACT INGREDIENT++

The Doctor leaned back and slapped the side of the microscope. 'Primitive thing. All they've done in twenty thousand years is add a few new buttons and a holographic readout point.' He looked at Sumner, as if it was all his fault. 'Can't your Federation invent something better than this? I need my TARDIS.'

It had taken Sam and Kyle nearly fifteen minutes to get out of the tunnels (pausing to look at the mucus wall which Reverend Lukas and company must have prised away from the outside with bits of shrubbery, going by the devastated wood and piles of leaves scattered about). They had then managed to wave down a hovercar and hitch a ride back to Carrington City.

They were thanking the pilot when Sam saw the Doctor and a couple of other people leaving the SSS Administration Building. He was too far away to hear her shout, so she ran like hell to reach him.

When he spotted her, he gave her a broad grin and held up his hand. 'I don't want to know, Sam, however exciting it is. Right now, I have to go to deal with the Foamasi, but you could help me.'

Sam was too out of breath to do anything other than try to attract his attention, but failed.

'Go to the TARDIS and get me the Lamerdine Spectral Bio-Analyser from the lab, will you? See you back here in ten minutes.'

'But... but Doctor...'

'Oh yes, sorry. The TARDIS is that way, turn left, right, straight on and it's by the big green park.'

As Sam tried to pull herself together, the Doctor got into a Carrington Corp hovercar with the two other people he was with and it went off.

She dropped to her knees. 'Right. I've got to get back into my running habit. I need to get fitter than this.'

'Hey,' said an angry voice behind her. 'I'm not made of credits and that hovercar cost me everything I had on me!'

Sam turned slowly and gave Kyle her patented 'Say one more word and you'll never need money again' glare.

Kyle shut up.

'The TARDIS,' she finally said. 'Now.'

Slowly – very slowly – they walked back to the ship.

The dining hall was dark, with just five candles illuminating odd corners.

Gielgud shuffled around, lighting the candelabra on the table, immediately casting a series of huge shadowy versions of himself on the wall behind him. Wherever he moved, briefly enlightened areas of brickwork become covered in shadow again, giving the whole room a rather Gothic feel.

Gielgud was pleased by this – it appealed to his flair for the over-dramatic.

As he finished lighting the last candle, he glanced over to the wall directly behind the head of the rectangular dining table.

'Will that be all, sir?' he asked in his cultured – but synthesised – English tones.

'Yes.' The voice came from nowhere yet everywhere. It was, however, unmistakably Green Fingers' voice. Gielgud was actually looking at a bizarre piece of Foamasi art that adorned the wall, but it certainly wasn't responsible for the reply.

'Very good, sir. When shall I return to clear up?'

'I will contact you. Please go.'

Gielgud bowed to his unseen master. He straightened the four jet-black, plastic, bowl-shaped seats, specially constructed to take Foamasi bulk, and shuffled out of the room, using his tail to close the heavy door behind him.

After a few seconds, a series of sections in each brick wall rotated on hidden hinges. Irregular spaces could now be seen, within each of which was a Foamasi.

One stepped into the dining hall.

'South Lodge presents Patriarch One.'

Another moved in from the opposite section.

'Dark Peaks Lodge presents Patriarch Two.'

'West Lodge presents Patriarch Three.'

'Twin Suns Lodge presents Patriarch Four.'

The Patriarchs took the seats nearest them and sat, casting wary glances at each other, and at the empty fifth seat at the head of the table, with its green crest at the top.

No one spoke, until finally the Twin Suns Lodge representative spoke. As a scholar on twentieth-century, human, 2-D movie actors, he knew he sounded just like Al Pacino in *Scarface*. To the other Foamasi, he sounded frequently unintelligible and rather ridiculous. But it was not good Foamasi manners to say so. Besides which, because, in theory, they were all working against each other, but in a very well-ordered structure, to pick an argument with an opposing number while attending one of the rare Gatherings, was considered unacceptable.

'So,' said the Twin Suns, 'why is we here at dis crucial time?'

'Typtpwtyp has been murdered. He was one of your agents, am I right?'

The Foamasi all stared at the empty chair, as if they could see someone seated there. That was custom.

The Twin Suns representative answered. 'One'a da boys, yeah.'

'He was murdered by the Dark Peaks Lodge, who are employing human agents in the Stadium.'

The Dark Peaks Representative swivelled around slightly. When he spoke, it was in the soporific tones of a mid-thirty-fifth-century Chelonian politician, lots of elongated vowel sounds and little dramatic pauses between inappropriate word breaks. He even underlined his meaning by poking at the air with his right hand.

'What evidence do you have to back up this wild accusation, Mr Speaker?'

'It is my job as Ambassadorial Representative to the Federation to know everything that goes on in Foamasi society. Especially on this world. You were told to stay away.'

The Dark Peaks representative shrugged. 'The Dark Peaks Lodge opted to ignore that recommendation, and note it *was* a recommendation, *not* an order. I draw your attention to the answer given by our Patriarch at the last Lodge Gathering on Liasici –'

'Don't quote Gathering minutes at me, Dark Peaks Representative.' The unseen Green Fingers was very angry now. 'I was there. I listened. I noted. And still, you were forbidden to attend. Why are you here?'

The West Lodge representative raised a hand.

'Go ahead, West.'

When he spoke, it was in a deep growling voice, like that of a Shistavanen game-show host, a curious mixture of bouncy rhetoric mixed with snarling lupine savagery.

'We were promised...' He waved his hand towards the others. 'We were *all* promised that the Dark Peaks would not be here to interfere with our transactions. But no, they have infiltrated a number of our operations, confounded and confused them.'

'Not true,' put in Dark Peaks, but West ignored him.

'We table a motion that the Dark Peaks representative return home to Liasici and face charges of treason and contemptible behaviour.'

'Seconded,' said the Twin Suns.

The South Lodge representative nodded.

Dark Peaks looked as his fellow Foamasi, angrily. 'None of you have what it takes to be Foamasi any longer. Ten centuries have passed since we last waged war against a common foe and tried to take a place in this galaxy that is ours by right. Since then the Foamasi have been content to pursue cheap and pointless theatrical crimes. Getting a reputation as the "bad guys" of the galaxy. Becoming something human mothers and Pakhar dames send their spawn to bed with, threatening them that if they don't sleep, the big bad Foamasi will eat them. Eat them! We're a joke! The Dark Peaks Lodge was formed because we realised that the other Lodges were weak, with no real ambition. Gambling, drugs, prostitution, oh yes, wonderful moneymakers.' He pointed to each of the Lodge representatives in turn. 'But where is the fire in your guts, eh? Where is the drive, the ambition to rule that our people once had. The Foamasi of today are weak. But next year sees the start of a new millennium and the Dark Peaks plan to ensure that the *real* Foamasi are ready to take control from the Federation. To acknowledge our birthright and –'

He never got any further as the heavy door opened and Gielgud shuffled in.

'What do you want, Twin Sunner?' snapped the Dark Peaks Representative.

'Just following my orders, sir,' said Gielgud and shot him dead with a single blaster bolt between the eyes.

The others watched in silence as Gielgud hobbled over, lifted the dead representative over his shoulder and carried him away. 'Apologies for the interruptions, sirs,' he called back, and then closed the door behind him.

'Fellow Representatives,' said the voice of Green Fingers, 'I have either just quelled a rebellion or started a civil war. It rests with you to decide which it is. Does any of you have any other business?'

The South Lodge indicated that he had, and spoke, or rather sang, his speech like an eighth-century pop star from the pre-stellar Menaxan civilisation. 'Sir, there appears to be a new drug going around the competitors at the Olympic Games. We understood that we had sole rights to drug supply on this planet.'

'Indeed,' said Green Fingers. 'And I am investigating this breach of protocol. My... sources suspect that there is an uninvited presence on Micawber's World which is being rooted out as we speak. I will call another meeting of the Lodge Patriarchs as soon as I have more news. Next?'

No one else had anything to say, so Green Fingers offered a few final words.

'Representatives, the Dark Peaks Lodge gains much power at home. We must decide to ally our own Lodges with it or against it. If civil war does break out, let it be known for posterity that it started here. I leave it to your own boards to decide their course of actions. Oh, and one last thing. Any Dark Peaks Foamasi are fair game. It'll give your assassins something to do until this drug business is sorted out.'

Muttering their thanks, the surviving Foamasi returned to the holes in the wall from which they had emerged. These led to small tunnels underground that in turn led to their respective bases – the locations of which were unknown to each other but had been set up by Green Fingers.

After a few moments, the heavy door opened and Gielgud showed Green Fingers and his guests in.

The Doctor crossed to where he had seen the Dark Peaks Representative die, while Ms Sox and Co-ordinator Sumner just looked at where the walls had resealed themselves, without a mark.

'Foamasi technology is very advanced,' Green Fingers said to their admiration. 'You can never spot exactly where we come in and out of a building.'

The Doctor frowned at him. 'Was the death of one of your people entirely necessary?'

'It is our way, Doctor. I did warn you that you may see things this afternoon which would alarm you.'

'You said the Dark Peaks were targets now,' added Ms Sox. 'Can you be sure that Micawber's World won't become a blood bath?'

'Assassins are very discreet, you know, Ms Sox. You won't even be aware of it happening. Now, everyone, with Commandant Ritchie's problem solved and my internal dispute solved in one fell swoop, let us concentrate on this drug business. It's really not on, you know…'

'Yes! I know what it must be!'

Ms Sox and the others stared at the Doctor. 'We know Sam has your sonic screwdriver, Doctor,' she began but he hushed her.

'I think I know what else is in those pills. Something so small that it's almost undetectable. My Spectral Bio-Analyser will confirm it, but I think our little recorder has the details.' He fished it out of his pocket.

++HELLO, DOCTOR++

'Right. You believed there was something else in those drugs, right?'

++CONFIRMED++

'Do you still have the analysis uploaded into your memory?'

++CONFIRMED++

The Doctor sighed with relief. 'I think it's a genetic code. It's the only thing small enough to be worth hiding in the pills. If it were a disease, then why hide it so deeply. If it were a series of mental commands… well, again we know our enemy is telepathic, so why bother? It has to be genetic. Using those parameters, can you speculate what it might be?'

++CONFIRMED. PLEASE WAIT++

'We don't have time,' shouted the Doctor. 'I need to know now!'

++GENETIC DECODER. THE TRACE ELEMENTS ARE MUTAGENIC IN ORIGIN. A COMPOUND PARASITE WHICH CAN RESTRUCTURE DNA AT THE MOLECULAR LEVEL++

'How fast do you think it can work?'

++INGESTION, THUS ABSORPTION INTO THE BIOSYSTEM OF MOST CREATURES ON MICAWBER'S WORLD, WOULD TAKE APPROXIMATELY TWO MINUTES++

'Oh no,' said the Doctor, his face suddenly ashen. 'Whatever's in that tunnel system, they're turning everyone taking part in the Olympic Games into alternative versions of themselves. Let's go!'

The three Foamasi assassins who had killed Chase Carrington and his driver a couple of nights before were in a small bar watching the opening parade come to its close on the holovid. With them were twelve humans from the Stadium workforce – the ones who had silenced 'George Sanders'.

The assassins were splitting their share of the profits.

'Where is our cut?' asked the dark-skinned man.

A tubbier man, George's contact, was more forceful. 'You better not have backed out, scale-face.'

'You were paid by Typtpwtyp,' said the Foamasi leader.

'That was on behalf of the Twin Suns Lodge. Killing him was on behalf of your lot, the Dark Peaks. So we want payment from you, too.'

The leader of the assassins thrust a self-elongating knife straight through the heart of the fatter man, also skewering two of the others standing behind him. Before the blade retracted and the three dead humans hit the floor, the other two Dark Peaks assassins had slaughtered the remaining nine. It was over in less than two seconds.

Dark Peaks assassins were almost the most efficient.

Unfortunately for them, a combined team of a West, South and Twin Suns assassins had been waiting at the bar, disguised as a Snarx, a Lurman and a Klepton. One of them tossed a cocoon grenade at the Dark Peaks group, and a moment later all three assassins were bound together by a tight white substance.

The three disguised assassins shed their skin suits and left them on the floor. If anyone else in the bar wanted to watch, or show any interest, they knew better.

The Dark Peaks assassins squirmed momentarily but all that did was tighten their bonds. The South Lodge assassin removed the retractable knife from the motionless claws of the lead assassin, aimed carefully and then released the spring, severing the back of each of their necks. Green blood began oozing out of the three trapped assassins and soaking into the cocoon substance, turning it vivid green.

Four and a half minutes later, the three Dark Peaks assassins were dead, completely drained of their blood. The West Lodge assassin kicked the corpses over and the cocoon soaked up the remaining blood on the floor.

The three Foamasi left their dead fellows behind as they walked out, knowing that the bar operator would invoice them for the mess later.

Sam unlocked the door to the TARDIS and ushered Kyle in. She smiled, imagining what his reaction would be, and was not disappointed.

The poor lad had been through so much in the last few hours that another shock merely added to his growing confusion with the world. He wandered towards the central console, listening to his feet clicking on the parquet floor and staring at the bust of Rassilon, then at the brass dials and switches and finally at the panoramic hologram on the ceiling.

He pointed straight up. 'Micawber's World,' he said simply.

Sam nodded. 'Where is your home, Kyle?'

'Iota 9. It's a small colony world on the other side of Sauron.'

Sam tapped in the name on the TARDIS databank. The ceiling blurred and Iota 9 appeared. It was one among about thirty planets, all circling a massive sun. 'Gravity here must have taken a while to get used to,' Sam said. 'It's obviously beefed up artificially to mimic the gravity on a much bigger world than yours.'

Kyle agreed. 'But after I'd been travelling to different places for a few months, my body got used to the changes. It takes about a day, and I'm OK each time Reverend Lukas moves us on...' He suddenly grabbed Sam's arm, but not too roughly.

'Can I tell you something?'

'Of course.' This wasn't getting the Doctor's thingumajig, but that could wait. Kyle needed to talk.

'For the last few years, all I have done is dedicate myself to the Church of the Way Forward, believing that what it stood for was right. But that... that thing in the tunnels. What it did to that newscaster, and Veronique and probably the others. Reverend Lukas said he believed it to be the Goddess, but it can't be, can it? I mean, the Goddess isn't like that, is she?'

Sam took his hand, gently stroking the back of it. Ever since she had begun travelling with the Doctor, Sam had been forced to grow up. To stop thinking about how the universe affected her, and how it affected everybody. Her time on Ha'olam had made her feel more mature, and she had been forced to cope alone with so much – people's traumas, people's depressions and her own guilt and all too frequent despair. But this was the first time she'd ever had to deal with a crisis of faith.

She remembered home again. The Sundays at church. Mum wasn't particularly a believer, but Dad was a sort of lapsed Catholic. Mum agreed to go along, taking Sam as well, to help him. To make Dad feel part of his church again. To do her bit, Sam had once gone to a confessional. She knew she shouldn't, that it was not something non-Catholics should do, but nevertheless she did. Not because she wanted to confess anything particularly, but because she had thought it might make her dad happy.

The priest had been very understanding. Incredibly so, as she explained why she was there, how sorry she was for not believing in God and wasting the priest's time.

But he said he understood and one day, she would look back on that moment and really understand why she had done it.

Perhaps now she did, standing here in the far future, away from home and family, facing someone else asking her the same sort of questions about a deity she had asked the priest: why he was believed in, why he let wars and suffering happen and why, if he was so all-powerful, there was hunger, poverty, human-rights violations and everything else she could think of still in the world.

Kyle didn't want to know those things, but here he was, having to question everything that in his life until today had been stable, neat, ordered and something he accepted without question, without hypocrisy or malice.

'I do not – I *cannot* – share your beliefs, Kyle,' she said softly. 'But for what it's worth, I don't believe that creature is your Goddess. I believe Reverend Lukas has made a mistake.'

Kyle shook his head. 'Reverend Lukas cannot make mistakes.'

'Of course he can. He's human, like you or me. He's fallible. He's searched for so long for answers, but become so wrapped up in the search, so scared of finding nothing, that he didn't *want* any answers. That's why this thing caught him like that. But the Goddess can't be down there, Kyle. Not your personal Goddess, because the purity and clarity you wanted to find, you already showed me you knew where it was.' She tapped his chest. 'You yourself told me that. Who am I, or who is Reverend Lukas or that monster to tell you differently?'

Kyle let go of her hand. 'Where are you from, Sam?'

Sam got up and twisted a dial. The hologram of Iota 9

shimmered and became her home. 'Earth.'

'No, really, where are you from?'

Sam chuckled. 'No, really, I am from Earth. But not 3999: 1997 actually. The Doctor and I travel in time.'

'Oh.' Kyle looked around the TARDIS again. 'I see.'

'You don't seem surprised.'

Kyle got up and began looking into the library, then at the wall of clocks. 'I can't deny the evidence of my own eyes, Sam. I mean, this was a blue box. Now it's a treasure cave. And I can see a corridor down there, so it must be huge. For anyone to build anything this huge they can be only one of two things. A god or a vastly superior being to everyone else on Micawber's World. And as you know, I don't now believe in gods or goddesses. Not any more, I don't think. So I have to accept the evidence and believe you.' He looked up at Earth. 'I've never been there. What's it like?'

'Now? No idea. But in my time, flawed, fractious, dangerous and beautiful. I miss it now and again.'

'If you travel in time, why don't you and the Doctor go back to 1997 then?'

Sam did not look at him, but stared instead at the representation of Earth. 'Just as the Goddess has been your mission, Kyle, so travelling with the Doctor is becoming mine. He does so much good, you know. And I'm so lucky to be able to see it with him, see and learn so much through him.' She smiled, sadly. 'How *could* I go back?'

She tweaked the dial and the hologram zoomed in, through the clouds, across Europe and on to Britain. It went further. England. Southern England. London. Finally it rested on the image of East London, near the Thames. Tower Bridge, the Tower of London and the entrance to the Rotherhithe tunnel could actually be picked out.

Sam breathed very deeply. Something inside her sank, but she couldn't say exactly what she was feeling. 'But maybe someday I should. Just to say hello. It's been such a long time now, and I feel guilty I never –'

The holographic Earth suddenly zoomed back out and dropped away until it was the size of a football. Then the hologram floated down from the ceiling and hovered in front of Sam. 'I never knew it could do that…' she gasped.

The hologram moved towards her, easing her backwards. And she laughed. 'Oh all right then, TARDIS. I get the message.' The hovering globe of light moved her towards the corridor.

'What's happening? asked Kyle, following her.

'I'm being reminded that I came to get something for the Doctor.'

They went into the corridor and into the galley area. 'The lab is through here,' she called over to Kyle, but then feinted to the left. The hovering globe followed and she pressed a button on the nearby microwave oven. The door popped open and the globe shot in. Sam slammed the door behind it, trapping the hologram. Sam turned the microwave on but didn't turn up the settings. 'That should scramble your circuits for a while.' She looked to the galley ceiling. 'Now, stop bossing me around, OK?'

Bewildered, Kyle looked up, but couldn't see who Sam was talking to. She placed the Meep toy, now looking a bit bedraggled, atop the microwave. 'And you, keep guard,' she said, and then walked on.

Kyle then followed her into a small ante-room, which was a miniature storage area, full of test tubes, Bunsen burners, welding kits, Petri dishes and every other kind of scientific hand-held paraphernalia.

'Biomolecular scanning whatnot… Here it is!' Sam showed Kyle something but he didn't recognise it. 'OK, Mr Dale, time to hit the road and help the Doctor win the war against the monsters.'

'Can he?'

Sam smiled and slipped an arm around Kyle's. 'Of course he can.

That's why I have faith in *him*.'

The Dark Peaks Lodge was where the action was, there was no doubt about that. His parents had been members of the South Lodge, but that was weak and pointless now. Any power it might have held once was long past. The Dark Peaks were the future. They were going to reclaim the economy, the standing, the honour and make Liasici a great planet once more.

And to add to that prestige, here he was, a young Foamasi – honoured by the mission to guard the human prisoners. Of course, they were well-fed, watered and exercised. The Dark Peaks Lodge weren't thugs, they were just doing what was necessary to ensure a better tomorrow for the Foamasi citizens.

If only his parents could see him now. They would be proud of him. Instead, they were just a pile of ashes on a street somewhere on Liasici, gunned down by members of a rival Lodge, accused of drugs-running, or prostitution pimping, or whatever. It really didn't matter – they had been in an opposing Lodge and one that had been competition for the Dark Peaks. They deserved their fate. But nevertheless, there were times when he wished he could tell them how well he had done. How far he had progressed.

He tapped his communicator. Where was the relief guard? No response. He tried a couple of other places – the guardhouse, the bar, the hidden headquarters.

And each time he looked at his viewscreen, all he could see were dead Foamasi – all bearing Dark Peaks tattoos on their shoulders.

Instinctively, he put his hand to his own, worn like a badge of honour. Of class.

But if the others were all dead, what was going on? Where was their Patriarch? Why wasn't he standing amid the carnage, declaring vengeance?

A cold chill ran through the young Foamasi. What if the

Patriarch was dead too? No, he couldn't afford to think that.

The only other place he could think to try was Carrington Corp. The two Dark Peaks insiders there might have some answers.

He was about to try to make contact with them, when three Foamasi came around the corner towards him. He took in the sight in an instant – each one had a different tattoo, and they were working together. West, South and Twin Suns.

'You can surrender your prisoners,' said the Souther. 'Or we kill you and take them anyway. The Dark Peaks are finished here, and back on Liasici too.'

The young Foamasi considered this.

With a shrug, he turned and unlocked the door, peeking in. 'You can come out, humans. You are free to go.'

With trepidation (and who could blame them?) the human woman led her young son out, staring around, blinking in the natural light.

'Your mate is at the Foamasi Embassy,' said the Wester to them. 'Go now.'

Without waiting for a second order, the two humans walked quickly away. In fact, as soon as they were past the other three Foamasi, they began running.

'I wish to join your campaign,' said the Young Foamasi to the three assassins. He felt his heart thumping wildly. Was it excitement? Fear? Concern? He looked at his chest. No, it was probably the sleek knife that had just embedded itself there.

'You change ideals too quickly,' muttered one of the other Foamasi. But he couldn't tell which one as all three were being swallowed up by some inexplicable darkness.

And it was *ever* so cold...

Sam yelled at the Doctor to stop as she came out of the TARDIS and he zoomed by in a hovercar. The car dropped to the ground. 'Get in. Both of you!'

With a sigh, Sam dragged Kyle to the hovercar and they squeezed in the back.

As it took off, Sam passed her trophy to him.

'Thanks Sam, but I don't need it now. I already know what secret the pills carry. A two-minute time-bomb that releases a mutagen in the carriers which then –'

'Turns them into greeny-brown slugs that can take over your body and change it in a matter of seconds the moment you get into contact with it. We know.'

'You do? How?'

'If you'd listened to me last time, I could have told you.' Sam began relating her and Kyle's adventures in the tunnels.

The doors to Chase Carrington's office were kicked in savagely. Both Carrington and Suki Raymond looked up from the pills in their trays.

'What do you –' Carrington started to say, but the West Lodge assassin yanked away his human head to reveal –

Not the Foamasi head the assassins expected to find, but a roughly Foamasi-shaped head, covered with pupal mucus of a Wirrrn grub. The other assassins grabbed Suki Raymond, ripping the whole bodysuit off. That Foamasi too was now almost completely covered in pupal mucus.

Despite this, the West Lodge assassin kept his cool, hurling the expanding knife they had taken from the Dark Peaks assassin straight at the Foamasi that had previously been Suki Raymond. It penetrated slightly, but then the half-Foamasi, half-Wirrrn snapped it off and dropped it to the floor.

The South Lodge assassin instantly drew a heavy-duty blaster and opened fire, but this only caused the Chase Carrington Foamasi/Wirrrn to shed a layer of skin.

With a nod to the others, the Twin Suns assassin ran forward and dived at Suki Raymond, sending both of them crashing into the plate-glass window and through it. Seconds later, both bodies smashed into pieces on the walkway far below.

Sensing the death of its compatriot, the Carrington hybrid tried to swing its mottled arm at the West Lodge assassin, but he ducked, grappled the hybrid to the floor and grabbed his blaster, tapping at the power pack.

The South Lodge assassin grabbed the pills from the table and then threw himself through the office doors, slamming them shut behind him just as the blaster overloaded with a flash of white and a large fizzing noise.

After a few seconds, he opened the doors to the office, which was empty – of everything. The walls, floor and ceiling had become like glazed marble, the contents of the room evaporated by the heat of the blast. The Foamasi and the hybrid had been atomised completely.

With a last look at the pills in his hands, the Foamasi assassin walked back out of the building, past the handful of terrified staff who just stared at him or the devastation and back to the Foamasi Temple.

Consort Ethelredd was standing at the side of the podium, on the grass, talking to Secretary Aigburth and Security Officer Gar when the explosion happened.

Ethelredd was looking past Aigburth (droning on about nothing as usual) and watching the Duchess nattering away with Edyth and Cait, her ladies-in-waiting. Just at the moment when Ethelredd decided that if you put the brains of the Duchess, the two giggling girls and Aigburth inside one head, you just might simulate the intellectual capability of a frog, a huge column of white-hot plasma vaporised the podium.

Ethelredd hardly had time to close his eyes before he was flung aside by the blast, and all he could hear was the repeated *crump!* of the explosion and the screams and yells of thousands of panicking spectators and athletes.

It seemed like an eternity, but was probably only a few seconds before he was lifted up – he would recognise Gar's powerful hands anywhere, so at least *he* was all right – and tried to open his eyes.

Slowly his blurred vision came into focus, but then he wished it hadn't.

The podium was a wreck: a few splinters of wood and plastic were all that was left. A collection of dead bodies fanned out from the base, people nearby who had been caught in the blast.

Ethelredd did not need to consider the Duchess of Auckland or her young ladies-in-waiting. Their bodies would have been atomised instantly. But De'Ath and Aigburth?

As his eyes focused on the dead body of Aigburth lying face down about ten metres from where they had been standing, the wail of De'Ath could be heard from the distance.

As he came into view, Ethelredd saw a miraculous transformation come over his favourite sparring partner. If Ethelredd expected the usual twee foppishness and camp vulgarity, he was disappointed. Instead, he saw a new Counsellor De'Ath, full of strength and sense, as he tried to help the injured and alarmed.

He caught Ethelredd's eye and looked meaningfully towards the podium. Ethelredd shook his head and De'Ath nodded.

Both of them would be held accountable for the Duchess's death, but that could wait. Right now, there was a disaster to help clear up, people to assist and aid to administer.

'Oh my...' Ms Sox put her hand over her mouth a they saw the pillar of white fire reach into the sky from the Stadium.

Although she couldn't see his face, Sam could imagine that the Doctor probably would have frowned. 'It's started,' he stated quietly.

'What has?' asked Sam.

'The final assault by whatever is in the tunnels.'

Sam recalled what the Doctor had said to her when she had seen him last. 'Ah. The Foamasi,' she said.

The large green reptile thing between her and Kyle started. 'There are Foamasi in the tunnels?'

Sam frowned. 'Aren't there, Doctor? You called them Foamasi when I saw you...'

Green Fingers tried to puff out his chest with pride, but in the cramped and overloaded hovercar, that was quite difficult. 'Young lady, *I* am a Foamasi.'

'And your thing in the tunnel didn't look like the Ambassador, did it?' added the Doctor.

'Er, no,' said Kyle, looking around the reptile at Sam for confirmation. 'More like a big insect thing. With pincers, and antennae and –'

The Doctor slapped his hand on his forehead. Sam thought it must have hurt. 'Surely I can't have been so stupid – yet maybe this is how it *really* began. The hatred for mankind...' Sam recognised this tone of voice. The Doctor would start rambling to himself if they weren't careful. She poked him in the back. 'Yes, right, thank you, Sam.' He looked at Ms Sox. 'Dr Mason's knowledge of chemistry and alien biology would be theirs, naturally.'

'Who?'

'An old enemy, if I'm correct. And I haven't got a clue how to stop them.'

Chapter Eleven
Dazzle

The Hovercar containing the Doctor's party touched down amid the ambulances and SSS agent carriers grouped outside the Stadium.

The Doctor ordered everyone out except Ms Sox. To her he gave a whisper. 'I need help. What I'm going to do is dangerous. Are you interested?'

But Sam overheard. 'Hey, you! What about me?'

The Doctor looked at her. 'They'll be expecting you. They know you. I'll be a surprise to them.'

'No you won't,' said Kyle. 'If they've absorbed Torin Chalfont's mind, they know all about you.'

The Doctor stared at Sam, frowning. 'I didn't know I was so famous.'

'I didn't know he was mentally attached to these bloody creatures, did I?'

The Doctor nodded. 'You're right, of course. I'm sorry.'

'Some people would be flattered that they were talked about behind their backs,' she grumbled.

He tapped her cheek. 'To be honest Sam, I'd be happier knowing you were here. I imagine there's a lot of good to be done here, and your experiences of disaster damage control on Ha'olam will come in very handy, all right?'

She looked like she might argue, but changed her mind. 'OK. But if you're not back in an hour, I'm coming looking.'

The Doctor winked at her and the hovercar took off.

Ms Sox looked down at the dwindling figures. 'I don't remember agreeing to come with you, actually,' she said.

'But, naturally, you will.'

'I have a choice?'

The Doctor looked concerned. 'Of course!'

'I was joking. Sort of. Let's go.' She gave a last look at the disaster-ridden Stadium. 'You control Miss Jones very well.'

The Doctor concentrated on navigating towards the tunnel entrance, which wasn't far but it was still quicker to fly than walk.

'Not at all. She'll follow us as soon as we go into the caves. They always do.'

'"They"?'

'Never mind. I just have to hope we can sort out the Wirrrn before she arrives.'

'Wirrrn? The insect things?'

The Doctor eased the hovercar to the ground, then opened the canopy. 'I think so, yes. The telepathic assault confirms it really. I'm beginning to realise that what I glimpsed in that must have been the Queen. She's down here.'

'Oh. And how do we find her?'

'I imagine we'll be met. I knew she knew about me regardless of Sam's encounter with her. Otherwise I would never have received that message so powerfully.' He grinned at her. 'This could be lots of suspense, lots of danger and very messy. Still want to come?'

'Of course I do. Isn't that what "they" always say to you?'

The Doctor laughed. 'You catch on quickly, Ms Sox. Let's go.'

Together they entered the dark tunnels.

Agent B'nel'ye't had been one of the first Pakhars ever to join the Space Security Service. Along with Sergeant Major Zzano'pt'll, he had joined up as soon as the SSS opened its door to non-human officers.

He was very proud of this fact – the rest of his litter were equally proud of 'our Benji' and regularly sent him pads and holos of the family and friends back home.

He had been intending to reciprocate this evening, when the events at the opening ceremony had come to a conclusion, but the sudden destruction that had just occurred put paid to that idea.

Benji knew that he was unlikely to get near his personal communicator for a couple of days now.

Shaking his head at the carnage he had seen inside, Benji was currently reporting in to Sergeant Major Zzano'pt'll on the troop carrier's holo unit. Zzano'pt'll said he was on his way over with more agents and some remote trackers to try to locate the bomber – or bombers.

After closing the communiqué, Benji was preparing to return to his fellows when he saw one of them sloping off in the opposite direction.

'Hey, Franks, where are you going?' he yelled.

But Franks clearly didn't hear, because he carried on walking. He seemed to be heading for Power House Building Three. Did he think the bombers were in there?

Benji scampered after him as fast as his little legs could go.

After a few moments he saw the Power House loom up, but he'd lost sight of Bobby Franks. Weird. Unless, of course, Franks had broken protocol and actually gone inside the Power House.

Slowly, Benji approached. He'd just drawn his blaster when the door to the Power House opened and Franks came out.

Benji's sigh of relief turned to shock as he saw what followed. A whole group of... of *things*. Yellow. Or green. Or brown. Or...

And they moved faster than Benji knew he could.

Within a few seconds, Benji had been enveloped by one of them, his muted shrieks for help lost.

The last thing he saw was the shape of Agent Franks, visible through the translucent mucus that now covered Benji's face, his nose and eyes, looking down at him, doing nothing, nothing at all…

Sam and Kyle were helping people towards the ambulances when the first scream of fear came.

'What now?' wondered Kyle but Sam was pointing.

The nightmare creatures she and Torin had seen in the tunnels were moving exceptionally quickly across the sandy terrain, swarming towards the Stadium.

SSS agents did not waste time – they dropped to their knees, taking aim and firing their blasters, while others ran around getting heavier weaponry out of the troop carriers.

Sam saw a group of agents led by a female sergeant take a defensive stance around the ambulances, giving other agents and some civilians the opportunity to keep loading the medical vehicles with the injured.

She told Kyle to wait for her and went over to join them.

'Hi,' she said to the female sergeant.

The woman glanced at her. 'Don't tell me – the Doctor's chum, right?'

Sam tried not to look surprised. 'Hey, I'm famous.'

'Ever fired one of those before?' asked a man whose name tag designated him as Agent Fenton.

Sam nodded, sadly. 'When it's proven necessary.'

'Good luck,' Fenton said and opened fire.

'There's a man with them,' said another agent – McCarrick.

Sam shrugged. 'They convert you to their side at a touch. He might look human, but he won't be inside. Not any more. He's one of them.'

An agent with a sort of binoculars affair held to his eyes was nodding. 'Sarge, he's covered in the same sort of stuff as the creatures. It's Agent Franks.'

'Trust me, Sergeant Dallion,' said Sam, glancing at the woman's badge. 'He's not one of you any more.'

'I hope you're right,' Dallion said, then raised a blaster rifle and fired, blowing most of Franks's upper torso away. 'It's court-martial time, otherwise.'

'Hey,' said Agent Clarke. 'Who cares? Ritchie's written us off anyway.'

The man with the binocular things lowered them. He was Agent Carruthers, apparently. 'The blasters are having no effect, Sarge. Slowing them a bit but they'll be here in moments.'

As Sam watched, the larval creatures were indeed shuffling across the rough ground at an alarming rate. She looked at the gun, then at the slugs. 'Well, I don't suppose I can very well *talk* you out of this…' she sighed.

She aimed and fired a concentrated burst, trying not to drop the gun. It had a far more powerful kickback than she had anticipated.

But her fire found its mark. One of the creatures was rearing up as it was hit and it seemed to slow momentarily. At first, Sam thought she had actually killed it, but it shook slightly and a whole body's worth of skin just sloughed off, revealing new skin beneath. The creature continued its relentless advance.

Across the way, Sam recognised her Regency-clad friends from the hotel, plus Gar the V'orrn. They were in danger of being swarmed over as they tried to bring more crippled people out of the Stadium.

'Cover me,' she said to an agent called Klein.

He did so, laying down enough fire to keep the creatures back as Sam raced across the way.

She rugby-tackled Consort Ethelredd to the floor, and smiled grimly as Counsellor De'Ath shrieked when he saw how close the creatures were.

Gar snatched the blaster from Sam's hand. 'Good to see you again,' he snapped.

'You too,' she said, pushing Ethelredd and De'Ath away from the battle lines. 'Go on, get away with these people.'

De'Ath started to move but Ethelredd stood his ground. Reaching into a nearby troop carrier he unloaded some blaster rifles, throwing one to Sam and another to De'Ath, who looked as if he had been asked to shoot himself.

Ethelredd powered the blaster up and silently stood beside Sam and Gar, joining them in firing at the creatures.

'Oh, what the hell!' said De'Ath, kneeling beside them.

One creature was very close, lying flat as it slithered over and Sam could see a slight hollow at the front, like a giant mouth.

De'Ath fired a long, unflinching blast straight down this indentation and a moment later the creature exploded into hundreds of little bits that stopped moving.

'I'm already nearly out of power,' he said.

Sam glanced behind her, feeling a draught as the ambulances took off. Freed from their medical obligations, more SSS agents joined the battle.

Dr Miles Mason shivered. He felt the power inside him, knowing he could not – indeed, would not – need to maintain his human body for much longer. He was destined to be a Swarm Leader, side by side with the Wirrrn Queen. But before he could take his designated place, there was a small matter to attend to. Beside him stood a number of athletes, from a variety of differing races. All of them had taken the red pills, believing that they would enhance their athletic capabilities. But it was all a lie, for the pills were little more than placebos, no stronger than basic painkillers. What the red ones in fact contained were the faster-acting Wirrrn agents, already at work inside them, disassembling and then rebuilding each user's DNA, creating a new Wirrrn.

He looked around for some of the takers of the blue pills. It would be months, possibly years, before they joined the hive-mind, but their fate was unavoidable. A Wirrrn would build itself inside each athlete, slowly, invisibly and implacably. And since the mutagens could be transferred genetically, Wirrrn numbers would increase exponentially.

'Now?' hissed a Werelox, staggering slightly.

Mason nodded. 'Now.'

His army slowly moved forward, merging into the crowd, deliberately adding to the chaos and panic created not only by Mason's bomb, but by the battle raging outside. SSS agents had sealed the Stadium entrances, thinking they had locked the Wirrrn out. But really...

Mason was interrupted by a scream – one of the Skirkon pentathletes had seemingly exploded in a shower of body parts, revealing a Wirrrn grub, which launched itself at the nearest spectators. Mason smiled as three more of his drug takers did the same thing, and within moments people were running blindly. All over the Stadium, more Wirrrn were bursting out from the athletes' twisted bodies, spreading the infection.

The SSS agents were panicking. They couldn't fire their blasters very easily for fear of taking innocent lives. Witnessing the new Wirrrn births was delightful, but it was time to move on and make his way back to his Queen.

He knew that the end was not far off, now. The gates had opened and extra SSS agents ran in, with more powerful weapons. New-born Wirrrn withered under the assault, but enough damage had been done. The Wirrrn would succeed.

With a final glance at the beauty of his victory, Miles Mason slipped past an SSS agent and back outside. Already he could feel his flesh pustulating and splitting as the Wirrrn cells in his body finally took control.

'We have to stop these things getting inside the stadium,' yelled what was obviously a high-ranking officer. 'There are thousands of civilians still in there.'

A white-coated SSS scientist was walking up behind the officer, and Sam suddenly remembered the Doctor's realisation about... what was the name? Mason.

'Dr Mason?' she shouted.

Sure enough, there was a brief moment when the man in white stopped, screwing his eyes up to look at her. The SSS officer did the same and then drew his blaster pistol.

He swung around, but Mason was almost upon him.

Shooting greeny-brown slugs was one thing, Sam decided. But this was a man. A human. She couldn't...

A blast from behind Mason took him squarely in the back, throwing him to the ground.

And Sam saw Kyle Dale, staring in complete shock, letting his blaster fall to the floor.

She wanted to go to him, tell him it was all right. But it wasn't, was it?

Kyle had devoted his entire existence to life and the spiritual well-being of the living, however misguided certain aspects of his beliefs were.

And now he had killed someone.

Or rather hadn't, as Sam saw Mason stagger up, his body almost exploding as the alienness inside him took control. Within seconds, like Torin Chalfont before, he was a man-shaped blob of viscous mucus. Only his head still had a vestige of humanity.

'Hear me, aliens,' he hissed. 'Hear me and prepare to be absorbed!'

The SSS officer blew his head off and the body sagged, then fell.

Sam waved Kyle over as a shout went up from Sergeant Dallion.

'Commandant Ritchie! They're retreating!'

The SSS officer who had killed the former Dr Mason turned, smiling. 'Good. Back to the tunnels where they belong.'

'But the Doctor's in there!' she yelled.

Dallion and her men started forward, moving as one, still blasting at the retreating monsters.

Few of the slugs appeared to have been killed, but many were presumably wounded, as a great many bits of shed skin lay scattered in the sand.

Sam slung her rifle over her shoulder and took off after Dallion, aware that Gar was beside her.

'Beats standing to attention on the *Space Pioneer*, anyway,' he grunted.

As if that wasn't enough, Sam realised that running to catch them up was Kyle. She was going to say something but he shouted to her first. 'I have to try to save Reverend Lukas, Jolyon and the others.'

A new mission for the young man, at least. At last.

Within moments the three of them had caught up with Dallion and her men. A look of respect passed between Dallion and the V'orrn – soldier to soldier.

How bloody macho, Sam thought. Typical. Meanwhile, those things are right behind the Doctor and that green woman, Socks or whatever she was called.

She pushed past the soldiers and looked into the dark tunnels. 'Well,' she said to everyone else. 'Anyone fancy a spot of potholing?'

Back at the disaster site, Consort Ethelredd was talking to Ritchie, Sumner and Green Fingers.

'If those things come back, we could use the weapons on the *Space Pioneer* to fry them.'

'The *Pioneer* has armaments?' Sumner was appalled. 'But there was nothing in the documentation about the Duchess arriving in an armed warship!'

De'Ath sighed. 'We were hardly going to transport one of the Royal Family in a ship halfway across the galaxy without being able to defend ourselves, Co-ordinator. There are people out there who would like to see Earth's First Family done away with.'

'Ourselves included at times,' muttered Ethelredd.

'So of course we were heavily armed.' De'Ath ignored his associate. 'Now, if we bring the ship here, we will have the firepower to stop them.'

'We could blow the tunnels to pieces,' suggested Green Fingers, but Ritchie shook his head.

'The conflagration would hit the power generator. Apart from vaporising about eight square kilometres, including the Stadium, Micawber's World would be bereft of all but a few safety backups. It'd be covered in ice in hours, dead within a day.' He looked at the two from the Royal Party. 'I think your suggestion is a good one. I'll have some SSS transport ships flown here as well. Let's do it and meet up here in twenty minutes. Is that enough time?'

Ethelredd agreed and dragged De'Ath away, saying all they had to do was drag their pilot out of whichever sleazy bar he had found for himself.

'I can pilot a ship like that,' De'Ath complained.

'I know,' retorted Ethelredd. 'Which is why I'd rather find a drunken pilot. You behind the controls is something I don't think I could bear to see…'

Their bickering faded as Ritchie looked at the devastation.

'I don't want to count the dead. It's too many.'

'It would have been a lot more if we hadn't been prepared,' Green Fingers said calmly. 'Let's be thankful for that.'

Madox and two other Teknix stalked through the corridors of the SSS building, heading for Ritchie's office. There were few people around to stop them and they were very good at hiding whenever anyone did approach them.

Taking the elevator, they reached the Commandant's office, and Madox went in first, sweeping the outer room with his blaster, ready to fire if he saw his target.

The room was empty.

His two fellows came in, and so Madox opened the door to Ritchie's private room.

Empty. Madox frowned and stared harder.

He then pointed to the far wall, where it joined the window.

The faint outline of a partition was visible and one of his Teknix shoved at it.

Sure enough, it slid open revealing a small walkway. And two humans being held captive by another Teknix, a blaster held against their heads.

Madox assumed this to be Ritchie's wife and son, presumably headed here to find the Commandant and instead met the alien-infected Krassix.

This all went through Madox's mind as the Teknix who opened the door was blasted lifeless back against the opposite wall of the office by the Krassix/Foamasi hybrid.

The human woman pulled her son to the floor suddenly and before Krassix could react, he was thrown a few metres backwards into the room. The other two Teknix had shot him squarely in the chest.

Madox pelted into the corridor, leaping over the frightened humans, knowing his partner would take them to safety. He saw Krassix stagger up, expecting to see the familiar Foamasi body bulging through the disguise.

Instead, the blast had revealed green bubbling mucus, and with a terrible high-pitched screech, whatever Krassix really was ran at him.

Calmly and methodically, as all Teknix were, Madox altered his blaster setting and calmly emptied the entire charge into Krassix's leaping body, blasting it into tiny pieces. As the noise abated, Madox regarded the bits of mucus splattered across the roof and walls.

Satisfied that it was completely dead and the honour of the Teknix was secure, he walked slowly over to Commandant Ritchie's family.

Finding the lair of the Wirrrn Queen had not been difficult. The orange glow seemed to suffuse the tunnel walls, creating an apparent invitation.

Within five minutes, the Time Lord and his new Jadean associate were facing a nightmare.

The Wirrrn Queen, bloated and writhing in pleasure, looked down at them, at least ten times larger than any other Wirrrn the Doctor could remember seeing. All those years ago, paradoxically in the future.

And he remembered what the Wirrrn had said then. How they had been forced to flee their homelands in the Andromeda Galaxy by humanity, who had entered their galaxy and hunted them.

So, why were they here, thousands of years previously? Of course, the Wirrrn were among the most intelligent and resourceful creatures he had encountered. Even back then, he had never felt quite that sure about their motives – they had been prepared to destroy everything that remained of the human race, stored and asleep in a vast space ark. Survival or revenge? He had never been completely convinced whether it was one or other, or a bit of both. But the Wirrrn had proven a relentless, opportunist enemy, outsmarting him and the tiny group of humans alive who had awoken on the ark. It had taken the last vestiges of humanity in an absorbed human to rid the ark of the Wirrrn by deliberately leading them into a damaged escape ship that exploded shortly after departure.

But what if the humans they claimed had hunted them were in fact themselves fighting back – from an earlier Wirrrn invasion?

Such as this one.

The Doctor raised his head gravely and looked up into the amber discs that were the Wirrrn Queen's eyes, seeing himself and Ms Sox reflected there. He breathed deeply as he spoke to her.

'I congratulate you, Your Majesty. Never have I seen such an audacious plan almost come to fruition. And one that is so wholly malevolent. You realise that I am here to put a stop to it.'

The Wirrrn Queen wriggled, presumably indicating some Wirrrn equivalent of amusement. With one of her long proboscises, she pointed downward.

Beneath her, a horrible tableau existed.

There were four Wirrrn grubs plus a miniature version of the Queen, a Swarm Leader, all moving slightly, as if ready to pounce.

Lying prostrate on the floor were two of the Church of the Way Forward, a man and woman, obviously unconscious. Beside them, smiling bizarrely, was the apparently untouched Reverend Lukas.

The most horrible thing of all was that drooping from the belly of the suspended Queen was an empty egg sac.

The Doctor glanced at the glowing generator. 'Of course, energy to keep her warm, and to provide succour for the breeding grounds.' He tapped Ms Sox's arm. 'Power source?'

'Self-generating.'

'Electrical?'

'Naturally, why?'

'They don't like it, Ms Sox.'

She shrugged. 'Oh, I can see that. I mean, that's why they live here, next to something they don't like.'

The Doctor kept his gaze fixed on the Queen. 'Absolutely. Needs must and all that. I presume it replicates the natural energy of a sun. Powers the planet, yes?'

Ms Sox agreed.

'How fascinating. What an amazing feat of engineering, to condense all that into one generator.'

'Carrington Corp spent billions developing it, Doctor. If we get out of here, remind me to show you the plans. They're top-secret.'

'Then why show me?' he smiled. 'After all, I might sell them to a competitor.'

'That's why I said 'if', Doctor. Frankly, I think we just committed suicide.'

The Swarm Leader moved towards them and for a fleeting moment, the Doctor could glimpse the pain-racked face of a human male, mid-fifties, superimposed over it.

'Torin Chalfont, I presume.'

The Swarm Leader spoke in a harsh, guttural voice, the last vestiges of its human vocal chords vibrating as intended, deliberately not wholly transformed to enable it to communicate in this primitive fashion.

'Hear me, Doctor. You will be absorbed. Your mind will be a very important addition to the Hive.'

The four grubs slithered nearer to Ms Sox, who involuntarily stepped back, creating a small gap between her and the Doctor. A grub moved immediately to fill that gap, but neither she nor the Doctor came into contact with one.

And then hell broke loose.

Blaster fire from behind the Doctor started, and Sam raced in followed by Kyle and some SSS agents, plus a very happy-looking V'orrn, who blasted away at the Queen.

'You're late' yelled the Doctor.

'And you told me not to come!' Sam retorted.

He gave her a thumbs up. 'A few moments more and the proverbial nick of time would have been a pretty deep gash!'

The Wirrrn grubs had reared up and dived towards the soldiers, trapping them by the small cavern entrance from the tunnel.

Ms Sox remembered that during their walk to this place, the Doctor had said something about how just one touch could make someone part of their 'hive-mind', or whatever. She realised she couldn't risk even getting near the…thing, so instead, she hurled her datapad at the Swarm Leader, hoping no one would charge her with damaging Carrington Corp property at a later date. Although it had little effect on the Wirrrn, the bump distracted it. Now, suddenly unfurling small wings, the Swarm Leader flew straight up, slashing at her with a pair of ferocious-looking talons at the end of its tail.

The V'orrn jumped down, blasting at the Swarm Leader, so it turned its attention to him, severing his head with one swish of its tail.

'No!' screamed Sam, but the Doctor tugged her closer to him.

'Sonic screwdriver, Sam. Where is it!'

But Sam was yelling obscenities at the Wirrrn, too distracted to hear him.

Then the Doctor saw Kyle jump bravely over a grub and pull the sonic screwdriver from his own robe pockets.

'Thank you,' said the Doctor, and pushed Sam towards Kyle. 'Don't let her do anything stupid!'

'How?'

'I was hoping you'd tell me that later,' the Doctor retorted.

Sam pulled away from Kyle and they both dropped down beside the dead V'orrn. 'Damn. Damn, damn, damn,' Sam was muttering, staring at her dead friend. Taking a deep breath, Kyle grabbed the dropped blaster and stood up.

The Swarm Leader dived straight at them but Kyle did not flinch. He saw it arch its tail, ready to lash out, but at the last moment he threw himself forward, under the tail, and swivelled around, firing straight into the back of its head.

The dead Swarm Leader crashed to the floor, lying across one of the grubs menacing Ms Sox.

Kyle pulled Sam up and back towards the soldiers trapped in the tunnel.

'The ones from the surface!' yelled Clarke. 'They're behind us!

They were hiding!'

'So that's why we couldn't find them,' muttered Sam. 'Clever slugs.'

Ms Sox suddenly dived towards the Doctor, probably thinking it was safer where he was, but Kyle saw the previously immobile Reverend Lukas punch her in the stomach, and she doubled up. Sam immediately dashed over to help her.

Kyle could see Jolyon and Phillipa, unconscious, but where were the others?

'Veronique! Max! Eldritch and Marcus! Where are they, Reverend Father?'

Reverend Lukas pointed at the four Wirrrn grubs in the cavern with them, taking fire from Sergeant Dallion's men.

No... He couldn't have given them to this... this...

Kyle pelted across the floor and started hitting Reverend Lukas, who just pushed him away, laughing.

'Don't you see, Kyle? The Goddess is here. All around us. This is the end of our journey. We have found salvation!'

While Sam helped Ms Sox up, the Doctor turned his sonic screwdriver on to the generator casing.

A maintenance hatch slid back and the Doctor made some adjustments. 'Come on, come on,' he said to himself.

'What are you doing, Doctor?' asked Ms Sox, her attention really on the horrendous figure of the Wirrrn Queen above her, who was now screeching angrily.

The sonic screwdriver ceased giving off sonic waves, and a thin red beam shot out of the end, cutting into some of the wiring, haphazardly.

A few wires shorted.

'So, that's how you do it,' Sam said.

'Get back,' he hissed to Ms Sox. 'Try to get that boy as near the tunnel as you can without touching the grubs. They're lethal!'

Ms Sox looked as if she was going to argue.

'Please! You're as bad as Sam!'

That did it, and Ms Sox dashed away, pulling Kyle away from the laughing Reverend Lukas.

'As bad as me. Thanks.' Sam smiled. 'You want me here because you want me to do something brave and stupid, don't you?'

'You always were a fast learner, Sam.'

'That's right, Doctor. I'm now a bloody expert. I threw away my Doctor's-assistant L-plates three years ago on the Mu Camelopides moon.'

The Doctor looked at her, as if he was seeing for the first time just how much she had grown up in the last few years. 'I'm sorry,' he said. 'I think we need to sit down and talk. About you, very soon. I've rather neglected you, haven't I?'

The Wirrrn Queen started to squirm, and Sam saw the walls shake slightly as she did so.

'God, you choose your moments, Doctor.' She pointed upward. 'Someone's getting tetchy.'

'Let's pray this works, Sam.'

Pray.

'Doctor? D'you believe in God?'

The Doctor stared at her. Then smiled. 'What did you just say about choosing your moments?'

But Sam just stared, oblivious to everything. 'I need an answer, but I don't know why.'

'Later, Sam. Later. Right now, I need you to attract Her Majesty's pincers.'

Almost mechanically, she thumped the Queen's tail. Instantly it flicked out, the talons missing Sam's face by less than half an inch.

And instead they rounded on the Doctor.

He stabbed his sonic screwdriver into the severed, live, sparking wiring in the generator, and ducked.

And the talons connected with the screwdriver, knocking it into another few wires and completing the circuit.

Exactly how many millions of volts went through the Wirrrn Queen's body at that second, Sam could not imagine, but the blue flash and acrid smell hit her a second before the blackness did.

Sam awoke because the Doctor was shaking her.

In her head, she could hear groans and mutters from the others and she opened her eyes. 'Hello. Did it work?'

'Sort of,' the Doctor replied, and Sam looked over to where they had been standing before the electric backlash had hit them.

The Queen was slumped, half torn from her sac in the wall. Reverend Lukas was lying completely still across the unconscious Phillipa and Jolyon.

The four Wirrrn grubs in the room with them were also quite still. One had ruptured and was oozing green pus on to the floor.

'The others? In the corridor?'

'That's where it went wrong. The tunnels didn't conduct the electricity like the coated floor of the cavern. They've escaped.'

'To the surface?' That was Dallion, staggering over and helping up Ms Sox.

'We must get after them. They're still dangerous.'

Sam looked around. Agent Fenton was dead, lying on his back, eyes wide open, half his face coated in mucus. Standing over him was Clarke, shaking his head, and from what the others were saying to him, Sam realised he had shot his own comrade to spare him the transformation.

Apart from that, shaken but not too badly stirred, everyone was OK.

Dallion grabbed her troops and headed off after the escaping Wirrrn grubs.

Kyle and Ms Sox looked at the Doctor and Sam.

'Well, what are we waiting for? It's not over yet.' The Doctor pointed to the tunnel. 'Thataway, I think.'

* * *

Commandant Ritchie was not expecting the sheer number of Wirrrn that poured out of the tunnel entrance, and neither were his troopers. They had thought the worst of it was over.

But Consort Ethelredd was prepared and he grabbed De'Ath and hauled him into the newly arrived *Space Pioneer*. 'Man the blasters,' he snapped.

Without argument, De'Ath went to do so.

On the surface, the Wirrrn moved on, ignoring the agents who blasted at them, snagging any that got too close – not enough to infect them, it seemed, just to cause confusion as the agents stopped firing for fear of hitting their friends.

Suddenly the Wirrrn changed course, and began swarming into two of the parked trooper carriers.

'Can they fly?' Sumner asked Green Fingers, as they watched, horrified, from closer to the Stadium entrance.

'Depends if any of the pilots are still in there.'

The start-up of the propulsion units answered that. The Wirrrn had claimed at least two more victims.

Just as the carriers started to rise, causing the ground troops to run away for fear of being caught by the powerful antigrav engines, Green Fingers gasped in horror.

'They're starting up the interstellar engines. They're going to try escaping the atmosphere.'

'Can they do that in one of those?' asked Sumner.

Green Fingers nodded. 'At least to get them to something bigger on one of the space stations or any of the nearer worlds.'

Seconds later, Dallion and her troopers were running out of the tunnel and, after a moment's hesitation to take it all in, piled on to the *Space Pioneer*. After a brief pause, that too took off.

Then the Doctor's party emerged.

'Good luck, Sergeant,' he said quietly.

The first reports from the *Space Pioneer* came in half an hour later. They had successfully destroyed one of the carriers but the other had docked with a deep-space cruiser after the *Pioneer* had lost track of it. By the time they realised what had happened, the cruiser was heading off, and the *Pioneer* was giving pursuit.

'It doesn't appear to be heading anywhere,' said the young holotechnician receiving reports from Sergeant Dallion.

'It is,' said the Doctor to Ritchie. 'It's doing the only thing it can. The Wirrrn's survival instinct is taking them home. To the Andromedan Galaxy.'

'I'll recall the *Space Pioneer*. If they stay chasing it for too long, they'll never have enough fuel to get back. And other ships can continue the chase.'

'That's up to you.' The Doctor shrugged and walked away. 'I'm going to have a rest.'

Chapter Twelve
There's A Planet In My Kitchen

The Doctor was shaking Ms Sox's hand.

'So, you have Carrington Corp to yourself now. I'm sorry that it had to happen in the way that it did.'

Ms Sox nodded. 'So am I. Chase Carrington was a good man, and I will ensure that his work is carried on. Micawber's World *will* recover, you know.'

'I understand from Events Co-ordinator Sumner that the Federation have suggested restarting the games in three weeks. Will you still fund them?'

Ms Sox nodded. 'Oh yes, Doctor. To let this tragedy overshadow the gathering together of all the species under one sun, as it were, would be a real disaster.'

There was a knock on the office door and Green Fingers trundled in. 'You'll be pleased to note, Doctor,' he said after the usual round of greetings, 'that your plan has worked.'

The Doctor nodded. 'Good.'

'Plan? Which plan was this, then?' asked Ms Sox.

The Doctor grinned broadly. 'The plan that involved me coming up not only with a neutralising agent to counter the drugs, but a retraction agent into the bargain.'

'Which will do?'

'Which will slowly unravel the hostile DNA that is embedded within each athlete's system, and at the same time bolster the immune system so that it will be safely broken down and eradicated.'

Ms Sox frowned. 'So will they be able to take part in the Games?'

The Doctor shook his head, sadly. 'Those who took the red capsules, well, maybe they'll be able to participate in the next

Games. But the ones who took the more powerful blue ones, I'm afraid not. I may have destroyed the Wirrrn DNA, but the cost to the atheletes' own bodies will be high. Most of them will need organ transplants, possibly cybernetic surgery, and I'm afraid all of them will have to be sterilised. Some of the weaker and smaller competitors such as the Morogs, the Kleptons and the Saurians may still die eventually as a result of all this. Their bodies might well collapse under the strain of the internal changes.'

'Some of us might be heartless enough to point out that if they hadn't taken the drugs, or wanted to cheat in the Games, they wouldn't be in this predicament.' Ms Sox tossed her hair back, and shrugged. 'I'm tempted to say they got what they deserved.'

'Are you, now?' The Doctor looked at her, sadly. 'Let's leave the sermons against drugs to the schools, shall we? I've had enough banner-waving and indoctrination from the Church of the Way Forward this trip, all right? I'm just glad I could ensure that no one will discover a Wirrrn eating them from the inside.'

The Foamasi Ambassador raised a clawed hand. 'I'm pleased you were able to help, Doctor, but there is another small problem. Commandant Ritchie's people have gone into the tunnels and found the cavern. The covering on the walls and floors has been easily removed and destroyed, as have the Wirrrn bodies. Except there was no sign of the Wirrrn Queen's body. It looks as if she managed to get away.'

The Doctor crossed to a window and looked upwards into the sky. 'I wonder...'

'All I have ever wanted is immortality!'

Unreadable eyes stared down at Reverend Lukas. No head movement. Not even a mandible trembled.

'I did it all for you, Goddess. Everything I have striven for over the years, the work, the sacrifice. You are the Blessed One. You are My Love.' He was on his knees before the Queen, gazing up, desperately searching for a sign of life. The welts on her chitin were blackened and cracked. Her antennae were drooped limply over her face.

'She's... dead... Father.'

Reverend Lukas did not turn at the sound of Jolyon's voice. 'I know. I know.' He wiped a tear from down the side of his nose. 'She is beautiful.'

'Why are... we here? Where exactly are... we?'

Lukas finally looked back at his two devoted helpers. They were lying on the acceleration couches, gripping each other's hand tightly. Phillipa was unconscious. Luckily for her. Lukas shuffled over on his knees, grabbing Jolyon's free hand, grinning widely.

'You, beloved boy, you are the future. The Goddess chose you. Both of you. An honour denied me, but you are so lucky.'

Jolyon tried to focus. He also tried to sit up, but realised he was strapped down. He pulled his hand free of Phillipa and tried to loosen the belt, but couldn't. Prising his other hand free of Lukas's fervent grip, he pulled harder but nothing gave.

Jolyon looked across as Phillipa, her chest rising slowly, a sign of deep sleep. 'Phillipa...?'

Lukas shook him, bringing his attention back to the Reverend. 'Enjoy your new role in the Church of the Way Forward. You will become a Beloved.' Lukas clasped his own hands together as if praying. 'Canonised, perhaps.'

'Where are we?' repeated Jolyon, somewhat more urgently. 'Why are we tied down?'

Lukas looked back at the dead Queen, propped against the wall. 'Going home, Beloved Child. Back to the stars whence we came, millions of years before.'

'Father... what are you talk –' Jolyon stopped. He looked at Phillipa again, then back at the dead Queen. 'No... no... oh Goddess, no...'

Inside him he suddenly felt it. It touched his mind, it touched every sense, every nerve, every thought. And if it was inside him, and he was strapped down, then Phillipa, strapped down as well must have one inside…

'Lukas! You bastard! What have you done to us?'

Reverend Lukas was on his feet, throwing himself at the carcass of the dead Queen, embracing it. 'They don't understand yet, Goddess. But they will. So soon, they will understand. Then they will lead us to new pastures, new temples, new followers.'

Jolyon was struggling violently, but to no avail. Lukas had strapped them down too well.

He could hear it, feel it, permeating everything in his body as it absorbed his mind, absorbed his consciousness. Devouring his history. His life.

He opened his mouth to spit more obscenities at Lukas, to cry out to his beloved Phillipa, in blessed sleep, unaware of what was growing inside her, engorging her…

But when eventually he found enough energy to make a sound, the only noise he made was one word, hissed as a mixture of terror and elation as Jolyon Tuck finally ceased to exist as a human individual.

'Wirrrrrrrrnnnnnn'

And the last thing his human eyes saw was Reverend Lukas smiling insanely at him.

The shuttle continued on its journey, deeper and deeper into space…

Kyle Dale patted the outside of the TARDIS.

'It's a marvellous ship, Sam.'

Sam nodded. 'Yup. More rooms than you can imagine, better facilities than you've ever seen and a machine that makes the meanest cup of Darjeeling you've ever tasted.'

'But no chapel? No place of worship?'

'I guess the Doctor never needed one. Or maybe there is, and

I've never found it.' A momentary flash of Stacy Townsend and Ssard zooming off to the stars zapped through her mind's eye. 'Then again, not even I know all the TARDIS' secrets.'

Kyle swallowed hard. 'You're going to ask me to go with you, aren't you?'

'Am I?'

Kyle nodded. 'But I can't. There's too much to do here. The Church needs a new Way Forward. Maybe I can help provide that path, show newcomers the right direction.'

Sam shrugged. 'I must ask you this, Kyle. Do you really have that right? To tell people what to believe in? And how to believe? After all that you found out about your "Goddess"? You told me that your faith, your absolute belief came from within. Lukas might have been your leader but he wasn't much more than a signpost on a map. You know your faith is within you. Why stay here just to prove it?'

Kyle laughed suddenly. 'You should be a politician. Or one of those holovid presenters, coaxing intelligent responses out of athletes.' He took her right hand in both of his. 'I know what you are saying, Sam, but my answer is no. You're right, I do know what my path is, where my heart and my faith lie. And they tell me that there is still much to be done here, and around the Federation. There is a new millennium dawning in a few months. I need to be here to see it in, to help celebrate the wonder that is eternity and the joy that the year 4000 will hold.'

Sam drew her hand back. 'And what if I told you the future? What if I told you I know what the next year will bring? What if I said that thousands will die in a galactic war, or maybe millions will perish in a terrible disease or that planet Earth will be vaporised in a space battle? Would that change your mind?'

'Do you really need to ask?'

Sam took a final look around Micawber's World. *The Utopia of the Next Millennium*, according to the advertising hoardings. Then she stared back at Kyle.

'Hey, Kyle, it was fun. Dangerous, terrifying and very, very tragic. But it was fun being with you. I understand you're staying here, and what you must do. But I've got to go with the Doctor, keep his nose wiped and his TARDIS working. He's *my* mission, if you like. No, that's patronising, I'm sorry. Your faith is more than that. But he's... He is what I must do. Does that make sense?'

Kyle reached over and kissed her on the cheek, then on the lips. Gently. Almost a brush, and she felt his touch like butterfly wings on her face, his breath on hers. And he moved back.

God, she was going to cry. Not at losing him, but at the sudden understanding of how pure he was. How untainted and unspoiled by the hypocrisy of his mentor, and by the terrible events they had witnessed. His God, or Goddess or whatever, really was there, inside him. An intrinsic part of his being.

She could never possibly be a part of that.

And that, she knew, was just plain sad. For all her family's going to church on a Sunday, singing hymns and praying, neither they nor anyone else had provided her with anything like the belief in the goodness of the universe that Kyle possessed.

'Goodbye, Kyle.'

'May your own God be with you, Samantha.' He bowed slightly and walked away, not looking back.

Sam heard the TARDIS door open behind her. The Doctor had waited. Had he watched? Probably.

'But I kept the sound off,' he said gently, giving her that smile that said he understood. 'Now, we must get to Kolpasha and finally have dinner with Stacy and Ssard – if you're up to that?' Sam nodded. 'Oh,' said the Doctor. 'One other thing.' He placed something in her hand and she brought it up to stare at it.

It was like the grass sculpture they had given Stacy and Ssard at their wedding. Only this time, the Doctor had made an image of Kyle.

'So you won't forget him,' he said quietly.

She nodded, but said nothing until Kyle was a dark spot in the distance. 'Thank you, Doctor. I appreciate this.' She gave a small laugh and held the grass sculpture up to the Doctor. 'Kyle Dale is now immortal, eh?'

The Doctor nodded. 'By the way...'

Sam frowned. 'What?'

'Follow me.'

She followed him, as requested, and before long found herself back in the kitchen. Galley. Whatever.

Still sitting on top of the microwave was the stuffed Meep toy. For a moment she considered chucking it out of the door, but it reminded her of poor brave Gar. And Consort Ethelredd and Counsellor De'Ath, their cynical exteriors hiding warm hearts. And a bittersweet pang for Kyle, and how much he never understood how wrong toys like this could be.

'You can stay. Until my conscience pricks my sentimentality,' she muttered to the toy. 'But don't tell anyone I said so, OK?'

Unsurprisingly, the toy did not reply.

The Doctor then tapped her on the shoulder.

'Care to explain how there is a planet hovering in my kitchen?'

She laughed and pressed the door switch on the microwave. Immediately it sprang open, and the hologram flew out. Then the image of Earth pixelated and exploded, the TARDIS absorbing every holographic particle. 'Whoops. Sorry,' Sam said. 'Still, if you rewired this time machine of your now and again...'

'The TARDIS, as well you know, has self-repairing circuits.'

'Anyone told her that, then?'

There was a notable rise in the pitch of the TARDIS hum. The Doctor cocked his head for a moment, as if listening.

'I see... Oh, all right, I am sorry.' He glanced over to Sam. 'You two are ganging up on me, you know. I won't stand for it.' He turned away in mock annoyance and headed back to the console room.

Sam waited a few minutes, then sauntered after him.

As she entered, her attention was caught by the holographic Earth once again back where it belonged, spread across the ceiling.

'A... little bird tells me you've been thinking about going home, Sam. Seeing your parents.' The Doctor didn't look at her, just kept staring up at Earth.

Sam shot a filthy look, the most evil one she could muster, at the TARDIS console, then walked up behind the Doctor and rested her chin on his shoulder, standing on tiptoe to do so. 'For "little bird" read "stool pigeon". And, yeah, I have been thinking about it. Just a quick hello and an explanation, face to face. But not to stay.'

The Doctor eased himself away and then turned. And smiled. That toothy grin, those grey-blue-green eyes... a thousand-odd-year-old acting like a toddler, wanting his own way again.

'But,' Sam said firmly – perhaps to herself as much as the Doctor – 'not yet. I'm going to write them another postcard tonight and maybe we could drop it off soon. But I'm still not quite ready for Shoreditch, rain, grime and the Jubilee Line extension at the moment. Maybe we could go back for the Millennium and see them then?'

'London. Midnight. 1999. Yes, I think we could manage that. London will be very safe that night, I've made sure of that. A few times, come to think of it.' The Doctor turned off the hologram of Earth. 'Kolpasha, then?'

'Do they do good vegetarian dishes there?'

'Naturally. Why do you think I recommended it to Stacy and Ssard?'

Sam stroked the TARDIS console. The last couple of years had been... interesting, there was no getting away from that. But right now, this was, well, home. 'And that is where my heart is,' she murmured.

'What's that?'

'Oh, nothing. Just thinking aloud.' Sam tapped into the TARDIS databank. 'Kolpasha. Fashion capital of the Federation,' she read. 'Well... better find something suitable to wear!'

Smiling, she headed off to her room, and within a few seconds, she could hear the usual wheezing and groaning noises reverberating through the walls as the TARDIS faded away from Micawber's World.

Kyle Dale sat on his bed, staring at the object he had found propped up against his door.

He traced the outline with his finger, letting a tear drop from his cheek on to it.

He reread the simple message that accompanied it, on a tiny scrap of paper, written, by hand, in classical script. A beautiful work of art in itself.

Never forget her.

'As if, Doctor.' Kyle kissed the object and placed it beside his bible.

It was a grass sculpture of Samantha Jones.

Well, it was a kind of immortality.

Watch out for Doctor Who on Video!

The following exciting adventures are currently available from BBC Worldwide:

THE LEISURE HIVE starring Tom Baker
THE AWAKENING/FRONTIOS starring Peter Davison
THE WAR MACHINES starring William Hartnell
THE HAPPINESS PATROL starring Sylvester McCoy
THE E-SPACE TRILOGY starring Tom Baker
TIMELASH starring Colin Baker
BATTLEFIELD starring Sylvester McCoy
THE MIND OF EVIL starring Jon Pertwee
HORROR OF FANG ROCK starring Tom Baker

Coming soon...

PLANET OF FIRE starring Peter Davison
THE ARK starring William Hartnell
THE ICE WARRIORS starring Patrick Troughton